MEMORIES OF LOVE

EILA TRENT

To my grandchildren for bringing a second wave of joy into my life. May we always be silly, laugh together and randomly dance in the driveway.
I love you. Xoxo... G-Nana & Ama

CHAPTER ONE

"Show me the box, honey." Hank said with a pained smile.

"Of course. You know I love that box and what it means. It's like our own time capsule, isn't it?" Betsy said, standing. She laid her hand on Hank's chest for a moment as he closed his eyes and drifted off. The medicine had that effect. She fought back tears as she listened to his steady breathing and felt the beating of his heart. Now was not the time.

Lady lifted her head from her position at the foot of the bed and eyed Betsy. "It's okay, girl," she whispered as the black-and-white dog crawled closer to Hank's hand and laid her head over his knee. She reached down and stroked Lady's silky coat, her furry tail thumping on the comforter.

Hank had surprised Betsy with the wiggly, bouncing bundle of puppy love a year earlier. The three of them enjoyed many walks through the meadow and into the woods by the house. They laughed at the rambunctious dog and her antics as she chased squirrels and rabbits and leaped at dragonflies. She would proudly return to their side as if she'd protected them from the fiercest of animals.

Lady became Hank's constant companion. She comforted him with her affection, for which Betsy was grateful. Her canine sense seemed to know when he wasn't feeling well, and she would nudge his hand with her nose as if to reassure him. She lay near him and even hesitated to go outside after long hours of keeping him company.

Betsy walked across the bedroom to her cedar chest under the window. She glanced out at the myriad of animals in the meadow and the budding trees. Soon the wildflowers would appear. She looked down, and there was a tug at her heart. "There are so many memories in this old chest," Betsy said as she placed her hand on the smooth wood. "Bits of my life."

She opened the heavy lid and picked up a delicate shawl in shades of purple that had once been worn by her grandmother. The stories of angels and miracles were told to Betsy and her sister long ago. Their grandmother shared with them about the long journey their ancestors had made as they emigrated from Europe. And after many years of searching, they eventually settled at the base of a mountain where magnificent wild irises grew in abundance. She told them the glorious purple flowers stretched toward the heavens and bloomed with the promise of spring and new life. It was those wildflowers that convinced their forefathers this new land would be their home forever.

Betsy placed her cheek on the shawl. "I miss you, Nana. But you're always in my heart." She laid the soft memory to one side carefully and picked up a large, rectangular item shrouded in a colorful cloth. With a delicate touch, she uncovered a wooden box and held the exquisite fabric up to the window. A smile crossed her lips as the gossamer material shimmered in the sunlight. Purple flowers with green and gold seemed to float against the ivory background.

Hank had bought the cloth as a surprise for her when they toured the street markets in Morocco. The trip was such an amazing adventure and too precious a memory for her to cut the silky textile into a dress. Instead, she used it to cloak the most cherished of all her treasures—the wooden keepsake box. Betsy rubbed her fingers across the top, feeling the outlines, ridges, and intricacies of the carved flowers. She smiled as she thought about the long hours Hank labored to find just the right wood upon which to carve the emblems of his love for her. Betsy marveled at the smoothness of the fine grain.

Only after he'd given her the box did she understand why he'd become so fascinated by and infatuated with the irises. It wasn't for himself, but for her. As children, she told him frequently how much she loved the purple blooms, which spoke of spring's arrival and long sunny days. They often played in a meadow near her house where the sea of irises grew. He came to recognize their beauty because of her. And Betsy came to appreciate him for that very reason. The flowers mattered in his life because she did. That was all she needed to know.

Hank coughed. "Betsy? Are you still here?"

"Yes, my love. I'm getting the box now." She draped the memory of Morocco over her shoulders, picked up the box, and returned to Hank's bedside.

"I guess I needed a quick nap. I thought I'd lost you," he said with a smile.

"Never." Betsy patted his hand. "Would you like some tea? I made some cookies for you, too."

"Chocolate chip?" he asked with a grin.

"What other kind is there?" She smiled back at him as she set the box of memories on the chair.

"That sounds wonderful. It just so happens I'm hungry,

and that's perhaps my favorite meal. We'll wait right here for you." Hank patted the bed and Lady moved up beside him. "That's my good girl." He rubbed her head as she adored him with her eyes.

Betsy smiled as her two loves shared a moment. "I'll be back in about ten minutes. Anything else you'd like?" she asked.

"Just more time, my dear. Just a little more time with you." His eyes were filled with sadness.

She leaned over and gave him a tender kiss on the lips.

"Are you my girl, too?" he whispered.

"Always," she said and stroked his cheek. Betsy took something from the box and handed it to him as Lady gave it a sniff.

"Here, hold this while you wait for me. It'll give you something to think about." She grinned as she left the room.

Hank looked at the pink satin ribbon, and as he rubbed the bit of silkiness, his mind filled with memories of long ago. The time when a young boy met a pretty little girl with pigtails seemed like only yesterday. The day Betsy came into his life. The day his life changed forever.

The nervous, gangly boy stood in front of the class, his eyes fixed on the yellowed, waxed tiles. He shifted from foot to foot and adjusted his glasses, although they weren't crooked. He kept his eyes on the floor.

"Class, we have a new student," Mrs. Purcell said as she looked around at the room full of curious faces. "Please tell them your name, dear."

"My name is Hank," he said without lifting his head.

"Please look at the class and say your name again so they can hear you."

Hank looked up at the sea of faces and his cheeks flushed as he repeated his name. He clenched his fists and swallowed hard.

"Thank you, Hank. You may take a seat back in the corner behind Betsy." The teacher pointed to a cute little girl with auburn pigtails tied with pink ribbons.

Hank hastened down the aisle and took a seat behind the girl as he looked down and exhaled.

"Hi, I'm Betsy. Glad to meet you," said the cheery face as she turned to greet him.

Hank glanced up and gave her a quick, weak smile before turning his eyes down again. Under his chair, he bounced his heels up and down as if to take flight. The fidgety boy was well beyond anxious about his induction into third grade at a new school.

"Okay, class. Everyone turn to page thirty in your spelling book. Hank, I'll have your book for you tomorrow. You can scoot your chair next to Betsy and share her book for today."

A terrified Hank widened his eyes as he hesitated. His face reddened again, his expression revealing he would rather have stood in front of a charging rhino.

"Go on, Hank," the teacher prompted. "She won't bite."

The class laughed at his look of terror. A couple of boys even pointed at Betsy. "Watch out, she has rabies," Matthew chided as he turned to a boy across the aisle. They snickered in unison.

"Oh, stop you two. Everyone settle down," the teacher said, annoyed by the disruption.

"Don't pay attention to them, Hank. They're always

teasing everyone," Betsy said as she slid her textbook closer for him to see and turned to glare at the class bully.

"Thanks," he mumbled. Hank was so uncomfortable he barely heard what was said in class. The pretty girl spoke to him, but he couldn't look up. With his head down, he just prayed it would soon be over.

When the bell rang, Betsy jumped up and hurried to leave the room. As something fell to the ground, Hank looked down. It was a ribbon from her hair. She was already gone, so he picked it up and shoved it into his pocket. He'd try to give it to her later.

CHAPTER TWO

The phone rang as Betsy walked down the stairs. She hurried to the kitchen counter, hoping it was news about Andy.

"Hi, Ben. Any updates?" she asked as she held her breath, her eyes wide with anticipation.

"Hi, Betsy. Yep, I just spoke with him and his plane gets in at three p.m. I'm here now waiting for him. Don't worry, I'll have him home soon," he said in a reassuring voice. "I'll call you when we're on our way."

"Thank you. I can't tell you how much we appreciate your help."

"Hey, that's what friends are for, right? Don't you worry."

"You're more than a friend, Ben. You're family." She was on the verge of tears.

"I know that, hon, and that makes my life so much sweeter. Tell Hank I'm bringing his boy home real soon. Okay?"

"I will, Ben. Be careful, please. Bye."

"We'll see you soon. Bye, Betsy."

She set the teapot on the stove and reached for the tray. By the time she'd arranged the cookies and plates, the tea was ready. As she pushed a lock of stray hair from her face, she glanced up at the handwritten note on the windowsill. Hank had put it there the day they found out he had cancer.

"Thank you for sharing your cookies with me. I will always love you, Betsy." -Hank

Tears spilled down Betsy's cheeks. She gripped the counter's edge, taking a deep breath and wiping her face. She couldn't allow the tears. "Hank is still here, and he needs me to be present," she scolded herself. "Thank you, Lord."

Her thoughts returned to Andy's arrival. It would improve her spirits and those of his father. It had been nearly a year since he'd been home, and he'd only recently been stateside. To their relief, his emergency leave had been granted quickly. She needed to remember to send a thank you note to his commanding officer.

Betsy gathered her thoughts and the tray, making her way up the stairs. She once again felt God's strength as she walked into the bedroom with a smile.

"There's my girl." Hank struggled to reposition himself.

"Here, let me help you, honey," she said, moving the pillows behind his back.

"I'm not sure, but I'd say seeing these cookies has made you feel better." She laughed as she set the tray over his lap.

"Yeah, a quick nap and cookies can do wonders, my dear. But you are the real medicine." He reached out and took her hand. "I love you, you know."

"Are you sure it's not just the chocolate chip cookies you love?" Betsy liked to tease him. She winked when he made a sad face. "Yes, I know and I love you more—and always."

They enjoyed their tea and cookies for the better part of an hour as they talked and laughed about how painfully shy he had been as a boy. They forgot about their troubles and only focused on the moment. Frequently, they would finish each other's sentences. Hank and Betsy had become one a long time ago. It all started with a chocolate chip cookie.

~

The new boy sat by himself in the lunchroom. Betsy usually sat with her sister, but hesitated. She looked toward Estelle, who had plenty of others to talk with, and then walked to Hank's table.

"Hi. Is it okay if I sit here?" She smiled as she looked at Hank.

He was surprised she'd come over to him. Not only did she speak to him again, but she asked to sit with him. No one ever wanted to sit with him during lunch or any other time, especially girls. He wanted to say yes, but the word wouldn't come out.

"I guess that means yes," she said, placing her tray on the table and sitting down.

"I promise I don't bite, and I don't have rabies despite what Matthew said. So where did you live before?" She picked up her fork and took a bite of meatloaf as she looked at the surprised face across from her.

"Uh, sure. I mean, yes. I, uh—" He stammered and blushed at the same time.

"Cat got your tongue? That's what my mom says to me, especially if I'm about to be in trouble. I'm usually trying to think of an answer that won't make her even more mad at me."

Betsy grinned and took another bite as she waited for him to answer.

Hank sat there, holding his sandwich in front of his mouth and unable to speak. He was shocked she had voluntarily come to sit with him. No girl had ever just started talking to him, unless it was to tell him to go away. That happened a lot. But no girl had ever just treated him nicely. He didn't know why, either. It was curious.

"I'm sorry. My mom says I always talk too fast and ask too many questions. So I'll just eat and give you time to think about your answers. No hurry. Take your time, Hank." She picked up more meatloaf with some mashed potatoes and quickly put it in her mouth. "Mmm, this is great today. When the other cook makes it, I don't like it very much. I don't know why. I just don't. I think my mom's meatloaf is the best in the whole world."

Hank took a bite of his sandwich and looked at her as he chewed. He swallowed the bite and said, "I like meatloaf." It was all he could do to speak those words. He had only said one word to her earlier in class.

"Great. Maybe some time you can come over to my house when my mom makes it. That might be fun. Would you like that?" Betsy looked up from her tray and grinned at him.

His childish heart felt something it never had before. He didn't know it then, but he had just fallen in love with the sweet, talkative red-haired girl. Hank finally smiled at her and found his voice.

"Thanks." He hesitated but was a bit more confident. "I'd like that, but I'll have to ask my mom." He had said more to this little girl than he'd ever spoken to a stranger before. But somehow, she didn't act like a stranger. Maybe she was a friend he just hadn't met. He didn't realize fate would make them friends for the rest of his life. But maybe somehow, they already knew that was their future.

"Okay, that settles it then. I'll ask my mom when she'll be cooking meatloaf and if you can come over. I'll tell you tomorrow." She smiled and continued to eat, as though she was just talking about the weather.

But for Hank, the sky was full of fireworks. He grinned and finished his sandwich. He tried several times to say more, but Betsy seemed content to just sit with him as they ate.

"Do you want half of my cookie, Hank?" Before he could answer, she had broken the chocolate chip cookie in half and handed one half to him.

"Uh, sure. Thanks. These are my favorite." He looked at her in disbelief. No one had ever given him half of their cookie, especially a chocolate chip one, his all-time favorite treat. That sealed the deal. He was most definitely in love. They both dunked their cookies into their milk, and as they did, they looked at each other and laughed.

The bell rang just as they finished cleaning their area.

"Thanks for having lunch with me, Betsy," he said with a shy smile.

"Sure," she replied with a grin. "I need to talk to my sister, so I'll see you in class."

And with that, the cute girl with one pink ribbon in her hair ducked through the doorway and disappeared. Hank had forgotten about the ribbon in his pocket.

CHAPTER THREE

Betsy remembered to take her phone upstairs, and Ben called just as she and Hank finished their tea. "Okay. Thanks, Ben." She smiled as she spoke. "We'll see you and Andy in about two hours. Bye."

"It'll be good to see Andy. I've missed that boy of ours," Hank said as he sat more upright and pointed at the foot of the bed. "Wrap that around your shoulders for me, honey."

Betsy stood, draping the Moroccan fabric around her body and neck and then over her shoulders. She turned and faced her husband.

He whistled. "As beautiful as ever—the cloth, too." He flashed her a crooked grin.

"You really know how to win and keep a girl's heart, mister." She gave him a quick kiss. He held her arms and kissed her again, but with a bit more passion.

"That's more like it," he said with a grin. "Now let's open the treasure box a handsome young lad gave to you. We'll take a trip down memory lane."

"I'd love to. It's been a long time since we've looked in here. Since before—" Betsy stopped, unable to finish her sentence. But even unspoken, the words hung in the air. She climbed onto the other side of the bed and put the wooden box between them. Looking at Hank, she squeezed his hand before opening the box filled with tokens of their love story.

"It seems like only yesterday..." Hank trailed off as he reached in, searching the bottom and pulling out a baseball-sized tin. When he held it up for Betsy to see, she laughed.

"This is one of my favorite stories. I thought you had to be the bravest boy at school, maybe even in the world." She grinned. "After all, I was twelve years old and wise for my age. And I was sure I was the envy of every girl in school." That caused them both to laugh as Hank removed the lid and ever so gently held up a single dried rose. It had lost some of its brilliant color, but not the meaning. They looked at the red flower and then at each other.

It was a bright spring morning as Hank walked toward Betsy's house. It would take him longer to get there because he took a different route on this particular day. A gust of wind blew his cap off and he chased it back down the side-walk. It might take even longer if that happened again. He was on a mission, having stayed up almost all night debating with himself about whether he should ask Betsy to be his girlfriend. Hank couldn't go to her empty-handed.

He had been friends with her and her twin sister, Estelle, for over three years, spending most of his free time with them. Their summers and school vacations were filled with days of swimming, camps, picnics, and hiking. Not to mention quite a few science experiments, which fortunately had not seriously injured any of them. As they got older, their parents had allowed them a wider range in which to explore.

They fancied themselves like the Three Musketeers, and people in town smiled and waved when they saw them. Parsons was a great town to grow up in. Little did the kids know their parents often received phone calls from those same friendly people as to their children's whereabouts. The town had a way of keeping their young ones safe and out of trouble—mostly.

Lately, however, Estelle had a crush on a boy in her neighborhood and now spent more time with Tommy or at home baking cookies for him. Hank was glad Betsy knew how to bake the same chocolate chip cookies as her mom. In his humble opinion, they were the best in the entire world. He had known the first time he met her she was a little more special than her sister. Most people couldn't see the difference between them, but Betsy had a kinder heart and he saw it in her smile. He could always recognize the twins by their smiles.

As he neared his target, he stopped to assess the best plan of attack. He was certain he wouldn't be seen if he crouched along the picket fence before he got to Mrs. Mathison's house. Then he'd hide in the tall bushes near the roses. Yep, that was a good plan. She'd never know, and she'd never miss just one. He glanced over his shoulder for cars or pedestrians. The coast was clear, and he dropped to the ground.

Mr. Adams had just set his newspaper on his lap and was looking out of his living room window. He reached for his phone. "Hi, Gladys. Just calling to let you know there's a young man crouched behind your picket fence at the corner of your house. I think it's the Walker boy. Yep, I'm sure it is. Now he's crawling beside your lilac bushes. Yep, you might want to ask him what he's looking for. Sure. You're welcome."

Mrs. Adams walked in and asked what was going on. "Do you think you should go over there?"

"Nope. Gladys can handle it. She's one tough old lady. I wouldn't want to be on her bad side," Mr. Adams chuckled. The two stood at their window and watched with an enormous amount of interest as the scene unfolded.

Gladys Mathison was a solitary person who kept to herself. She and her husband had no children, although they would have welcomed one. Since Mr. Mathison's death many years earlier, her greatest love and joy in life was growing roses. However, she had been allergic to the sun since childhood and forced to adjust her lifestyle. She loved her garden but only tended to it far into the evening after sunset, when most others prepared for bed. She preferred the cooler temperature and didn't mind the darkness as she wore a head lamp to navigate around the yard. Quite a few of the townsfolk were curious how she had always grown the county's prize-winning, blue-ribbon roses since no one ever saw her outside. Even Mr. and Mrs. Adams had wondered about that.

By now, Mrs. Mathison had stepped out of her front door, quietly over a squeaky stair, and into her front yard. She slowly turned on the faucet and picked up her garden hose. As sShe stood in front of her lilac bushes in disbelief, two hands came through the foliage, grabbing a large rose and cutting the stem with a small pocketknife. The hands and rose disappeared into the bushes.

"No!" Mrs. Mathison shouted as she stamped her foot. "You come out of there right now, young man. If you don't, I'm going to drown you with my hose before I call your mother."

Hank was so startled he dropped his pocketknife. He wanted to run but was terrified of the old woman. It was rumored at school she was a witch who practiced black magic at night. Some kids said they had heard moaning and cackling noises coming from her house and strange lights in the darkness. Hank didn't want to be turned into a toad or drowned, so he covered his face with his cap and pushed his way through the branches.

"I know who you are, so put the cap down this very instant. If you don't, I will drench you. Do you hear me, Hank Walker?"

Hank widened his eyes in terror. It must be true. How else could she know his name? No kid had ever seen her face, only her shadow through the windows. He wasn't going to look into her eyes for fear of her witch's powers. "Look at the ground. Look at the ground," he told himself out loud as he lowered his cap.

"Why in the world did you cut my rose?" Mrs. Mathison asked. "And look at me when I talk to you."

This is it. I'm a dead man—or a toad. He looked up at what could have been a very sweet-looking grandma with a furious face. Fortunately, he did not turn into an amphibious creature.

"I—I—uh," Hank stammered and swallowed. "I wanted to give the rose to Betsy when I asked her to be my girl-friend." The words gushed out of his mouth as he exhaled. He'd been holding his breath. "I'm sorry. I'm so sorry. Please believe me, Mrs. Mathison. It won't happen again. I prom-ise." He pleaded like his life depended on it, which it very well might have.

"You're darn right it won't happen again. I'm calling your mother right now. You follow me, young man." The furious old woman turned and grumbled to herself as she marched toward the house and up the porch stairs.

Hank had already angered the woman enough. At this point, he was more afraid of not doing as she said. And he was really glad it was daytime and not night.

Without words, she pointed to a chair on the porch. Hank stepped on the middle stair and jumped when it squeaked. He had never been so afraid. She went inside to talk to his mother. He looked at the red rose and shook his head. Hank looked up, glancing across the street. Mr. and Mrs. Adams were standing in front of their living-room window, grinning. It all made sense. The town was full of spies.

In the end, he was allowed to keep his life in human form, but he would have to pull weeds every Saturday for a month as penance. Also, he was to write an apology to Mrs. Mathison that included the reason for his crime and how poor decisions and consequences affect your life. The letter was to be no less than five hundred words, in legible cursive. He almost wished the old woman had cast a spell on him instead.

Hank's mom came to pick him up, and she also apologized for her son's misdeeds.

"What were you thinking, Hank?" she said when they got in the car.

"It's all ruined now. All I wanted was a rose for Betsy because you're always so happy when Dad gives you flowers." Hank's eyes brimmed with tears, and he lowered his voice to a whisper.

"I was going to ask her to be my girlfriend." His face flushed, and he turned to look out of the window, only to see Mrs. Mathison glaring back at him. He dropped his face into his hands and shook his head.

"Well, a very nice thought," his mom said in a stern tone, "but poorly executed. Next time, talk to me first and we'll see what we can do to save you from a life of crime. Okay?" As the corners of her mouth curled up, she looked over her left shoulder. "When we get home, you need to tell your father what you did."

"Oh man, now I wish I was a toad," Hank mumbled under his breath.

"What, Hank? A toad?"

"Sorry, Mom. Nothing. Okay, I'll tell Dad." He exhaled, resigned to his fate.

Fortunately for Hank, his dad was not terribly upset. He had already been forewarned by his wife about his son's indiscretions. Hank was sent to his room for the rest of the day, and there was still the matter of his punishment to be performed.

Later that evening in private, his parents had a good laugh at his expense. And in the darkness that night, Mrs. Mathison could've been heard humming as she tended her garden. She was relieved the boy hadn't damaged any of her special hybrid flowers, which were certain to be the blue ribbon winners that year.

The next day, Hank's mom handed him the stolen rose, which she had put in water and tucked away in the refrigerator.

"Here, Hank," she said. "There's no sense in wasting a perfectly beautiful rose. Now go do what you had intended and make Betsy a happy young lady. I hope it all goes well. Mind your manners and please don't get into any more trouble."

In all the ruckus he'd caused, Hank forgot about the rose. He left it on the chair at Mrs. Mathison's house. But how did it get home?

"I don't understand. How'd you—"

His mom smiled and kissed his forehead. "It's magic, son." She patted his cheek. "Now I want you home no later than noon, okay?"

"Yes, ma'am," he said. Before he walked out of the door, he turned. "I love you, Mom."

"I love you, too, son."

CHAPTER FOUR

"I remember how nervous you were as you stood there on my front porch with that rose," Betsy said, smiling.

"And I remember how much I wanted you to be my girl-friend. Even at that young age, I knew you were the one." His face exploded into a crooked grin. "Besides, I'd battled the powers of darkness to get that rose."

They both laughed at the thought of children's fantasies and rumors of witches.

"Okay, now it's your turn, honey." He pushed the box closer to his wife. "No peeking, Betsy," he said in a playful voice.

She pouted as she reached into the box and felt for something specific. Betsy searched carefully until she found what she wanted. Her face lit up as she pulled out two movie tickets.

"I had a feeling you'd find those," Hank said and grinned. He reached out and gave her a hug and a quick kiss.

"Back by special demand." She laughed and held up the decades-old passes. "My mom couldn't believe that at fifteen years old we actually went to see a black-and-white movie. She said we were old souls for appreciating the classic films."

"They always had such great story lines. It was just a different era in moviemaking. I think Casablanca will always be at the top of the list." He spoke as if to convince his wife.

"You have always been a romantic. And I believe, sir, that was our first kiss if my memory serves me well." She gave her husband a coy smile. "A very memorable night for more than just Bogart and Bergman." Hank slapped the bed as his laughter filled the room. "You're my best medicine, Betsy."

"After all these years, I still marvel at how patient and restrained you were. Always the ultimate gentleman." She shook her head. "I told Mom I didn't think you were ever going to kiss me." She scowled for a second, then grinned.

"Well, Mama said I should mind my manners, so I took her seriously. Besides, I asked her one day how she knew my dad was the one for her. She told me he was patient, kind, and never made her feel less than respected. So I waited because I wanted you to see me like that." He paused and his voice struck a serious note. "I wanted you to know you meant more to me than anything in the world and I would never hurt you. That takes time. And when I asked her how she knew it was love, Mama said, 'When your heart, head, and God agree.' It took a while for me to understand her words, but one day I just knew I wanted you in my life forever."

Betsy sat with tears in her eyes as she looked at him. "And that is why you've had my love and my heart all these years." She held his hand and kissed him. Then she sat back and laughed. "I just wished you'd kissed me sooner. Estelle and all of our friends had already been kissed. They used to tease me, and they were a merciless bunch."

"I remember that night like it was yesterday," he said. "After we crossed the street from the theater, I knew it was the right time. It was then or never."

"It was a warm evening, and the breeze was filled with the scent of lilacs. We held hands while we walked, then you stopped and turned to me."

He took her hand. "I wasn't nervous at all when I asked if I could kiss you. I remember how you blushed and didn't say a word. You just nodded." He grinned.

"I had waited so long for that moment I was speechless when it finally happened. You lifted my chin up and spoke those immortal words—"

"Here's looking at you, kid," they both said in their best Bogart voices and laughed.

"It was the sweetest kiss," she said. "I felt as though I really would swoon, but I put my arms around your neck as I kissed you back. It was so incredibly romantic. Every young girl's dream. I'd waited a long time, but it was worth it." She grinned and waved her hand in front of her face, giving an enormous sigh.

They both laughed and looked at the tickets. "This is still my favorite movie ever," he said in a reverent voice.

"Mine, too. And that's why we've watched it year after year. It's fun to celebrate our anniversary with Sam and Ilsa. Theirs was one of the greatest romances of all time, right?" She paused. "I wonder if anyone else has done that?" She laid back on the pillow and snuggled next to Hank. "You seem to be feeling better now, honey. Do you want to continue this downstairs?"

"Yeah, I'd like to greet Andy and Ben when they get here. Besides, the recliner is comfortable, and maybe we can sit by the fire after dinner. I've got a bit of a chill. I'm not sure what last night's temperature was, but there's still lots of snow on top of the mountain." He pulled his wife closer to him.

Betsy reached her arm over his chest to give him more of her body heat. "Is that better, my sweet husband?" She looked up at his smiling face.

"Yup. All better." They stayed snuggled for a while and rested in the synchrony of their breathing. They each had a contented smile, which spoke of the many years of their love and the many miles in their lives together.

A bit later, Hank got up in a slow, deliberate movement.

"Do you need me to get something for you?" Betsy sat upright and waited as she watched him.

"Nope. Well, yes," he said as he walked across the bedroom. In the far corner by the love seat was an old record player. He put a well-used vinyl on the turntable and carefully set the needle to an exact spot. There was a slight crackling noise before the song began. He turned toward Betsy and spread out his arms. "May I please have this dance, my lovely lady?"

"Why certainly," she said as she walked into his waiting arms.

In a familiar embrace, they hummed and swayed to the sweet strains of the melody. The song had become their anthem as the years went on. As it ended, they kissed. And as if on cue from deep within their souls, they whispered to each other, "We must remember this always."

CHAPTER FIVE

Hank sat nearby with Lady in attendance as Betsy tended to dinner preparations.

"Mmm... that smells heavenly." He pointed his nose up as he inhaled the savory aroma. The dog also had her nose in the air.

Betsy laughed. Hank opened his eyes and realized what had amused her. "I guess you have two hungry admirers." Their furry friend had crept just a tad closer to the stove.

"Okay, Lady, don't crowd the cook." He patted his leg. The dog hesitated a second longer to breathe in a little more of the intoxicating air before she returned to his side. She wagged her tail and laid her head on his knee. He stared down at her big brown eyes. "I love you, too." He rested his hand on her soft head, and she sat as she swished her tail across the floor.

"A woman could almost be jealous, you know," Betsy said.

"You're my first love. Doesn't that count?" he shot back as he grinned. "So my sweet, what's on the menu tonight?"

"Something easy, but delicious. It's a new recipe with a

Mediterranean flair, a chicken-and-rice casserole. I got the recipe from Estelle the last time we had lunch together. I know you'll enjoy it. Oh, and I told Ben he'd be eating with us."

"That sounds great, and I'm glad you invited him to stay. It's the least we can do for his shuttle services. He's been such a good friend all these years." He thought for a moment and shook his head with a roguish expression. "I don't think I've told you half of the mischief we've gotten into."

"And I'm sure I probably don't want to know, either," she said with a snicker. "I'm not sure about the statute of limitations, but I certainly wouldn't want to be considered an accomplice, and neither would Estelle."

He laughed. "Heck, he's the sheriff. I don't think he'll be arresting any of us soon. Besides, by now I'm sure old man Potter has forgiven us for putting his cow in the school gymnasium." He slapped his leg as he laughed again and Lady jumped to her feet from a sound sleep. "Sorry, girl. It's okay. I didn't mean to startle you." He patted her side, and she relaxed as she lay down. Soon her feet twitched as she chased squirrels and rabbits in her sleep.

"How's Estelle doing, honey?" he asked as Betsy made magic with the food. "I've missed seeing her. Where's she been?"

"Oh, she's fine, but busy with inventory and a couple of buying trips. Last week she was on the East Coast hunting for specific antiques. There are quite a few clients now from the big cities she caters to. They tell her what they want and pay good money for it, never quibbling about the price." Betsy nodded with a look of pride. "She's done a good job of building up her business and reputation. I'm thrilled for her."

"Do you think she'll ever move? I mean, since it sounds like maybe a chunk of her revenue is coming in now from the cities."

"Nope. She's a Parsons girl through and through, just like me. Besides, we're a packaged deal. There's no separating us, you know that," she teased and winked. "Once twins, always twins. And these twins will never leave this mountain."

He laughed at his wife's joke. "Yeah, there's no denying that. You two have always been double trouble. Everyone in school knew not to get in your crosshairs," he said with a grin. "Even though Ben and I towered over both of you, we were mostly terrified a good part of the time." He ducked his head and laughed as she tossed the dish towel at him.

"Oh stop, we weren't that bad." She grinned at him. "We just played a wicked game of good cop, bad cop. And it worked out well for us. I even seem to remember a time we rescued a couple of boys in the school hallway."

"Hey, we could've taken care of that ourselves," he protested as he winked at her.

As Estelle and Betsy walked down the hallway to their next class, loud voices came from around the corner. They stopped to listen and assess the situation.

"So what is this," a mocking voice said, "a giraffe convention?" Several other voices laughed and chimed in with more insults and mockery.

"Hey, please just get out of the way so we can get to class before the bell rings," another voice said.

The girls whispered to each other about the identities of the voices they'd heard. Their faces almost matched the color of their auburn hair. They rarely got mad, but this was an exception. The twins took their positions and jumped around the corner at the same time. With their hands on their hips, their eyes squinted, and their lips tight, they looked formidable—in stereo.

"And just who do you think you are, all of you?" Estelle said in a low growl as she looked each of the four bullies in the eye. "What, cat got your tongue, you weasels?"

"Let's not hurt them on school property, Estelle," Betsy reminded her, "or we'll get in big trouble." She held her sister's arm as if to keep her from lunging at the wide-eyed, frightened boys.

"Well, they need to be taught a lesson. And we're the ones who can do it. Right, boys?" Estelle sneered as she glared again at each of the bullies.

"I'll tell you what," Betsy said, as the negotiator. "We'll meet you guys across the street, on the other side of the park, after the last bell rings. You can show us then how tough you are while we school you in better manners." She took a step toward the mouthy boys.

"Or maybe you'd just like to apologize to Hank and Ben for being such jerks." Estelle narrowed her eyes as she spoke. "Did you all forget about what the principal said at the last school assembly? You know, the part about not bullying. Or you just decided not to remember, Matthew? You and your sniveling minions need to find another hobby." As she leaned toward the pack, they reacted by leaning back in unison, their feet glued to the gray linoleum.

"Okay, yeah, sure. Sorry," said the pack leader to his intended victims. "No harm, no foul. Come on, guys." But the other three boys had already backed away and turned to run. "Hey, wait for me," the ringleader cried as he scurried off.

"You'd better run, Matthew. I'll be talking to your mom this evening," Betsy yelled after them. The girls broke out in hysterical laughter. Meanwhile, Hank and Ben stood speechless and somewhat terrified.

"Oh, that was worth it. And I bet they'll never admit to this having happened." Estelle doubled over with laughter. "This could come in handy later."

"That was the best, Estelle. You've really perfected that bad cop skill."

The girls looked at each other and laughed all over again, oblivious to the puzzled looks on the victims' faces. They were startled out of their reverie as the bell rang.

"Hey, we'll see you boys after school. Come on, Elizabeth." Estelle pulled at her sister's sleeve and they hurried away.

"Yeah, okay," Hank said as the girls ran off.

"What just happened?" Ben's eyes were glued to the girls' backs.

"I'm not sure." Hank shrugged. "But we'll have to wait a couple of hours to find out. I think we were just rescued by two cute girls much shorter than us, but cute just the same." He laughed and gave Ben a quick slap on his back. "Yeah, I hadn't told you yet about the twins. Best advice—don't cross them. I swear they can read each other's minds. They are double trouble with red hair. Let's go."

CHAPTER SIX

Hank and Betsy laughed as they remembered how she and her twin sister had saved Hank and Ben from the hallway bullies.

"You know, to this day, if Matthew is walking toward me in public, he'll avoid me and won't make eye contact," she said as she grinned. "And I didn't even talk to his mom that day."

"Well, you two had a pretty fierce presence when you needed it," he said. "That was only Ben's second day at our school, so he was really confused. I'd just told him I was happy there was another tall kid in school when the bully gang showed up." He grinned and widened his eyes. "Then the dynamic duo appeared like superheroes." They both laughed.

"Well, you know what they say. You never get a second chance at a first impression."

"We still laugh about it to this day. I think he was more traumatized by Estelle than anything." Hank grinned at her. "Later that day, I showed him the two karate trophies you girls won at the state tournament. That helped him understand why Matthew and his gang were in such a hurry to get to class."

Just then, Lady jumped up and ran to the door. She barked once and wagged her bushy tail as she waited for a response from her people.

"That must be Ben and Andy." Betsy's eyes sparkled as she gave Hank a quick kiss on the cheek as she passed by on her way to the door. "You stay here, honey. We'll all come join you in the kitchen, okay?"

"Aye, aye, Captain." His wife weaved her way around the chairs and into the living room. "You have the grace of a dancer, my love." He put his elbows on the table and rested his chin on his folded hands.

"Thank you, God, for this time with my loved ones," he breathed. He looked out the window at the cloudless blue sky and the trees swaying in the cool breeze. He gazed upward at the snow-covered mountaintops. "And thank you for this glorious day."

Snow still lay in patches under the window in the shade. But where the sun shined, the green sword-shaped iris leaves pushed their way through the warm, damp earth. Spring was on its way and once again the mountain would be clothed in purple flowers—and hope.

Several hundred heartbeats later, Hank looked toward the door. Lady barked and then came the sound of Ben's truck, followed by voices and footsteps on the porch. As he stood to greet his son and his best friend, the front door opened.

"Hey, Dad, where are you?" Andy said as he walked toward the kitchen.

"In here, Andy." Before he could take a step toward his

son's voice, he was already in front of him. He reached out, and the two stood in a long-awaited hug. Lady bumped their legs with her nose and waited for her turn as she furiously wagged her tail.

"I got here as fast as I could, Dad," he said as he clung to his father, who had taught him how to be a man.

"I know, son. You're here now and that's all that matters." He clapped his hand on Andy's back a couple of times. "You know I love you, right?"

"Absolutely," Andy said with a big grin. "And I love you right back." They shared a familiar, crooked smile.

"Let me look at you, boy." He held his son out by the shoulders and gave him a solid inspection from head to toe. "I swear each time you come home, you've grown, and now you're an inch taller than me."

Andy grinned and patted the top of his father's head. Betsy and Ben walked in at that moment and laughed as Lady bounced around the table.

"Hmm, seems your little boy's not so little anymore," Ben said, grinning. "Military life must agree with you. At least the meals do."

The men continued to laugh as they pulled out dining chairs, but before they sat down, Betsy interrupted.

"Dinner will be ready in about ten minutes, so maybe you should all go wash up. Hank, do you want to sit at the table?" Her brow furrowed slightly.

"Sure, I'm feeling pretty good tonight. But maybe we can take dessert into the living room later by the fireplace. That would be nice."

"Of course, honey. I'm glad you feel up to it. And by the way, dessert will be a rerun," she said with a wink. "More chocolate chip cookies."

Hank grinned. "It's at the top of my favorite-foods list."

CHAPTER SEVEN

"Mmm, this is so delicious, Mom," Andy said as he took another bite of the chicken casserole.

"I second the motion." Ben scooped up a forkful of the tender rice and smacked his lips.

"Yes, please let Estelle know the men in this family wholeheartedly approve of her recipe," Hank said as he reached for another bite. Lady popped her head up from underneath the table as she sniffed the air. "I think even Lady agrees." When no one offered to share, she lay back down with a sigh.

"Well, she'll be happy to know you've enjoyed it," Betsy replied with a curious smile and an arched eyebrow. "I think there's a story here. She got it from a small restaurant in New York she visited recently. She sent her compliments to the chef via the waiter and was shocked when he came out to thank her personally."

"He must have really liked her—enough to give away his recipe," Andy said with a wink.

"She did mention he was very handsome. I'll be interested to see if this develops into anything. Hmm..." She tilted her head and tapped her finger on the table.

"I was just about to ask you how Aunt Estelle was doing these days. Obviously, she's doing well." Andy grinned in between bites.

"Actually, I was glad to hear her speak about him. She rarely remarks about any of the men she's met. I hope this is someone she can allow into her life, or into her heart," she said.

"Why is it she's never married?" Andy leaned forward.

"When her fiancé died in a car accident, that part of her heart kind of shut down. It really broke her spirit, so she turned to her work. She went to Europe for a couple of years to study antiquities and heal. When she came back to help care for your grandparents, that's when she opened her antique store."

Betsy glanced at her husband. "I just told your dad she's built an impressive clientele over the years, and quite of few of them have deep pockets. All in all, she seems happy and has a lot of friends in Parsons and across the globe as well. She enjoys traveling and helping with the different causes in town. Her shop is quaint, but don't let that fool you. Your aunt is an expert in what she does, and now she gets to reap the benefits. I just wish she had someone special to love."

"Well, she deserves to be happy," Ben said. "She's always been a good friend to me and was an occasional accomplice in our younger days." He chuckled.

"Oh, those were the days, weren't they?" Hank grinned and shook his head. "We were all quite the rascals and pranksters in town."

"Yes, but it was good fun. Embarrassing maybe, but not hurtful. I just want that clear," Betsy added with a smirk.

Hank reached across the table and patted Andy's hand.

"You look good, Andy. On a more serious note, are we winning?"

"This is a difficult war, Dad. I'm not sure we aren't losing just as many battles as we win. But it's not my call. I do the best I can to keep my men safe." He sighed, and his smile returned. "But right now, right here, it's really good to be off the field. I plan on sleeping a lot the next few weeks, when I'm not spending time with you and Mom, of course." His face relaxed.

They finished their meal and pushed back their chairs as they talked. "Hey, let's take this conversation into the living room and get more relaxed," Betsy said. "Andy, will you please build a fire for us?"

"Sure, Mom. After I do that, I'll come help with the cleanup. After all, you cooked the amazing dinner." He stood and gave her a quick hug.

"That was a terrific dinner, Bets. Thanks for the invite." Ben's words expressed his gratitude, and his eyes showed his affection.

"You're certainly welcome, Sheriff. Hank, I think your recliner is waiting for you. Ben, you can help clear the table, right?" She nodded and looked at him.

"You got it." He already had an armload of dishes and was headed to the sink. He noticed

the large wooden box and smiled in recognition as he passed by.

"Is it just me, or has she gotten bossy in her old age?" Hank said as he winked at Ben.

"I'd be careful about any 'old' comments if I were you." Ben darted his eyes toward Betsy, amused by his humor and always ready to instigate a ruckus.

"Yes, you best watch what you say to a woman who knows where all the sharp knives are, mister." She laughed as she scrunched up her face and glared at her husband.

"Hey, did you hear her just threaten me, Sheriff?" he said in mock fear. "Aren't you

going to arrest her or something?"

"Nope. I didn't hear or see anything. Don't know what you're talking about, Hank." Ben whistled as he continued to the sink.

"Hey, whose side are you on?" Hank said.

"I'm on the side with the dessert, buddy." They all roared with laughter, especially Betsy.

"Traitor." Hank grinned at his lifelong friend. And with that, he retired to the living room and Lady jumped up to provide him an escort. Andy had just lit the kindling. Lady ran over and kissed his cheek before she took her place beside the one who needed her most.

"It should be good in a few minutes, Dad. I'll come back in and add some more wood."

"Thanks, son. I'll keep an eye on it." Hank took a deep breath and sighed as he leaned back in the chair. "It's sure good to see you, boy."

"Same here. It's been too long." There was a tinge of sadness in his voice.

"Well, you're here now and that's all that counts." He smiled at his son as he stroked the soft fur on Lady's ear.

"Is there anything you need before I help Mom in the kitchen?"

"Yeah, send that Benedict Arnold in here to keep me company. And maybe I'll have my trusted companion here bite him." He made a disgruntled face that made them laugh.

As Ben left the kitchen, he noticed the wooden box again and smiled.

CHAPTER EIGHT

"Thanks for lighting the fire, Andy," Betsy said as she rubbed her son's shoulder. "Your dad seems to get chilled pretty often these days. Although it's warmer during the day now, it's still cold at night and he's lost some weight. I'm sure that contributes to it." Her face showed her concern as she turned to put the leftovers into smaller containers. "We'll use the dishwasher tonight, honey. So you can load it for me, please."

"Sure, Mom." He picked up a plate as he spoke. "I noticed he was thinner. What's the latest from the doctor and when's the surgery?" He stopped for a moment to look at his mom.

"There was a cancellation in the doctor's schedule. Surgery has been moved up a week earlier—it's in four days." She sighed, worried. "Dr. Chandler said if all goes well, that should buy your dad more time. He's not sure how much, but we're just praying it goes well." Her shoulders sagged as she exhaled. She wanted to always be strong, but that strength eluded her.

Andy set the plate down when he saw her fight back the

tears. He wrapped his arms around her as he whispered, "I'll always be here for you, Mom." He rubbed and patted her back. "I'm praying, too. Dad's a tough guy and I know he's not ready to give up." When she lifted her head, he released her. He stepped back with a tender smile. "Who'd want to leave all this?" He spread his arms wide and waved them in a slow semi-circle. "Besides, he has you to take care of him." She looked up with an appreciative smile.

"Thank you, honey." She wiped her eyes and put on a brave front again. "Now let's get this cleaned up so we can get back to some fun conversation and dessert. It's not good to leave those two alone for very long. They're always thinking of ways to get in trouble—despite one of them being the sheriff," she said with a snicker.

"Yeah, from the stories I've heard, they have a way of getting into a lot of mischief. And they're pretty creative with their pranks."

"I'll have to remind them how Estelle and I got back at them once—you'll enjoy the story." She dried her hands. "I'm going to go ask them if they want coffee with their dessert."

While Betsy and Andy took care of the kitchen cleanup, Hank and Ben had their own conversation by the fireplace. Lady was asleep by the chair, her paws twitching as she dreamed of chasing squirrels and running through tall grass.

"How are you feeling, Hank?" Ben said, leaning forward.

"Well, Ben, I'll tell you—I have good days and then I have better days." He shrugged with a slight smile. "The doctor says my operation should buy me some more time and improve my quality of life. So that's what I'm placing my bet on. Dr. Chandler comes highly recommended. He's certainly thorough and a nice guy. "Let's just say he's young enough to be knowledgeable on the latest medical research and techniques, but old enough that he hasn't had a paper route in a couple of decades."

Both men laughed at the imagery. "That's reassuring. But is there anything that you need me to do for you?" Ben asked. "You just need to call me, okay?" His words were heartfelt.

"Yes, I know that. Thanks. You'll be the first I call if I need help. Betsy always seems to have everything under control, and with Andy here for a while, he can do any heavy lifting or run errands for his mom." He frowned. "She didn't take any bed-and-breakfast reservations this year because of me. That kinda breaks my heart because she loves sharing this house with her guests. It's what she's always wanted to do. And oh, how she loves telling stories about this mountain. I knew I had to build this for her—to make her dream come true. You know, I thank God every day for that woman." He gazed out of the window. "She's a pillar of strength." He paused and smiled. "With the mind of a comedian. Not a day goes by that she doesn't make me laugh, no matter how hard it gets."

"Yeah, she's an excellent remedy, no doubt." The corners of Ben's mouth curled up into a huge grin. "But I wouldn't want to be on the wrong side of her, especially if Estelle joined in." The men got a good chuckle from that, along with memories to prove the point.

"Did I hear my sister's name mentioned?" Betsy said as she walked into the room. Both men turned toward her, faces frozen and wide-eyed.

With a sheepish grin, Ben said, "I swear, woman, nothing gets past you, does it?"

"Nothing sinister going on here, I promise." Hank grinned and held his hands up as if in surrender.

"I knew you two would be up to no good," she said, pretending to scold them. "So tell me, what dastardly deed have you devised, Sheriff Ben?"

Hank snickered at her words and the look of guilt on his friend's face.

"First time I've ever seen you speechless, Ben. You may as well confess," he said, highly amused by his wife's accusation and his friend's reaction.

"You're not helping," Ben complained. "I just told your husband I'd never want to be on your bad side—or Estelle's. You two are a force of nature." He slowly shook his head and glared at his friend.

"And don't you forget it." Betsy placed her hands on her hips to emphasize the suggestion. "I may be small, but I'm determined. You're just lucky Estelle's out of town or she'd be here, too."

The good-natured banter made them laugh as they harassed each other. They'd been friends as long as they could remember and shared all their good times and not-so-good times. That's what forged such a strong bond among them—they had laughed and cried together for decades. Through the years, from childhood to adults, their respect, trust, and love for one another had also grown. No truer friends could be found.

Betsy needed the release the lighthearted revelry brought. It was medicine for her soul. "Okay, now that we're straight on who's boss," she said as she winked at Hank. "Who wants coffee with their dessert?"

Both men nodded and grinned. "You need some help?" Ben offered, perhaps hoping to speed things along.

"Thanks, but Andy's riding shotgun for me tonight. We'll be back in a few minutes." Her countenance glowed with the warmth and love that surrounded her. Only one thing could improve her life. She sighed as she walked to the kitchen.

CHAPTER NINE

"I'll take the dishes to the kitchen, Mom," Andy said as he stood and gathered the dessert plates. "Sip your tea and enjoy the company. I'll be back in a flash to hear more stories about the terror your gang wrought in the community." He laughed as he walked to the kitchen to deposit the last remnants of dinner.

"Hey, we weren't that bad, young man," Ben called with a huge grin and a mischievous look in his eyes. He turned to his lifelong friends. "We had some fun times, though, didn't we?" He shook his head and rolled his eyes. "And the kids around here wonder how I know what they're up to."

"Does anyone want more coffee?" Andy called from the kitchen. "And don't make me feel like I'm missing something really interesting in there."

"No, we're all good. Thanks," his dad said. With a loving smile, he turned to his wife. "You did a fine job teaching our boy some manners."

"I think we all helped with that. You two showed him what real men are, and I'm grateful to you. It wouldn't have been easy for a mother to teach him those things. I think he got a pretty well-rounded education and good examples from all of us, including his Aunt Estelle. I couldn't be any prouder of him." Her face was flushed with pride.

Andy came back into the living room, and as he sat near the fireplace, Lady jumped up and nudged his hands with her wet nose. He stroked her head and looked into her eyes as she wagged her tail and licked his hand. He smiled and scratched behind her ear, looking at his family with a grin. "Did I miss anything? I'm taking notes, you know, to be used as blackmail later. So leave nothing out." He had an evil smile as he shook his head. "I can't believe that after all these years, I'm still hearing stories for the first time."

"That's the joy of getting together—our collective memory. The older we get, the more we depend on the others to remember details," his dad said as he laughed. "It's funny how facts change with age."

"We all remember events just a little differently," Betsy said in a slow, emphatic manner. She nudged Hank with her elbow and gave him a sideways look.

Ben laughed so hard he got the hiccups and laughed even more. He held up his finger as he held his breath. He finally spoke. "She's got a point. It's best not to argue any details with her. We know women have better long-term memories than men."

"I'll second that." Andy grinned from ear to ear. "Mom probably knows what she fixed for dinner twenty years ago."

"Roast beef and baby carrots," Betsy said without missing a beat. "With a fresh loaf of bread, salad, and strawberry pie for dessert. And I think you had a scoop of ice cream with your pie, Andy." The men howled with laughter. She grinned like the Cheshire Cat, an expression perfected just for such occasions. She and Estelle had often used the look when they dealt with their male friends, Hank and Ben in particular.

"Okay, you win, Mom. I surrender. I don't doubt for a minute that could actually be true."

He knew from his childhood that his mother had a keen memory for details. That attribute helped keep him from making poor judgments while growing up. He appreciated the importance of just how much his parents had influenced his decision-making abilities. There was never a time when he'd chosen poorly that his parents made him feel unloved, but they allowed him to learn from the experience. They had taught him a basic law of physics—for each action, there is an equal and opposite reaction. In "kid speak," for every decision he made, there would be consequences, hopefully good, but sometimes unintended, and it was at those times he felt their support. This is what his mom and dad referred to as life experience. He had learned early on to weigh all the options.

"Hey, so tell me, Mom, did you and Aunt Estelle ever prank these guys?" Andy said with a huge grin and eager eyes. "I've heard some stories about how they tormented you girls."

"We certainly did. Your dad and our esteemed sheriff here were fond of constantly making us girls scream. It seemed to be their delight and mission in life to startle us. They'd pop up out of nowhere and catch us off guard. One day, Estelle and I decided it was time to give them a taste of their own medicine. We knew they'd planned a two-day fishing trip with their dads. So we—"

"I can't believe you girls got our dads to go along with it," Hank interrupted, seemingly still indignant decades later as he wrinkled his forehead.

Ben shook his head. "Just goes to show how persuasive

the female species can be." He leaned forward, his eyes wide in anticipation of the story. He bounced his foot as he waited.

Betsy winked at Andy and continued. "So your Aunt Estelle and I explained to the aforementioned dads just how much their sons had terrorized us over the years." She stopped and inhaled deeply. "Of course, we may have exaggerated our distress a bit, but these boys needed to be taught a lesson. A girl can only stand so many fake spiders, snakes, and rats in their lockers, gym bags, and such. Not to mention all the times they jumped out from behind the bushes. No amount of pleading on our part seemed to discourage them from their so-called fun."

Betsy shook her head as she clucked her tongue and darted her eyes from Hank to Ben. "So upon recruiting adult help, an elaborate scheme was devised that we hoped would scare the dickens out of them. In fact, their moms even offered to assist." A slow, devious smile crossed her lips. The men stared intently as they listened to her words, the tension growing. As they leaned in, Hank and Ben waited to relive their shared childhoods again. This memory had only gained more traction through the years and was a source of great embellishment by all.

Betsy waited for a moment, as all talented storytellers do, before she spoke. Her voice dropped low in dramatic fashion. "We agreed, including the parents, that this would be a life-altering event." Her voice was barely audible. Then she grinned. "Not to mention it was going to be fun." She gave a quick wink and nod to Andy.

"Not so much fun for us," the older men said almost in unison and with perhaps yet a tinge of a grudge.

"Well, you both deserved it, according to all six of us. It was unanimous," she emphasized her words. "It seems both your mothers had come across quite a few inanimate creatures strategically placed to elicit their screams. Wherein you boys were immediately scolded. But that didn't dissuade you, did it?" She smirked at the now-grown boys. "Now then, where was I? Oh, yes, it was time to plan."

She glanced at Hank. "It was your father who came up with the first inspiration. He'd lain the groundwork in your minds with a story about four miners long ago who went missing near the camping area. Rumor had it only two bodies had been found near a mine decades later, just after the snowmelt. One skeleton still clutched a gun in his bony fingers. It was suspected that the other two miners had stolen all their gold and left the two men to die from wounds they'd suffered in a struggle. The hunters who found the remains felt it best to bury the bones where they lay." Betsy stretched and leaned back in her chair.

"I can't believe Dad told that story with such a straight face," Hank said as he shook his head. "He waited until Ben came over for supper a couple of days before we went camping. He also made certain he told us no one had been brought to justice for those murders."

"And don't forget he said that strange things had been seen at night near the lake—ghostly images," Ben added. "I remember feeling that maybe we should go camp somewhere else, or not at all." Even after all the years that had passed, the memory still seemed to stir up a trace of anxiety in his voice. He squinted as he grimaced.

Betsy fell forward as she laughed. "Your dad said both of you sat motionless at the dinner table with eyes as wide as the plates in front of you." She looked again at her son and continued. "Your grandfather told them it was just some silly old wives' tale, but added in his most bloodcurdling voice that folks said tortured souls that can't rest will haunt the place of their demise."

Hank snorted. "I was pretty sure by that time I wished we wouldn't go at all."

"Me, too. I couldn't stop thinking about the dead miners—and ghosts. I ran all the way home from your house that night." Ben shivered.

"Why, Sheriff Murphy, you look like you've seen the bogeyman," Betsy taunted as she reached over and slapped him on the shoulder.

"I'm telling you I suffered some PTSD from that story and a moonless night," he said in his defense. "But it certainly made me swear off scaring people." He scowled. It was apparent he wasn't exactly joking.

Betsy continued to speak with a glint in her eyes and a devilish grin.

CHAPTER TEN

"Hello? Oh, hi, Mary. Is Ben ready to go camping today? Uh-huh. Oh, yes. I'm sure they'll have a great time. What? No, I've heard nothing about that. Don't be silly. Of course there aren't wolves in that area."

Hank's mom was talking and laughing on the phone with Ben's mom when he brought his gear downstairs. She smiled at him and pointed to the back door. He nodded and stepped outside in the cool, early morning, his dad in the driveway.

"Good morning, Dad. I have all my things in this duffel bag, including the flashlight, like you said."

"Hey, son, that's great. Wanna give me a hand loading this equipment?" Mr. Walker said as he grabbed a tackle box.

"Sure." He reached for the sleeping bags and handed them to his dad. "Dad, are there any wolves where we're going?" he asked, worried.

"Not that I've ever heard of. Why?" He stopped and looked at his son.

"Oh, no reason. Just curious. What time are we leaving?

Maybe I should call Ben to make sure he's ready when we stop to pick him up."

Mrs. Walker stepped out of the screen door with a paper bag in her hand. "I just spoke with Mary. She said Ben was up and ready to go as soon as he's finished with breakfast. Oh, and here are some sandwiches in case you boys get hungry while on the road." She stretched out her arm from the top stair and dangled the bag.

"Okay, that's good to hear. Thanks, honey. I'm sure we'll need those after we unload and set up the tents. The plan is to get camp secured before we go fishing. We shouldn't be driving for long. I'm pretty sure I know where to go. I haven't been there before, but I hear it's a great place to camp." While his son's back was turned, he gave his wife a big grin and a wink.

Hank spun around, his expression contorted. "You've never been there before?" His voice cracked.

"Nope, but the guys at Drake's Hardware said the fish were biting big time and usually no one else was camping there this early in the year. So we'll have the place to ourselves." He laughed and patted Hank's shoulder. "Nothing like being out in the wilderness all alone, huh?"

"I-I guess so," he stammered as his eyebrows knitted together. He was anxious.

"It'll be fine. We won't be that far from town if it rains us out or you boys catch your limits. There should be some terrific rainbow trout in that lake," his dad said, grinning.

"It'd be great for you boys to catch enough for at least a few dinners. I haven't had trout since the church cookout last summer. I'll be good and ready to eat some fish by the time you get back." Mrs. Walker nodded as she licked her lips and rubbed her belly. She winked at her husband as she laughed at herself.

"I'd say we better not come home empty-handed." Mr. Walker smirked at his wife. "Well, it looks like we're just about packed up here. Did Mary say if John was still

coming out later after he takes care of some business?"

"Yep, he'll be a couple of hours behind you. Mary said he's really looking forward to a boys' camp out. He's excited about going to a new lake and maybe he'll do some exploring in the woods, too."

"Well, I'd like another cup of coffee and to explore one of those donuts I saw you had hidden in the cabinet." He laughed and gave his wife a big hug. "You know better than to hide the sweets from me, honey. I've got a nose like a bloodhound. Come on, son, you can have a donut too before we leave." Even Hank laughed as they walked back into the house.

"I'll put some on a plate," his mom said, turning around to add, "after you wash your hands, that is."

"We never get away with it, do we?" Mr. Walker poked his son with his elbow. "I think your mom has eyes in the back of her head."

Hank grinned.

"I don't know how I did it, boys, but it seems I've taken a wrong turn. But that's okay, we're not in a hurry," said Mr. Walker. "Hey, let's stop up here and have some of those sandwiches your mom made."

"Wow, you got lost, Dad? That's the first time I've ever seen that happen." Hank looked at Ben and they both snickered.

"Good thing we're not on foot," he said, pulling the truck off the road and into a small clearing. "Grab some sandwiches and sodas, please. We can eat here and enjoy this sunshine. Hmm, I must have turned off the main road too soon. But we'll get there in plenty of time before your dad, Ben. We'll get camp set up first and then try to outwit some hungry fish." The boys nodded.

"Sounds good to me," Ben said just before he stuffed the corner of a sandwich in his mouth. "I'm just glad I don't have to mow the lawn this weekend." Both boys laughed.

"Hey, that's right—no chores," Hank said. They seemed pretty content to be in the woods and not at home. Mr. Walker grinned from ear to ear. The boys didn't notice his slight nod.

Three would-be campers soaked in the sun and enjoyed an early lunch. Unbeknownst to the boys, a small army of vigilantes prepared the idyllic lake setting for their visit. This would be an adventure like no other.

"Ah, this is the right place," Mr. Walker said. He turned the truck onto a gravel road. "Now I remember—Carl mentioned a tall pine tree, fire charred and split in half. Well, we still have plenty of daylight. We'll get set up first. Then we'll see how worthy our opponents in the lake will be. It should only take about thirty minutes to get there now."

"I'm really excited to try out the new fishing pole I got for Christmas," Ben said with a big smile. "I bet I catch the biggest rainbow."

"Nah, I'm going to," Hank said as he shoved his shoulder against his friend's.

"Wanna bet?" Ben pushed back.

"Sure. If I win, you mow our yard next weekend," Hank said, smirking.

"Same. You're on." Ben reached his hand out so they could shake on it. They grinned at each other, and Mr. Walker laughed and continued to smile.

A large lake came into view as the truck crested a small hill. The bright blue water was as smooth as glass and mirrored the billowy, pillow-like clouds above. There were no other campers or fishermen, and the area was void of any other living creatures. The tranquility belied what was to come later that night.

The boys cheered and expressed how good it would be to stretch their legs, immediately challenging each other to a rock-skipping contest.

"You two can do that right after camp is set up. Tents first," Mr. Walker said.

"Sure thing," the boys said simultaneously as they high-fived.

An hour later, just as the last of the tents, tarp, and all things from the back of the truck had been put in place, Mr. Murphy arrived.

Ben ran to meet his dad and helped him carry the fishing gear.

"Hey, John, glad you made it," Mr. Walker said as he patted him on the shoulder.

"Thanks, Andrew. Yeah, good to be here. A little late, but I got all my business taken care of," he said with a grin and a wink. "Looks like you boys have been busy here. I need to eat a bite, though, before I think about challenging any rainbows." The men laughed and sat down next to an ice chest.

"I have just the thing for you. Julie made some sandwiches for us. She knew we'd need strength to reel in all those big fish. Here you go," Mr. Murphy said and grinned as he handed the bag to John. "Hey, boys, you want more sandwiches?"

"No thanks," both boys shouted out as they ran for the water.

The men watched their sons as the boys picked up rocks, skipped them, and counted out loud. The boys teased each other about who had the most skips.

"So, we're all set then?" Hank's dad asked with a gleam in his eyes as he turned toward John.

"You bet. The girls will show up at ten tonight, park beside the high road, and walk down the trail to that stand of trees. It only takes about ten minutes. We tested it this morning before you left your house. It took us just over an hour to set up all the surprises. Estelle, Betsy, and our wives are beyond excited about this. I must admit it's going to be hilarious revenge and fascinatingly frightening." He grinned as he shook his head.

"I'm sure I wouldn't want to be on the wrong side of all those females. I've seen now how they think, and it's pretty scary." Mr. Murphy widened his eyes in mock terror just before the men burst out in laughter.

"I don't know about you boys, but I'm ready to crawl into my tent and dream about catching more fish tomorrow," Mr. Murphy said. He stood up and doused the campfire. "You two put a flashlight beside your sleeping bags in case you need to get up during the night."

"Okay, Dad," said Hank. "Let's hit the sack, Ben, and we can tell each other some scary stories." They grinned in agreement and ducked into their shared tent, falling asleep after a long while.

The two men smiled at each other—it would be show time soon.

"Good night, John. See you in the morning, bright and early."

"Good night, Andrew."

And with that, both men slipped into their tents. A while later, the whispers and laughter in the boys' tent died down. The boys were fast asleep, and the darkness fell silent.

Mr. Murphy crept away from his tent and into the tall pines. Mr. Walker reached for the recorder in his gear and tiptoed to the far side of the tents, away from the trees. He waited for several minutes before he pushed the button. A loud howl pierced the silence and startled the boys awake. Hank reached for his flashlight just as something scratched hard and loud on the side of their tent. Both boys yelped and recoiled from the sound.

"Whoa, what was that?" Hank whispered as he fumbled to find his flashlight.

The boys stared at each other. Another howl made them jump to their feet and crash into each other. Their eyes were enormous, and their faces were taut.

"Run, Hank! Run, Ben—hide in the trees!" One of their fathers screamed from somewhere on the lakeside.

Another howl flushed the boys from their tent and toward the forest. Hank struggled with his flashlight. It wouldn't turn on. In the dim moonlight, both boys ran for their lives as they followed the narrow, tangled path. They hadn't seen their fathers, but they hadn't stopped to look. Fear was etched on their faces as they ran through the shadows. Branches tore at their clothes and scraped their cheeks as they ran through the shadows.

The howling continued, and loud footsteps came from behind them. Soon after they had passed into the woods, a pair of glowing red eyes appeared from behind a tree about ten feet away in the dense growth.

"You took my gold," the eyes screamed. "I want my gold." The eyes came toward them and shrieked again. "You stole my gold!" The voice sounded deep and angry.

"Agh!" both boys yelled and ran even faster as they followed the path into the dark night and shadows.

Ben tripped, and a skeleton dropped from overhead.

"No," he cried as he rolled away from the bony remains. Hank reached down and grabbed him up as they raced on.

They ran farther and faster away from the demons. Hank looked over his shoulder. The red eyes were following them. Branches cracked and the thud of heavy footsteps was behind them.

"Run, Ben," Hank shouted as he pushed his fourteen-year-old breathless body to the limit. "Hurry."

As they rounded a curve, two weathered wooden crosses and two empty graves appeared. Bony hands clawed in the dirt as if to escape the dark holes. They gasped as a skull rolled down a freshly heaped mound of dank soil. But they didn't see the two trip lines.

As they both screamed at the horror in front of them, Hank was the first to fall. Two steps later, Ben went down. Their falls were unusually soft, even spongy. As the boys struggled to sit up, they realized the path was covered with snakes. They rolled off of the trail and away from the dreadful creatures, only to find themselves covered in spiderwebs. Panic ensued as they tried to escape their heinous dilemma.

"Agh!" they yelled. Any shade of color vanished from their faces. The boys flailed their hands and arms to rid themselves of the evil, loathsome webs.

Their obvious fright and ghastly calamity caused giggles and snickers just ahead. A beam of light shone on the boys' faces and they squinted. They jumped to their feet, confused and shaken as they still swiped at imaginary creatures.

"So, have you had enough?" a female voice said in a sassy tone.

"Who is that?" Hank said as he looked down at the lifeless snakes and stepped forward as he attempted to peer into the darkness.

"What's going on?" Ben asked as he grimaced and pulled webs from his hair.

Footsteps approached from behind and the boys turned to their fathers as they walked toward them. As they got closer to the light, they saw the men were grinning at each other.

"So girls, I'd say tonight was a success. Wouldn't you agree?" one father said.

As the light in front of them got closer, it also revealed their moms and the twins.

"No wonder you two have scared us for years. It's fun to watch," Estelle said with a smirk.

"I'll second that," Betsy and the moms agreed in unison. The girls giggled and clapped.

The terrorized boys were still confused.

"You—you mean this was all a prank?" Ben said as he looked from one female to another.

"Why did you do this to us?" Hank said, his voice shaky and indignant.

The twins looked at each other and sighed. They shook their heads and turned to the boys' moms for guidance.

"Think about all the times you two have had your fun at our expense, scaring all of us girls," Hank's mom said as she put her hands on her hips and tapped her foot with a bit of annoyance.

"We just gave you a taste of your own medicine," Ben's mom chimed in as she pursed her lips and straightened her shoulders.

Hank and Ben shook their heads, each picking up a rubber snake as they grimaced.

"I thought we were goners," Hank said as he relaxed his shoulders, exhausted from the marathon. He looked at his friend and cohort in crime.

"Me, too," mumbled Ben, still pale and sweaty.

Estelle and Betsy stared at the boys. "And?" they said.

"I'm sorry," Hank said as he darted his eyes from mom to mom and then to both of the girls.

"Me, too... sorry," Ben said as he bit his lip and looked down.

"That's all we wanted, boys," the twins said and the moms nodded.

And with that, Betsy and Estelle joined arms and skipped away back toward camp. A melody could be heard in the darkness and distance. The words the girls sang hung in the air before they drifted into the shadows. The familiar lyrics were from the inimitable Queen of Soul herself about a certain thing called respect.

CHAPTER ELEVEN

"And that is why women should rule the world," Betsy said, her voice triumphant. The room was filled with such loud laughter, Lady jumped up and excitedly turned in circles. "I think Lady agrees." She laughed as she stroked the dog's soft fur.

"I enjoy that story every time, even more than the time before," Hank said and glanced at Ben. They shook their heads and grinned at each other.

"The moral to the story, Andy," Ben said as he let out an enormous sigh, "is don't doubt for a moment women aren't the superior ones." He laughed even harder as he slapped his knee. "And trust me when I say—they keep count, too."

"That was a remarkable and devious scheme," the younger man said as he turned to his mom. "Too bad there wasn't video." He grinned as he looked at his dad and the sheriff. "How long before you didn't need your nightlights when you went to bed?" Andy chided the chastised culprits.

"What do you mean? I still need it," Ben said with a shrug and a smirk.

Betsy laughed until her eyes watered with happy tears.

"Well, that was a lot of fun, but I think I need to get on home and let you all get some rest. Laughing and reminiscing is hard work," Ben said as he stood and stretched.

She had gained her composure and reached out to give him a hug.

"Thanks for bringing our boy home and sharing your evening with us."

"Are you kidding? And miss that terrific meal? Not a chance." The sheriff beamed.

Ben and Hank shared a quick hug and pat on the back.

"Call me if you need something."

"You got it, buddy." Hank nodded with a smile.

As they walked to the front door, Ben stopped and turned. He stood beside Andy and placed his arm around his shoulders.

"Keep an eye on these two. They're pretty suspicious characters. I expect a full report in the morning," he said with affection as he glanced over his shoulder at his friends. They smiled back at him with the same warmth and love.

Andy laughed. "Yes, sir, Sheriff Murphy."

~

The next morning, Betsy brought a tray with coffee and blueberry muffins into the bedroom. As she suspected, her husband had just awakened.

"I have coffee for you, my love," she said with a bright smile.

"You are too good to me, Betsy. What did I ever do to deserve you?" He sat up in the bed and adjusted the covers. His hair was tousled, remnants of sleep still on his face.

"That's a simple question to answer," she said, placing

the tray on the bed. "You love me more than I could ever have imagined possible." She bent down and kissed his forehead. Their eyes met and spoke volumes of their devotion. She patted his hand. "How do you feel this morning?"

"Tired from our late visit with Ben, but it was so worth it." He paused and smiled. "He's the best friend anyone could ever want."

"That he is," she agreed. "That he is. It's hard to even remember a time he hasn't been in our lives. They are so intrinsically intertwined." She gazed at the sunlight that had just peeked through the far window. For a second, she wished this moment would last forever.

"Coffee with a view, sir?" she said with a grin and a slight curtsy.

"Of course, my dear. And shall you join me?" he replied in his best British accent, mirroring her humor.

"Yes, I should very much like that." She patted his cheek as he passed by.

"I'll join you in a few moments, my sweet, with a more proper appearance befitting a queen."

She giggled and walked across the bedroom to the two overstuffed chairs near the window. As she set the tray on the small table, she glanced up in time to see a deer walk across the meadow below. Betsy took a deep breath and slowly exhaled. She never tired of the view or the peace it instilled in her heart. "Thank you," she whispered as she poured the steaming coffee into the cups.

A few minutes later, Hank appeared again and sat in his favorite chair. "I know this chair is frayed and worn, very much like me, but that's what makes it so comfortable." He grinned and rubbed the arm.

"Unlike the chair, dear, you have only grown more handsome." She looked at her husband with admiration. "I see the way women still look at you. You haven't lost your looks or your charm, Mr. Walker."

"Flattery will get you everywhere, Mrs. Walker." He winked at his wife.

She took a sip of her coffee and frowned as she shook her head. "I don't know how you put up with me through our high school years. Every time another girl looked at you, I was so jealous. I'm sure you must have had your doubts about me." She looked up at him, the man she'd loved her entire life, a slight smile on his face.

"Let's just say I was glad when you finally realized, as corny as it sounds, I only had eyes for you," he said in a gentle voice. "I talked a lot with Mom, and she told me to be patient, that you needed some time to gain your self-confidence. She said it was a hard age for girls, many of whom have low self-esteem." Then he broke into a crooked grin. "She also told me to pray—a lot." He laughed and almost spilled his coffee.

"Well, she was right on all counts and a wise woman," she said with a grin. "You've never given me a reason to doubt your love and faithfulness. Thank you for being such a wonderful husband and example for our son." Her voice softened. "I thank God every day for you, Hank Walker."

"You're an easy person to love, Betsy. I've always considered myself a very lucky man. But I'll have to admit, I still get tickled when I think about Natalie. It was all I could do not to tell her the story when we went to her wedding." He smiled as he rubbed his chin.

"I just knew you'd tell her in front of all the wedding guests and I'd be so embarrassed I'd have to run and hide. Thank you for your restraint." She had a sheepish grin as she reached over and patted his knee.

"Well, some things are just not meant to be shared, my

dear." The look on his face was one of sheer delight as his eyes twinkled. "I don't think I've ever seen you so angry. It's funny now, but only because time has made it so."

~

"Mom, I'm going to walk over to Hank's house if that's okay with you," Betsy said as she stood at the bottom of the stairs and looked up. She waited for her mother's footsteps above and her face to appear.

"Did you finish all your homework? And your essay is completed?" Her mom leaned over the railing as she spoke.

"Yes, and yes. I'm all caught up, and I even put away all the dishes."

"Well, then it sounds like you'll be walking to Hank's. Does he know you're coming over?"

"Nope. I thought I'd just surprise him. I'll take some cookies I baked. You know how much he loves the chocolate chip," she said. "Thanks, Mom. Call if you need me for something."

"Okay, honey, have fun. Be sure to tell Hank and his folks I send my regards. Oh, and maybe ask if there's a day next week they'd like to come over for dinner."

"Sure thing, Mom. Thanks, and I'll be home by six. Love you," she called out as she grabbed her purse and the bagged cookies and headed out the door. "Oh, wait," she said. She stopped, backing into the house and walking to the living room.

Sitting in a rocking chair in front of the large window was Betsy's grandmother. Her cat, Harvey, was curled up in her lap as they both napped. She stopped, not wanting to wake them, but as she turned around to leave, she heard her grandmother's voice.

"What is it, my dear?" asked the gray-haired woman, her gentle eyes now looking at her.

"Oh, I'm so sorry, Nana. I didn't mean to wake you."

"Nonsense. Harvey and I were merely resting our eyes," the old woman said with a

loving smile as the cat stood and stretched on her lap before circling and lying down again.

"I was just leaving, and I wanted to say goodbye and give you a kiss, that's all."

"That is the best reason I can think of to be roused from our catnap. Don't you agree, Harvey?" she said as she stroked the soft fur.

"I love you so very much, Nana." She walked to the rocker, wrapped her arms around her grandmother's neck, and kissed her cheek.

"And I love you, my sweet girl. Where are you off to?"

"I'm going to Hank's house to surprise him with cookies," she replied with a big smile.

"I'm pretty certain that boy is already hooked—you needn't any more bait," the wise old woman teased with a wink.

Betsy laughed. "Oh, Nana, you're so funny. I love you. Bye-bye. I'll see you at dinner."

A brisk, twenty-minute walk brought Betsy to Hank's front door. Before she knocked on the screen door, she heard his voice. He was on the phone, talking in the hallway.

"Natalie, you looked so beautiful in your new dress," he said. His back was turned toward her, but she heard his words clearly.

Betsy froze, all the color draining from her face. She

widened her eyes and stopped breathing. She tensed and her smile faded as rage took hold.

He continued. "Yes, you're my girl. What? Will I marry you?" He tipped his head back and laughed. "I'll have to think about that for now. Okay? Yes, I love you, too. I'll see you soon, honey."

She couldn't contain herself any longer. "Who are you talking to, Hank Walker?" she hissed through the screen, her voice cold and angry. "How could you?"

He turned around right before Betsy ran down the front walk and out to the street.

"Betsy," he yelled. "Betsy, come back. What are you doing?" He dropped the phone and ran out the door toward her.

She stopped and turned around to face him. "No. The question should be, what are you doing?" Her eyes filled with tears as she shook her finger at him and glared.

"What are you talking about?" He stood in front of her, his face filled with confusion. "Why are you here? And why are you suddenly so angry at me?"

"Here," she growled through tight lips as she stuck the bag of cookies in his face. "I brought these for you. And I hate you. Goodbye," she huffed. "I never want to see you again."

As she turned to leave, he grabbed her arm. "Wait. Betsy, what do you think you heard?" He released her arm as she pivoted back to him, her eyes filled with fury.

"What did I hear? I heard you tell another girl she was beautiful. I heard you tell her you loved her. And you're going to marry her. That's what I heard, Hank Walker." Her face grew red and her hands became fists. "I should never have trusted you. Now I know you're a two-faced jerk."

His face relaxed as he grinned. "Wait, it's not what you think. Really."

"Don't you laugh at me." She glowered at him, her hands on her hips. "I know what I heard, and it was you talking to your other girlfriend. We're done. I'm going now." She spun around to leave.

"No. Wait. Betsy, you're my girlfriend—my only girlfriend. Honestly," he pleaded. "I was talking to my cousin!" he shouted at her back.

"What?" She turned and looked at him again as she gasped, her face flooded with shock.

"No, it's not what you think. Natalie is only four years old. I saw a picture of her as a flower girl at a friend's wedding recently. Really, Betsy, I'm telling the truth. Mom handed me the phone because Natalie wanted to talk to me. I swear. She always says we'll get married when she grows up. Come on, give me a chance here. Let's go back to my house and I'll have my mom explain. Please," he begged. His grin had been replaced with a somber expression and pleading eyes. "Betsy, please," he whispered as he held both hands open and extended toward her.

Her demeanor changed in an instant. The anger was exchanged for embarrassment and shame. She unfurled her fingers from their fists and her tight lips relaxed to form a silent "oh." Betsy's shoulders slumped at her exaggerated overreaction to an innocent conversation. She had let her imagination run rampant before Hank could defend himself.

"I-I thought..." she stammered, just before she burst into tears. "Hank, I'm sorry. I'm a dreadful person," she blurted. "You deserve another girlfriend, not someone like me." She continued to sob into her hands and repeated her apologies.

He stepped closer and took her into his arms. "It's okay,

Bets. I get it. I accept your apology. It was just a big misunderstanding."

She sobbed into his shoulder. "I wouldn't blame you if you told me to go away forever. I acted horrible and said terrible things to you."

He patted her back and let her cry. His mom had told him once that girls sometimes needed to do that. After a few minutes, he put his hands on her shoulders and looked into her swollen red eyes.

"Betsy, I promise I'll tell you if my feelings for you ever change. Okay? I won't ever betray your trust. You're my best friend," he said and smiled down at her.

"I feel so stupid," she said as she shook her head. "And ashamed for thinking you could do such a detestable thing. Right now, I don't think I'm anyone's best friend."

"Betsy, stop," he said in a quiet, stern voice. "We all make mistakes and misjudge situations." His face reflected no malice. "So we'll forget this ever happened, okay? And years from now, we'll get a good laugh out of it."

"It's going to take a lifetime to forget how poorly I just treated you," she said, wracked with guilt. "Thank you, Hank, for being so forgiving and patient with me." She couldn't continue to look at him.

He raised her chin up so their eyes met. "Hey, you need to be patient with yourself, too. God's still working on all of us. And I suspect He'll never be finished." He grinned. "Now let's go inside for some milk to go with these cookies."

CHAPTER TWELVE

"Good morning, Andy," Betsy said as she descended the stairs with a tray in hand. "I'm so happy to see you sitting there," she added with a warm smile.

"Good morning, Mom." He walked over to take the tray for her. "Here, let me get that."

"Thanks, son. Your dad should be down soon. Are you hungry?" She kissed him on the cheek.

"Funny you should ask." Andy flashed a crooked grin. "I inhaled two of those tasty blueberry muffins with my coffee already."

"Well, that's exactly what I had hoped you'd do. I can make some omelets for us, too. A man can't live on muffins alone," she said as she gathered ingredients from the fridge.

"How's Dad this morning?" Andy's voice was serious.

"He's feeling pretty good, only a slight headache. But it's unpredictable and the pain usually increases throughout the day, as does the dizziness. He's ready to have the surgery. If all goes well, it'll relieve his symptoms and prolong his life." She sighed as she looked to the window, her eyes moist. "I know it sounds selfish, but I want your dad around for a lot longer."

"It's not selfish, Mom. We all want more time with him, and I think God understands our prayers." Andy smiled at his mom. "Dad's the best man I know. And I only hope I am even half the man he is."

"You are, son—and more." As Betsy turned and looked up, she smiled as she saw her husband.

"Hey, why's it so quiet in here?" Hank said with a grin as he walked into the kitchen.

"Good morning, Andy. You're a sight for sore eyes, boy. Did you sleep well?" He put his arm around his son's shoulders and gave him a firm hug. His smile radiated across the room.

"Good morning, Dad. Yes, I did. Thanks. You're looking good this morning. I was afraid that a late-night visit with Ben would wear you out. Are we still on for going to see Leroy today?"

"Absolutely. I have papers to sign before I have my surgery. Did your mom tell you I'm selling the construction company to Sunny?" He nodded, a satisfied look on his face. "He's been my right-hand man all these years, so he knows exactly how to handle any job. And all the folks in town know and like him. I think it'll be an easy transition."

"I bet he's happy to have this opportunity," Andy said. "Yeah, he's a great guy. He's been like an uncle to me since I was a little kid. It'll be good to see him again. It's been too long."

"His two boys started working with us this last year, too, so he's already been training his crew," Hank grinned. "They're hard workers, just like their dad. I think the business will do as well for him as it has for us."

While the men talked, Betsy cooked some toast and

omelets. Now she headed toward them with steaming plates.

"Andy, will you please put some napkins and silverware on the table? This is ready to eat. Then you fellas can get on the road." She smiled at her husband. "I've fixed a thermos of coffee for you, honey. I set it by the truck keys."

"You're too good to me, Mrs. Walker," he said as he wrapped an arm around her waist with a smile.

"You deserve every bit of what I do for you," she replied. "Now, who wants some homemade salsa on their omelet?"

"Mornin', Hank," Leroy said as the men walked through the office door. "And Andy, mighty fine to see you, young man." He got up from his desk and walked over, giving him a quick hug and a pat on his back. "You're looking healthy. Military life must agree with you."

"No complaints from me. And you don't look a day over—"

"One hundred," Hank interrupted and grinned at Leroy.

"Now why would you want to insult your lawyer, Hank?" Leroy asked and slapped him on the shoulder.

"Sit, gentlemen. Want coffee?" the attorney asked as he grabbed his cup for a refill.

"Nope, we're good. Betsy just fed and watered us and sent us down the road to take care of this business," Hank said. "Sorry for the rush, Leroy. I hope this didn't interrupt your work on something else."

"Nope. When you called, I was finishing up your paper-work. I'm pretty sure I followed all your requests. Changes can be made, if needed, and we'll have everything completed before your surgery. I was a little surprised how quickly that was going to happen, though. But I've only ever heard good things about your doctor. I'll keep you in my prayers, my friend." Leroy's expression was filled with compassion and sincerity.

"Thanks. That means a lot to me," Hank said as he nodded. "I'm at peace with whatever the outcome will be. This sale gives me peace of mind, knowing Betsy and the B&B will be completely taken care of with no financial worry on her shoulders. And I feel good that this way Sunny can continue to take care of his family."

"You're a good man, Hank," he replied.

Just then, the door opened again and a tall, muscular man with dark hair with sprinkles of gray walked into the office.

"There he is, the-soon-to-be owner of Parsons Construction Company," Leroy said with a grin. "Good morning, Sunny."

"Good morning, guys." Sunny smiled, looking from one to the other. "Hey, Andy, I didn't know you were home. Good to see you." Andy smiled back and stood up as Sunny took a couple of steps toward him. The two men hugged for a moment, their friendship etched on their faces and each with a huge grin. Sunny grabbed Andy by the shoulders and held him at arm's length.

"I'm pretty sure my boys are taller than you now," he said. "They'd sure be happy to see you if you've got time. They ask about you a lot."

"Yeah, I'd be happy to spend some time with them, too," Andy said with an enthusiastic nod.

"Okay, gentlemen," Leroy said. "Let's get on with this, shall we? I have a date with a hot turkey sandwich in just about an hour." He and the others laughed. "As we discussed on the phone, I've changed a few dates, but other than that, the papers are the same as our last meeting." He handed a stapled batch of papers to Sunny. "Here, look these over, Sunny."

As Sunny began reading through the contract, Hank handed his papers to his attorney.

"It all looks good to me, Leroy. Where do I sign?" He picked up a pen from the tray on the desk.

Andy watched his father's face as he signed the documents.

"Yep, this all looks right, Leroy," Sunny said as he laid the papers on the corner of the desk. "Just show me where I need to sign, please."

When the two men set their pens down, they stood up and shook hands. Hank put his other hand on Sunny's shoulder.

"I couldn't have found a better person to take over my business. You're gonna do well, Sunny. In fact, I'm sure you'll be able to hand it over to your boys some day."

"Funny you should say that. I was talking with my wife last night about how good that would be. And they're both really eager to learn everything there is about contracting work. The oldest boy loves math and his brother loves building—a perfect match." He laughed. "I think their future looks bright in this business. I'm happy to have them learn by my side. Hank, I can't thank you enough for helping to make this happen."

"Well, you've always been my friend, Sunny—never my employee." The men shared a smile of deep respect and years of friendship.

Leroy gathered the paperwork and tidied up his desk. "Well, gentlemen, I think we're all finished here. I'll have the final papers and copies to you this week," he said. "And now it's just about time for my lunch date at the diner. Maggie always sets aside a plate for me because she knows how much I love her hot turkey sandwiches. Can't keep her waiting now, can I?"

He grinned as he shooed the men out of his office. His work was done for the day, his stomach growling like a beast as he locked the door.

CHAPTER THIRTEEN

While her men were in town, Betsy called her sister.

"Hello Betsy," said Estelle in a cheery voice. "Glad you called. I was just thinking about you. Is Andy home now?"

"Hi, sis. Yes, Ben brought him home from the airport for us yesterday. We're so glad everything worked out so he could be here, especially now. It's an enormous relief for all of us."

"That's good, and I'm glad he's with you, too. I'm eager to see him," Estelle said. "And I don't know what we'd do without our sweet Sheriff Ben."

Betsy laughed. "I don't think he'd much like that rumor getting around town. It doesn't lend to his tough law man's reputation." They chuckled.

"Yeah, I think you're right—that'll stay between us then. I'm happy you called. I wanted to catch up on what's been going on while I've been gone and ask how Hank's doing."

"He's feeling the same, no better but no worse. It's tolerable with medication. The big news is that his surgery date has been moved up to this week, in just a few days. He does pre-op tomorrow. I'll let you know all the details as soon as I know them," Betsy said. "Please keep us in your prayers."

"You're all always in my prayers, especially now. And how are you doing?"

"Prayer, Hank's love, and Andy being home now. Those are all helping to keep me strong. It's all in His hands." She sighed and fought back tears.

"You're tough, Betsy, but don't forget, I know you. I'm always here for you, whatever you need."

"Thanks. I depend on that. We've come through a lot together, haven't we? Funny how when I look at you, I see myself. I don't know what I'd do without you."

"That's what twins do, right?" she said. "What are your boys up to today?"

"They're in town completing the sale of Hank's company. He's glad to get that taken care of before his surgery. He was anxious about it because the schedule had been so drastically changed. But Leroy has it all handled. He's come through again, as usual."

"That's wonderful news. Are you up for some extra company this evening? I feel like there's a lot more we can talk about. I'm unpacked and ready for a home-cooked meal, too." She laughed at her invitation.

"We'd love for you to come over. I know Andy's eager to see you." Betsy instantly brightened.

"I'll come early. What can I bring?" Estelle said, joy in every word. It had been weeks since she'd seen her family.

"Not a thing—just your fabulous self. You'll be medicine for all our souls," she said with a grin.

"Just the same, I think I'll bring a bottle of a new wine I discovered while I was in New York."

Estelle smiled. All their lives, they had been caretakers

for each other. They shared everything—their looks, their birthday, their thoughts, and their love and strength.

～

As the men drove back home, they caught up on each other's lives since Andy's deployment.

"How does it feel not to have your company anymore, Dad?" Andy asked. "It's been part of who you are for most of your adult life and all that I've ever known." He hesitated, his eyes questioning and uncertain. "I watched your face as you signed the papers—you seemed happy. How come?"

Hank smiled at his son's questions. He continued to watch the road as he spoke. "I know it was the right thing to do and at the right time. So I'm happy with my decision. The business will continue to support a lot of families," he said. "Well, it will be different not to have that responsibility. But the biggest part of who I am regarding my responsibilities has to do with your mother. First and foremost, she is the love of my life. Always has been, always will be. And with that came my promise, not only to love and care for her heart, but also to make sure she is provided with all she could want and need. Her happiness has always been my heart's desire. Selling my company ensures her bed-and-breakfast will be maintained, and she'll continue her ministries in the community for as long as she lives." His expression said it all as he glanced at his son.

Andy nodded. "That makes sense. That's why you and Mom are the best example of what love, partnership, and marriage should be. Hopefully someday, I'll find the right woman to share my life with." He turned toward the window and sighed. "I guess my first attempt wasn't the right choice." His words were melancholy and there was sadness in his eyes.

"When it's right, you'll know, son," Hank said. "But it still takes a lifetime of prayer and constant work not to let the flame die out. But every hour of every day with your mother has been a blessing, even when we didn't agree. God knew who I needed." He paused, forming a crooked smile before he spoke. "Just remember to keep Him in the loop," he said with a smirk.

The truck cab was quiet for a moment before both men laughed at his last word and the gloom on Andy's face disappeared.

"That's the modern version of asking for His guidance, I suppose," he said with a grin. "Yeah, sometimes I think I can make the big decisions by myself, and that's when I get into trouble." With a serious tone and slight hesitation, he finished his thoughts. "It hurt a lot to get that Dear John letter, but deep down, I know the right person will come into my life. I just hope I recognize her."

"You will, Andy. Trust me, you will."

It was a sunny day during spring break. As Hank sat at the table eating his lunch, he looked up at his mom standing at the sink.

"Mom, how did you know Dad was the right man for you?" he said in between bites of his thick ham-and-cheese sandwich.

"That's a mighty big question for a teenage boy," she answered. "Is there something I should know about?" she said. She grinned and turned toward her son. But he was deep in thought.

Hank took a big gulp of his milk and set the glass down. He paused, concerned. "Nope, I don't plan to get married soon, not until I've finished high school and done a few years in the military." He looked directly at his mom, his eyes intent. "It's just that some of my friends' parents have gotten divorced recently. So I wondered what keeps some marriages together and others not. Were those people not supposed to have gotten married in the first place?" he said, his face showing the seriousness of his question.

His mother sat down at the table across from him as she dried her hands on her apron. She put her elbows on the table and rested her chin on her folded hands.

"Hmm... let me think about this a moment," she said, before she offered her explanation. "When I met your father, I instantly wanted to know him better. After several months of social gatherings and dating, we'd become good friends. And in that time, I'd seen how kind and patient he was to other people." She stopped and smiled. "That's the test of a wonderful human being—respect and regard for others, not just the person of their interest. That's not something you can see if you're in a rush."

"You mean he never got mad?" Hank's voice jumped an octave higher as he stopped chewing and looked confused.

"Oh, there were times he was angry and might not agree," she said, "but he didn't allow that to make him treat other people without respect or lose control. There's a fine line between disagreement and disrespect, and your father knew the difference, even at a young age. I admired him for that."

"So that's it?" Hank said in disbelief as he set his sandwich on the plate.

"No, that's just a small part of knowing," his mom said. "It takes time to build a relationship and to discover if that person is the right choice for you. How your father treated me, as well as other people, showed me the type of man he was and how he thought. When he told me my happiness was more important to him than his own and acted in kind, he showed me his heart. But when he told me he prayed, he showed me his soul. That's when I knew."

Hank was quiet for a few moments as he contemplated what his mother had just told him. She watched his face for any sign of understanding. He nodded and pursed his lips.

"So basically, you're saying you needed time to know his head, heart, and soul." He looked toward the ceiling while he chose his words. "You needed to see the whole person—and Dad passed the test." He grinned at his mom. "Right?"

"I'd say that's quite precise and succinct, young man." His mother paused for several seconds. "Did I mention I also needed your grandparents to agree?" Her expression was as good as any successful poker player's.

Hank was speechless, his face frozen with shock. It was several seconds before he realized the joke and she grinned. Their laughter floated through the screen door, into the blue sky, through the puffy white clouds, and up to the heavens.

CHAPTER FOURTEEN

"Aunt Estelle," Andy called out cheerily as he walked into the house and gave her a warm hug and kiss on the cheek. "I'm so thrilled to see you. How's my favorite aunt?"

"Let me look at you, boy," she said, giving him a last squeeze and backing up a little. "My... you are even more handsome than the last time I saw you, Andy. There's a strength and confidence in your eyes now." She studied him a little longer. "You've experienced a lot of life while you've been gone. I guess I shouldn't call you a boy. What stands before me now is—a man." She patted his cheek. "Just seeing you makes my heart happy." She smiled at him, but there was a hint of sadness in her eyes.

"You make me happy, too," he said. "And you can always call me boy because I know you love me." He laughed and winked at his aunt. "You're like my other mom."

Estelle patted his cheek again and grinned. "That's my good boy. Your parents taught you well—always the diplomat."

He laughed as he walked over to give his mom a hug,

too. "And how's the best mom in the world?" he said as he gave her a big hug and kiss.

"Always better when my son hugs me," she replied with a smile. "Would you mind lighting the fire, please? Seems chilly in here since it clouded over. Dinner is still about an hour away, so we can sit in here and chat."

"Sure thing, Mom. I'll go out and bring in more wood, too."

"Estelle brought wine," Betsy said. "Any takers? Or something else?" As she waited for responses, Hank walked over to his wife and wrapped his arms around her.

"I'll have you, please," he said as he kissed her lightly and gave her a wink.

She smiled and gave him a quick squeeze. "I think you need to sit down and rest," she said, shooing him toward his chair. "You've had a busy day and have probably done more than you should have. It's time to relax, my love. Besides, Lady has missed you."

"As you wish," he responded with a low bow and strode toward his chair. But midway he stopped and looked at his wife. "I love that you take such good care of me, Betsy. Thank you." He let out a gigantic sigh as he sat down. "Yep, this feels mighty good." He reached down and stroked Lady's head as she laid it across his knee. Her eyes stared into his, as if to sense what his next move might be. "Go ahead, my sweet girl. You can relax, too. I'm not going anywhere." Lady thumped her tail lightly on the carpet as she closed her eyes.

Betsy smiled before heading into the kitchen. "I'll put some hot water on for tea, but I know we girls are having wine." She looked at her husband. "Tea?" He nodded.

Estelle was already seated on the couch in the large

living room. She smiled at the interaction between her sister and Hank.

"I knew when we were still in grade school the two of you were made for each other," she said with an affectionate smile. "After all these years, it still holds true." She nodded in approval. "I couldn't have asked for a better or kinder man for my little sister."

Hank laughed out loud. "You're older by two minutes, Estelle. But you really know how to play that card, don't you?" He winked at her.

She laughed with him. "I've used it so many times on Betsy, but she's always been a good sport about it. Well, except when we were young and the oldest of us got first pick what chores we'd do." Estelle grinned. "She really hated toilet duty."

Andy came back into the house, his arms loaded with firewood, and Lady jumped up to greet him. She bumped his leg with her nose and he laughed. "Let me put this down first, then you can have some rubs, okay?" She sat and waited, almost patiently. "I've missed you, too, girl." He freed up his arms and knelt by the fireplace. Before tending to anything else, he gave Lady her just due as promised. She looked at his face as he rubbed her ears and patted her sides before rolling over for more. Andy laughed and obliged a while longer.

"Okay, Lady, come here before that fire goes out," Hank said with a grin as the dog returned to his side.

"This wood should last a few days, since we only need some heat in the evenings," Andy said, laying some larger kindling over the small fire he'd started earlier. "This should make it nice and comfortable in a few minutes." He walked to the kitchen just in time to help his mother carry the wine and hot tea.

"I'll have some tea with Dad," he said. "And let me get that tray for you, Mom." Pride spread across her face. "Thank you, son."

As the fire crackled and the drinks were served, everyone settled in for a pleasant visit.

"Ah," Betsy said. She drew her legs up under herself on the couch and leaned her back into the soft cushion. "I wish we could stay just like this in this moment." She closed her eyes and relaxed with another deep sigh.

"Yeah, this feels good, Mom," Andy said, but his face reflected some sorrow.

"Mmm, yes," whispered Estelle, her face calm and body relaxed.

It was quiet for only a minute when Hank laughed and said, "How about if we stay just like this after dinner? I'm starving."

Everyone laughed, appreciating Hank's hunger and humor.

"Hey, just being honest here." He shrugged with a grin. "And what is that heavenly aroma coming from the kitchen, Betsy?" He looked at her with wide-eyed expectations.

She grinned. "That would be the prime rib to go with Estelle's new wine. Which is quite good, by the way." She held her wineglass up in an air toast, to which her sister responded. "It's less than an hour to dinner. Can you wait that long?" she said and winked at her husband.

"I suppose I'll have to." He made a sad face. "But that's just about enough time to tell the story about our anniversary trip to Italy." His sadness instantly faded.

"Oh, Hank, I'm sure these two have heard that a thousand times," Betsy said, but only in feeble protest. It was one of her favorite love stories about them.

~

Hank and Betsy waited by the edge of the sidewalk as a taxi appeared. Raising his arm, he signaled for the vehicle to stop. They got in and were quickly seated as the taxi lurched forward, causing their door to slam shut. Betsy gasped, but the driver laughed.

"Is okay. I'm good driver," the man said with a huge smile and even bigger accent.

"Where?" he said as he looked over his shoulder at his new riders and back to the narrow road in time to dodge an oncoming car. He shook his fist at the other driver and yelled a few words in Italian as he honked his horn.

"Scusa," the cabbie said as he smiled again and looked in the rearview mirror. "Uh,

where?" the man asked, as he gave his words some thought for translation.

Hank grinned back into the mirror and told the driver, "Un ristorante romantico, per favor." Pleased with himself for having recited his new language, he sat back and squeezed Betsy's hand.

"Ah, yes, trattoria is better," the man replied and glanced at Betsy. "I know a good place." His head bobbled as he directed his vehicle at full speed through the maze of cars and streets, his curly dark hair barely contained under his bright blue cap.

After ten long minutes, and many near misses, the taxi screeched to a halt in front of a small eatery. There were several tables inside and just as many outside on the open cobblestone patio. The diners talked and laughed between bites of food, expressing their thoughts with hand gestures. People, many of whom were couples, strolled past in no particular hurry. The night had just begun as the city exhaled its day. The moon shined a message to slow down, relax, and enjoy love. Nearby was a three-tiered fountain, into which two small children threw coins. A man stood guard as the woman smelled the fragrant flowers in the bushes surrounding the tiny plaza. The taxi driver jumped out of the cab and opened a rear door.

"Per favor," he said to Betsy and held out his hand for her. As she stood upright, the man kissed the back of her hand.

"Oh." She blushed. "Thank you. You are very kind." The man grinned and nodded.

He closed the door, held her elbow, and walked her to Hank. "Come, I talk to owners for you, yes?" He waited only a moment, and before they could respond, he said, "Good."

The couple followed their new guide into the small establishment. A bright yellow-and-red sign hung above the door with the name Trattoria Gino in bold print.

"Ciao, Lorenzo," a pleasant older woman said to their escort as she came from around a small counter. She was a lovely woman who held herself with pride as she strode to the man with open arms. She air-kissed both his cheeks and gave him a fond smile.

"And who have you brought me tonight, my dear cousin?" She turned to Hank and Betsy with a bright smile and twinkling eyes. Her expression, warm and welcoming, and her demeanor no less than charming.

"Buonasera—good evening to you. My name is Anna. How may I serve you?" the woman said.

"Buonasera," they answered and smiled back.

"My name is Hank and this beautiful woman is my wife, Betsy. I told your cousin Lorenzo to take us to a romantic restaurant, and it seems this is our destination. We're here to celebrate our tenth anniversary."

"Splendid. You will not be disappointed." She turned to Lorenzo and spoke in Italian to him. He kissed her cheeks, bowed to Hank and Betsy, and grinned as he stood up to leave.

"Amore," he said to them in a gleeful voice. He brought his right fingers and thumb together, raising them to his lips, kissing them lightly, and joyfully tossed them open into the air. He laughed and walked through the doorway back to his taxi. Seconds later, his vehicle bolted into the traffic and was gone.

Anna continued to watch with a smile until the taxi was out of sight. "So, it is a romantic dinner that brings you to me?" She stepped back and studied them for a moment, looking into their eyes and noticing they held hands. Her smile widened. "Yes, I see you are very much in love."

Betsy blushed and glanced up at Hank's face. His cheeks also had a rosy glow.

"Ah, that says everything." Anna's eyes expressed her gladness. "Follow me. I have a special table for you. You are lovebirds, yes?" She grinned and spun around, her skirt twirling at her ankles. The soft colorful fabric danced and swished as she walked. She took them to a side door, opening it and leading them to a single table with two chairs in a small courtyard. There was a soft, ambient glow from small rope lights attached to the trees. They were hidden from view by the same flower bushes they'd seen on the sidewalk in front, and the fountain was visible from the table.

Anna spread her arms out theatrically and smiled. "You like, yes?"

Betsy stood mesmerized by the scene, her eyes wide and

her lips parted in a half smile. Hank glanced at his wife's face and grinned at Anna. "Yes, this is more than perfect."

"Ah, splendid," she said and reached into her pocket. "This will add that special radiance to your eyes—and lips." She flicked the lighter and lit the candle on the table, looking pleased. "Sit. I will bring wine now." She smiled and spun on her heel with a flutter of her skirt. Within moments, the soft melody of an Italian love song wafted from the cafe window.

When they were seated, Hank looked at his wife with an eager expression. "Is this what you had in mind, honey?"

She sighed and leaned forward, the candle's glow on her face. "I want to remember this moment forever, my love." She reached across the table and placed her hand on his.

"You are so good to me. Thank you." The candle flame flickered and cast small shadows across her face.

"You are my world, Betsy Walker. My heart revolves around you—only you—forever."

Anna appeared with wine and glasses. "I think this wine shall please your palates." She set their glasses down and held up the bottle. "It is Barbera d'Asti, direct from the winery. My husband and I have family who are winemakers in the Piedmont region. This year is the most delicious." Her face expressed a familial pride as she opened the bottle and poured a small amount for Hank to taste.

"Yes, this is very good." He smacked his lips and turned to his wife. "You'll love it, Betsy."

Anna grinned and poured the ruby-red wine into their glasses. "I know the chef very well," she said with a wink. "My husband makes the best lasagna in Italy, if not the world. Would that appease your appetites this evening?"

"Oh, yes," said Betsy, her enthusiasm palpable.

Hank laughed as his wife blushed at her response. "I'm

afraid my wife is close to starving. Lasagna sounds just as good to me, thank you."

"I will bring that out shortly, then. Enjoy your wine, music, and the evening while you wait." As she turned, she stopped to look up. "I think the moon tonight is filled with magic," she whispered to them.

~

"Ah, I see you were both hungry," Anna said with a smile as she collected their plates. "My Gino will be pleased you enjoyed your meal."

"Yes," Betsy said with a satisfied smile. She hesitated. "Delizioso." She beamed at her skill with her new found word.

Anna and Hank laughed. "Yes, my compliments to the chef and his lovely wife," he said.

"Grazie mille," Anna replied as her cheeks glowed. "You both are very kind. I shall return in un momento." She whisked away with her arms full of dishes.

Through the bushes, an older couple stood by the fountain. The man gave a coin to the woman. She smiled, kissed him, and threw it into the water. They looked at each other and strolled to a nearby bench to sit. The water danced and sparkled in the moonlight. After a time, with much difficulty, the old man stood up with his cane and carefully plucked a flower from a bush. He returned to the woman and bowed to her as he presented his gift. She looked up at him and held his hand with the flower in both of hers. They shared a smile that reflected a lifetime of love and kindness.

"That will be us someday," Betsy whispered as she squeezed Hank's hand.

His eyes mirrored the love. "I should be the luckiest

man in the world, then." He gazed at his wife. "You look simply radiant tonight, my dear."

"It's the work of candlelight—and your love."

Anna returned with a small platter of bite-sized desserts and coffee cups. Behind her was a man dressed in white, including a white apron, a red scarf tied around his neck. He carried a small silver coffeepot.

"This is Chef Gino," Anna said proudly as she set the cups and desserts in front of their guests.

The chef smiled and bowed his head slightly. "I am honored you are here tonight," he said in a gracious and noble tone. "Please allow me." He poured coffee into their cups. "Enjoy with my compliments."

"Chef Gino, I'm Hank and this is my wife, Betsy. We are very honored to make your acquaintance."

"And may I say that your wife is right? You make the best lasagna in the world," Betsy said with a grin and turned her attention to the pastries. "I can hardly wait to sample these."

"Grazie mille." Chef Gino bowed his head as he gestured to the waiting confections. "Anna," he said as he extended his bent arm to his wife.

"Please, take your time," she said to the couple. "Food is meant to be savored, as is love."

Hank and Betsy both grinned as they nodded, eager to taste the sweet delights and espresso. With a quick wave, Anna and her chef returned to their other guests.

Before taking a bite, Betsy sighed and looked at Hank.

"I love you so much, my dear husband. Thank you. This has been a magical evening."

Hank grinned. "Anna said there was magic in the moon tonight."

CHAPTER FIFTEEN

Betsy grinned at Ben as she set the pan of cinnamon rolls on the table, mostly in front of him. Lady took her position on the floor next to Hank's feet. She held her nose up and inhaled, then sighed and closed her eyes.

"I told Hank this morning that you'd be here," Betsy said with a grin.

"I always come to visit on Wednesday morning. You know that." He grinned and winked. "I can't help it if you always cook cinnamon rolls then. Coincidence, I think." With a big laugh, he scooped out a hot roll and set it on his plate. "You make the best, Betsy. Where's the—"

The men laughed as Betsy set the bowl of extra cream cheese frosting on the table before he could finish his sentence.

"And you're a mind reader." He grinned and drizzled more frosting on the steaming roll. His eyes were wide in anticipation, and he licked his lips.

"Oh, my dear sheriff, you are so very predictable." She chuckled and sat down at the table. "If ever there is a cinnamon-roll heist in town, you'll be the first suspect. You know that, right?"

He laughed out loud and turned to his best friend. "Any plans for today, Hank?" he said in between bites.

"Nope. I'm all caught up on my list of things to do before surgery." He paused and looked at his wife. "I think I'll just stay home with my family and rest today."

"Sounds like a good plan. If there's anything I can do for you, let me know, okay?"

"I will. I promise." Hank smiled at his friend and took a sip of coffee.

Andy had been quiet and engaged in only one task—eating. "Mom, I agree with our sheriff. This is absolute perfection." He took a huge bite of his roll and closed his eyes, his face a portrait of contentment.

After the cinnamon rolls had almost been depleted and the coffeepot emptied, Ben commented on the ornately carved wooden box.

"My... but that brings back so many memories," he said as he gazed at the corner. "It seems like a lifetime and yet only yesterday that we were in wood shop together." He looked at Hank with a smile. "That box represents one of the greatest lessons in my life." He slowly shook his head. "And one that I've never forgotten. In fact, I think about it every single time I go fishing and when the cold makes my arm hurt. And I thank you for that, Hank."

Hank smiled back at his friend and nodded. "We all need to understand that lesson," he said in a quiet, earnest voice. "The heart can love many people at the same time."

~

"Hey Hank, how 'bout some fishing today? I heard they're biting real good at a place we've never been to," Ben said on the phone.

"Nah, I'm still working on that box for Betsy." Hank sighed as he stretched and spoke into the phone. "Mr. Connelly said he'd be at the school, so I could come in if I wanted. I've been working so long on this project, but I'm almost finished. I know Betsy's gonna love it. Not to mention, Connelly seems really impressed with my efforts. So A+ here I come." Hank laughed, not noticing his friend wasn't also amused.

"Oh, okay. Yeah, that's great," he said with a hint of disappointment. "I'll see ya at school on Monday, then."

"Okay, thanks for the invite. I promise we'll get to those fish soon." Hank laughed again and hung up the phone.

Ben put the phone down with some force. He was rejected yet again. He'd invited his best friend to go fishing at least four times, and he'd declined each time. All of Hank's days were now dedicated to his girlfriend. They'd all been close since childhood, but as they got older, Hank and Betsy's relationship became romantic. That's when he felt sidelined.

"Of course he doesn't have time for fishing," he muttered.

"What did you say, Ben?" his mom called out from the laundry room.

"Nothing, Mom," he answered in a brusque tone. "I'm going fishing. I'll be home by three o'clock so I can help Dad with the garage."

"Okay, honey," his mom said. "Is Hank going, too?"

He bristled at her question. "No, not this time or maybe ever," he said under his breath.

He grabbed some cookies and a couple of apples from

the counter and put them in his backpack. His temperament had soured since the last phone call. He was even more determined to catch some fish—with or without company. As he opened the back door and reached for the key to the old red truck, the door banged against his knee. He was angry at the door. He was angry at Hank.

Ben stopped by the feed store and tackle shop at the edge of town. The fish would be hungry and biting on worms.

"So, Ben, where are you going fishing today?" Mr. Wiggins said as he peered over his gold-rimmed glasses and put the small container of worms into a bag.

"I'm gonna try a new spot," he answered with a scowl. "I heard they're biting at the fork of Russell's Creek. At least that's what I'm thinking for now, anyway." He was annoyed he'd been asked. It wasn't anyone's business. He just wanted to be alone for now.

He paid and picked up his bag to leave. He almost smiled, glad to be on his way out of town.

"Is Hank going with you?" the old man asked as his face wrinkled into a smile.

"Why does everyone think Hank should go with me?" Ben snapped. He immediately regretted he'd said that, but didn't apologize. "No, he's not." He turned and stomped out of the store.

Mr. Wiggins watched as the boy left. "I wonder what's troubling him today?" he said to the next person in line.

"Who knows?" said the lady. "He's a teenager."

Ben parked his truck just below the road and near a dirt path that led down to the water. Finally, he would be by himself, all alone—again.

"I guess I just need to learn to do things by myself anyway," he mumbled as he carried his gear toward the creek. "At least I'll know who's going to be there." He kicked a rock.

At the water's edge, he stopped and studied the current. He looked for areas where eddies formed and for drop-offs, boulders, and overhanging trees and bushes. The fish might hide in those places. He'd walked upstream and downstream a way before he saw a good place to cast his line. It was a bit of a distance from the truck, but he had plenty of time to get back home.

He'd been fishing for a while with no luck, so he tried a more difficult spot. He'd seen a fallen tree near some large boulders. If he could get a line in just below the rocks, he might catch something. He worked his way through some thick brush and walked partway onto the fallen tree toward the rocks. He stopped to cast, and as he shifted his weight a little, his foot slipped on some moss and he fell backward off of the tree. As he fell, his arm became wedged between two large rocks and snapped. The pain was excruciating. He'd also hit his head on a rock but could keep his face just above the waterline. He couldn't release his arm and struggled to keep his balance on the rocks below the surface. He clung to the face of a large boulder with his free hand.

"Help," he shouted. He hadn't seen anyone else around, but he yelled anyway. He hoped against hope. "Someone help me, please," he cried. After what seemed like an eternity and his voice became hoarse, he quit calling out. He was soaked and cold to the bone as the water swirled around and past his body.

His arm hurt beyond any pain he'd ever felt before, and the water was freezing. He tried desperately to find a higher footing so he could lift his arm out of the rocks, but he found none. It was hopeless. His family didn't know where he was, and it was somewhere he'd never been before. He shivered and lost consciousness, but each time his free hand slipped on the wet granite surface, he woke up. Despite the increased pain in his arm, he moved and leaned his back against a rock to stabilize himself. He was exhausted and shook himself awake several times, only to relapse into the darkness again. His last thought was one of time. The sun was no longer overhead. And he was supposed to be home soon. But no one knew where to find him.

"Don't worry, I'll find him and bring him home," Hank said to Ben's mom over the phone. He rushed to the kitchen where his mother had begun dinner.

"Mom, I have to go," he said, his eyes wide with panic. "Ben went fishing and hasn't returned. He was supposed to be home two hours ago and it'll be dark soon."

As he grabbed his car keys and looked for a flashlight in the hall closet, he decided he should make a call.

"Betsy, Ben's missing and I have to find him before dark." His voice was filled with urgency. "I have to —"

"Wait, Hank," she said. "Stop and pick me up. I can be a second set of eyes. And I'll bring our first aid kit." Concern had replaced her cheery voice.

Once she was in the car, he told her their friend had gone fishing and hadn't returned.

"Do his parents know where he went?" Her voice quivered.

"No, they don't, but I think I might have a way to find out." He gripped the steering wheel with both hands, his knuckles white. "Ben would've needed bait, so let's stop by the feed and bait store. Maybe he said something when he was there."

It only took a few minutes to drive to Wiggins' Feed Store and Bait Shop. Hank explained the situation to the owner and hoped he had some information.

"You know, Hank, I think Ben told me, but I can't seem to remember at this very moment," Mr. Wiggins said as he reached up and scratched his balding head. "You're lucky you got here when you did. I was just about to close up shop for the day. Business slows down after four, you know." He paused. "The boy seemed to be in a bad mood. That's kinda unusual for him."

"Anything you can remember might help." Hank struggled to be patient as his anxiety began to surface.

"I remember asking him where he was going. Let me think—" The old man rubbed his head and smoothed the few hairs that remained. "And I remember he bought worms. I'll walk over to the register and maybe that will jog my memory. It's not what it used to be. Happens when you get older. You'll know some day what I mean." Mr. Wiggins walked to the counter and stepped behind it. He scratched his head again and rubbed his chin. "Yeah, yeah, I asked him where he was going fishing and he said—" He hesitated and adjusted his gold-rimmed glasses. "I got it, by golly. He said he was going to Russell's Creek. I remember now because I thought to myself that not many people fish there. But I'd heard spring was the best time thereabouts."

"Thank you, Mr. Wiggins." As Hank turned to leave, he stopped and looked at the old man. "Thank you so much.

You may have just saved my best friend's life." As he fought his tears, he rushed out and jumped into his vehicle.

~

"There—over there," Betsy shouted as she bounced on the seat. "There's his truck."

"Thank God," Hank said as his breath escaped his lungs. He'd thought about a couple of different locations where the fishing might be good early in the year but still close enough for Ben to be home in time to help his dad. The first place had shown no sign of him. Hank felt desperate—and guilty. He realized he'd put off spending time with his friend much more than he should have.

He slammed on the brakes and parked behind Ben's truck.

"I've got the first aid kit," Betsy said as she jumped out of the vehicle.

"And I've got the flashlight. Hopefully, we won't need it."

Once they reached the creek below, Hank made a strategic decision. "We'll do better if we split up. You go upstream and I'll go down. Yell my name if you find him. And I'll call out your name three times when I hear you, okay? You do the same," he said as he gently held her arm. "And be careful, Betsy."

She gave him a quick smile of determination. "Don't worry, I know we'll find him."

The two went in opposite directions and called out Ben's name as they scoured the creek and banks. Daylight was almost in the past when Hank heard his name being shouted out.

"Hank, Hank, Hank!" Betsy yelled out as she

approached Ben. "Hank, Hank, Hank!" she called out again at the top of her lungs.

"Ben. Ben, can you hear me?" she said to the limp body of her dear friend. "Ben, nod your head if you can hear me." She positioned herself on the bank by the fallen tree and resisted the urge to go further. Hank didn't need to rescue two people.

"Betsy, Betsy, Betsy!" Hank cried out when he heard her shout his name. He ran to the sound of her voice. His heart raced as he braced himself for what he might see.

"Oh, Ben, I'm so sorry. Please be okay. Please be alive," he said into the approaching darkness as he got closer to Betsy's location.

"Ben. Ben, we're here now. Please, please let me know you're alive." As tears streamed down her face, she pleaded to the lifeless body. "Oh, Ben, please don't die. I love you. You're my brother, Ben. Please nod your head or open your eyes."

As Hank's footsteps approached, Ben moved his head.

"Yes. Yes, Ben!" Betsy grinned and shouted excitedly. "I see you. You'll be okay."

"Is he alive?" Hank said as he crouched down on the tree trunk.

Betsy could only nod wildly and smile.

"Ben, I'm coming for you. Hang on, buddy," Hank said in a calm voice. "I'm coming for you, Ben. Help is here."

He made his way carefully on the tree trunk toward Ben and then through the water. The frigid water was up to his chest, but he found a much higher rock on which to stand.

"Ben, can you hear me?" He wrapped his arms around his waist and under the trapped arm. "I'm going to lift you and your arm at the same time. Okay?"

Ben managed to open his eyes and nod once before he fell motionless again.

"It's gonna hurt—big time. I'm sorry, but it's the only way," he said. "On the count of three. One, two, three."

Ben screamed out. His friend, the one who wouldn't go fishing with him, had released his arm and freed him from an icy night and potential death.

On the ride to the hospital, Ben lay in the back seat, his knees folded up and his head on Betsy's lap. She had wrapped his arm between two pieces of wood and given him some ibuprofen from the first aid kit. Her Red Cross first aid course had been put to good use. All the while, she cried and repeated, "Never scare me like this again, Ben Murphy. We love you."

Once his arm had been stabilized, and he'd warmed up, he could speak again. "How did you know where to find me?" He looked from Betsy to the back of Hank's head.

"You're my best friend, Ben," Hank said. "We've been friends so long I know how you think." His voice caught in his throat. "And I can't imagine life without you in it. I know I hurt you. I'm sorry."

Ben looked surprised and then sad. "No, I'm just a jerk." His words faltered. "Betsy's your girl. I—"

"Wait a minute," Betsy said, her voice stern. "We are all best friends—got it? There's room for all of us in our lives. I won't have it any other way."

The car fell silent as her words hung in the air. The boys were quiet for a few seconds before they burst out laughing.

"Ow, ow—don't make me laugh. It hurts," Ben said as he tried to stifle his laughter.

"If all of this," she said as she waved her hand over Ben's arm and at the back of Hank's head, "is because you two couldn't figure out that you were best friends... Well, I just might not be speaking to either of you for a very long time."

Silence filled the car again before the boys erupted into laughter.

~

Ben shook his head as Betsy cleared the remaining cinnamon rolls and bowl of frosting from the table. Sheriff Ben had done a fine job of downing four of the sweet pastries.

"Nothing like a scolding from a girl much shorter than you to set you on the path to righteousness," he said as he grinned and wiped his mouth.

Hank laughed and nodded. "Yep, seems she did that a lot before we finally figured it out."

Ben raised his coffee cup. "Here's to having room in your heart for a girlfriend and a best friend," he said. "Thank you, Hank."

CHAPTER SIXTEEN

"I always enjoy the good sheriff's visits," Betsy said with a grin. "And over the years, I learned to double the batch of cinnamon rolls." Her men laughed out loud.

"I think he ate more than me, and that's saying a lot," Andy said. "That man has truly perfected the art of eating those rolls." They all laughed and nodded in agreement. Lady jumped up from her nap, shook herself, and nudged her nose under Hank's hand.

"I think Miss Lady needs a trip outside," he said. When she heard those words, Lady spun twice and ran to the kitchen door.

"Let me take her out, Dad," Andy said. "I need to stretch my legs and breathe in more of this amazing mountain air. I've missed it—and this place." He stood up and Lady knew instantly who would take her out.

"I swear that dog can speak English," said Betsy with a smile. "She just knows things and I'm uncertain how." She watched as her son walked to the door. When it opened, the black-and-white tornado bounded out and spun several circles before she dashed to the trees. "She's so in tune with every sound and movement. Sometimes I think she's reading my mind, silly as that sounds. She's an amazing companion and a definite member of our family."

"It's interesting how she's made it a point to be near me since I haven't felt well," Hank said as he sighed. "She'll often just sit in front of me and stare for a moment or two and then place her paw on my knee, as if to comfort me. She wants me to know she's there."

"I'm so happy she came to live with us." She smiled at her husband. "And it's all thanks to you, my love." She bent down and gave Hank a quick kiss. "Now, why don't you go rest in your chair by the fire?"

"Brilliant idea as usual." He kissed her hand.

No sooner had he'd gotten comfortable in front of the fireplace than Lady bounded into the room. She stopped just short of crashing into his leg and gently placed her paw on his knee as she stared into his eyes.

"Yes," he said with a smile. "I love you, too, my Lady." He stroked the top of her head as she thumped her tail ever so lightly on the carpet. After a minute, she sighed and lay down beside his chair closest to the warm fire. She was content that all was well with her world.

Andy walked in the door as Betsy finished the kitchen cleanup. "There's barely any snow left out there," he said and removed his boots. "Won't be long and the flowers and trees will be in full bloom." He gave his mom a tender smile. "I saw a few iris stems coming through the dirt by the house. I know that makes you happy."

"Yes. Yes, it does." She smiled back at her son. "You know me well." She dried her hands and hung the towel by the sink. "Let's go in and sit with your father."

"That's exactly what I had in mind." He waited for her

before he walked toward the living room. "It's such a peaceful room, especially filled with your love, Mom."

Betsy walked beside him and wrapped one arm around his waist. "You and your father are very easy for me to love, Andy."

Lady jumped up and led them to their chairs and the warmth of the glowing embers.

When Andy sat down, Lady promptly sat in front of him and waited for more rubs. He laughed.

"She's such a remarkable dog. I told her it was okay to go run, but she stayed by my side most of the time. She did her business and came right back. I told her several times to go on. But she insisted she needed to make sure I didn't get lost," Andy said and laughed.

"That's her herding instinct," his dad said. "But I think it's more than that. We're her family and she wants to be near us and defend us. You're new to the pack," he said with a grin.

Lady took her position by Hank again as if she knew his words were about her. She rested her paw on his leg and looked at him.

Betsy laughed. "I've never known a dog who wouldn't break a stare with you and never blink. Maggie told me that's what this breed does to the animal it's herding. It's called 'giving the eye' and she knows how to use it well on any of our chickens that get out of their pen," she said with a grin. "And when she stares at you, it's almost as if she knows your thoughts without them being spoken."

She slowly shook her head. "I know she wouldn't hesitate to take on a bear if she thought we were in danger. When I walk out into the woods with her, she leads me and stops every so often to listen and sniff the air. She'll look back at me as if to say it's all clear and safe to move on, but never very far ahead. She's done that since she was about seven months old. I guess that's when she decided we were her charges." She smiled at her husband. "I'm so happy you brought her home for me, honey. I fell in love with that little bundle of fur the moment she ran across the kitchen and into my arms."

"Yep, that one's all love and loyalty for sure," Andy said. "We should all be so lucky to have a friend like her."

At that moment, Lady walked to the center of the room and sat upright with her front paws in the air, swishing her tail back and forth. She appeared to smile at her humans. Border collie families had often said their fur friends had a certain expression that quite accurately looked like a smile.

"Okay, Lady, now you're just showing off," Hank said as they all laughed. "And did I mention she's a clown?" Their furry friend barked once and ran off to find a toy. She was only gone a minute when she returned with her squeaky squirrel. She lay down by Hank's chair and chewed and licked the little creature with great vigor. Soon enough, she tired of her inanimate friend and laid her head down for a quick nap.

"You must have gotten her just after I left for my last deployment," Andy said. "Where did you find her?"

His dad smiled. "I think she found us."

Hank threw the bags of feed into the back of his truck. Just as he opened the driver's door, someone shouted his name.

"Hank," Maggie hollered. "Hank, you're just the man I need to talk with." She waved her hand above her head to get his attention as she stood beside her pickup across the street.

"Good morning, Maggie," Hank shouted back as he walked over to meet with her. "So, what can I do for you on such a fine day?" He flashed his crooked smile.

"Well, you're always giving my Birdie lots of love when you see her and saying what a fine dog you think she is," said the cheerful older woman dressed in blue coveralls and a pink-checkered shirt.

"Yeah, where is she today, by the way?" he said as he glanced toward Maggie's truck bed. He didn't see the usual black-and-white furry head looking at him.

"Just so happens she's at home tending to her passel of puppies. She's got eight pups that'll be needing homes soon. Do you think you and Betsy might be interested?"

"Well, with Andy gone now, I know so much of Betsy's maternal instincts have been left unused." He shook his head with a grin. "And I can only be mothered so much." He smirked.

Maggie burst out laughing. "I can just picture that," she said with a huge grin. "The pups will be ready to go in a couple of weeks. You're the first person I've spoken to because I wanted to give you the first pick. The sire is Beau, our best herding dog, and he and Birdie have thrown a mighty good-looking bunch of little border collies. This breed is so smart and willing to do whatever you ask just to please you."

"I think I'd like to come see them. When can that happen?"

"Today—right now, if you'd like. I'll be headed home from here if that's good for you."

"Sounds like a plan." He nodded and smiled. "I'll be headed up the mountain right behind you."

Maggie waved out of her window as she drove off. He pulled onto the street and followed her truck to the farm.

Twenty minutes outside of town, and a short way up the mountain, he could see the house, barn, and pens. The dots of white across the hilly meadow got larger as he approached. Maggie and Mitch had worked hard for years to establish profitability with their growing flock of Merino sheep, which now counted over one hundred. They had found an artisans guild whose members purchased all their fine wool to create and carry on the traditional methods of their handmade crafts.

Maggie parked and motioned for Hank to bring his truck up beside hers. She grinned and pointed toward the hill behind the barn.

"You're just in time, Hank, to watch Beau bring in that small part of the herd we had grazing up on the hill today," she said as she motioned toward the higher ground.

He looked out at Mitch and Beau on a grassy knoll. There was a whistle, and Beau bounded up and over the hill to the right. Within moments, a small herd of white wool trotted toward home with Beau behind them. The dog would quickly cut left or right as needed to keep the sheep in a tight pack and headed in the same direction. The docile animals were calm as they followed instruction from their black-and-white compass. Mitch walked toward the main pen as Beau guided the woolen creatures to their proper destination. He saw Hank and waved. He called Beau to his side once all the sheep were penned, and they walked to where Maggie and Hank waited.

"Hello, Mitch," said Hank with a smile and a nod. "That's mighty impressive. It never ceases to amaze me what your dogs can do. I think they're brilliant."

"Yeah, old Beau knows what I need before I do," he replied with a laugh. "It's good to see you, Hank. What brings you out our way?"

Maggie spoke up before Hank could answer. "Remember, we wanted to offer Hank one of Birdie's pups?"

"Oh, right," he said. "It's our way of saying thank you for all the help you've given us over the years. So you thinking of a present for that lovely wife of yours?"

Mitch looked at Maggie and winked. "That's what I did for my Maggie here. I brought Birdie home for her and I got the best dinner in return," he said and smirked. "She even made a peach cobbler for me."

"Well, I think Betsy needs another companion—a furry one," Hank said, grinning.

"Let's walk over to the barn," she said. "I've got them in a stall to keep them contained. They're a lively little crew now, you'll see." She grinned at Hank.

Inside the barn, a chorus of yips and small growls could be heard. Before Maggie walked up to the stall, a flash of black-and-white fur jumped over the short door. Birdie snuggled against Maggie's leg as she swished her tail through the air in a furious motion.

"How's my Birdie?" Maggie said as she bent down and rubbed her face against that of her favorite fur friend. "I brought a nice man to look at those babies of yours," she said to the affectionate dog. "He's a good guy." Birdie looked up into Maggie's eyes and licked her cheek. She glanced at Mitch and wagged her tail at him. Next, she leaned over and sniffed Hank's pant leg. Birdie stared into his eyes without blinking for several seconds. He returned her gaze.

"She's right, Birdie. I am a good guy," he said in a gentle voice, "and we'll take excellent care of your baby."

Birdie stepped over to him and sat in front of her new human friend. He reached down and stroked the top of her head. "That's a good girl. Now let me look at that noisy bunch of fur you made." Birdie thumped her tail and lifted a paw to him as if to shake on it.

"It seems you've struck a deal with her, Hank," Maggie said. They all laughed and shook their heads at Birdie's apparent understanding of Hank's words. "I told you these dogs are smarter than us."

Birdie walked back to the stall and hopped over the door with ease. Her pups rushed her as she laid down to give them a warm snack. The sight made Hank smile. It had been years since he'd watched the magic. There was something about the miracle of life that always lifted his spirit.

As the group walked into the stall, Hank knelt down and was bombarded by a whimpering, wiggling, and squirming mass of black-and-white with wet tongues and puppy breath. Each pup was more excited than the next, except for one. It was the last to lift its head away from its lunch. When Mitch and Maggie knelt on the floor behind Hank, the cluster of fur balls tumbled over each other to get to them. The lone puppy kept its eyes on Hank's face, barked once, and walked straight into his open hands. It had waited its turn to be the center of Hank's attention.

"Well, aren't you quite the clever one? Glad to meet you, too," he said as he sat on the straw-laden wooden floor. He scooped up the puppy and at the sound of his voice, it erupted into a wriggling mass of fur. It licked his face once, shy at first, but then with complete abandon. The soft body was all tongue and paws as the pup thrashed and contorted to get closer to its new friend. Hank laughed and pulled the puppy to his chest, where it continued to bathe his chin. He kissed the top of the furry head and it twisted and pushed upward in order to be face-to-face with him. The puppy looked into his eyes and barked.

"Well, I think you've just been chosen, Hank," Mitch

said as he laughed. "That's a little girl, and I'm pretty sure she's the smartest of them all. The only one brave enough to approach the sheep is her. She even touched noses with one. That one's got courage and intelligence in abundance."

"Definitely," Maggie agreed as she nodded. "She's the one that sees all that's going on, no matter how hungry she may be. Smart as a whip, I tell you. I can almost hear her thinking sometimes. She's so young to be that observant. She'll be a wonder to train and a fantastic companion. I put food in two bowls and all the pups but her will run to the first bowl I set down. But she waits because she knows she'll have the second bowl to herself for a short while." She snorted. "I guess you're the second bowl, Hank."

At the sound of Maggie's voice, the puppy stopped moving and looked at her. She barked once and wagged her tail. They all laughed at her perfect timing.

"She just thanked you for your sales pitch, Mags," her husband said with a grin as he lifted his cap and scratched his head.

"That was mighty ladylike of you," Hank said as he rubbed the puppy's ear between his fingers. "Hey, that's a perfect name for you—Lady." No sooner had he finished his words than he was once again inundated with puppy kisses. "Little girl, I know you're going to make my Betsy a very happy woman."

CHAPTER SEVENTEEN

"I need to make some phone calls and check my messages," Betsy said as she stood up. Lady lifted her head to assess the new movement and returned to her nap beside the one who needed her most.

"Can I get you something, honey?" Betsy said, as she stroked Hank's arm.

"No, I'm good, but thank you, my sweet," he said as he laid his hand on hers. "Andy and I can visit and catch up on life while he was away." He grabbed a peppermint from the bowl by his chair and popped it into his mouth. Then he tossed one to Andy, who caught it mid-flight. The men smiled.

"Okay, Andy, I'm leaving you in charge of your father." She grinned and nodded at her son.

"I can do that," he answered and smiled back at her.

She left the comfort of the smoldering embers. The sun shone through the windows and warmed the interior of the house, filling it with hope.

"Tell me how you're really doing, son," Hank said, his expression filled with love and concern.

"It's been tough. War changes so much in you. It changes the way you see yourself. I've seen things I'll never be able to forget. Images burned into my subconscious. Every day is new, and each day brings a new danger. Keeping my mind focused on my men and my mission helps me get through each hour. It's when I try to sleep that those pictures in my mind haunt and torment me. I do my best to keep them locked away, but sleep makes me vulnerable." He looked at his dad, the pain visible in his eyes.

"I know, son," Hank said in a solemn but gentle voice. "I still have dreams, but not the vivid nightmares that would wake me from a sound sleep and leave me gasping for air anymore."

"Does time help?" Andy's brow furrowed in agony.

"Yes, for me it did. But I also sought counseling—and prayed. I prayed I would be the gentle and loving man who left your mother, but stronger. And I prayed my hell with war would not negatively affect our marriage." He stared out of the window, the sunlight on his face. "It was difficult for a few years, but your mother is the most caring and compassionate human being I've ever known. If not for her love and understanding..." His voice trailed off to a distant memory and pain.

"Thanks, Dad. It helps to know that life can be normal someday." His voice quavered. He cleared his throat and straightened his shoulders. "It was a tough blow when I got my Dear John letter. I've just put those emotions on the back burner for now."

"Sometimes we see best in the darkness." He returned his gaze to his son. "You have to believe there are no coincidences. For whatever reason, that relationship wasn't meant to be. But your person is out there somewhere. And when you least expect it, she'll be there in the right place at the right time. You just need to make sure your head and heart are ready for her. It won't be easy coming back to civilian life, but if you find a woman like your mother—it'll be worth all your effort. I can't imagine my life without her." He shook his head. "Life is full of battles, son. You just must choose which ones you're willing to fight."

Andy nodded and sighed. "You and Mom make it look so easy. I can't remember one instance of hearing you two having an argument."

Hank laughed. "Oh, there were times." He grinned and rubbed his chin. His eyes sparkled. "We just chose to settle our differences in private. When you bring two lives together, they're never going to agree all the time. But, and this is important, we always respected each other. Communication is key. If you don't talk, you don't know, and anger is the result. We always listened to what the other had to say. And your mom had a lot to say." He smiled and nodded slowly. "But we brought balance to one another."

"But where do you start?" The young man's shoulders sagged, and he shook his head.

"You start—and end—with being friends. Love and life fall somewhere in the middle. But you always keep that friendship alive. That friendship and respect curbs your tongue, tempers your attitude, and picks up the one who's fallen. There's no greater number than two. Two built this house. Two built this life. And two built you." His smile was filled with love. Then he flashed a crooked smile, the one Andy had inherited. "Let's go raid the kitchen."

His son laughed and Lady jumped awake, dashing to the kitchen.

"I swear she knows what you're saying," Andy said with a grin.

As the men foraged in the fridge, Betsy walked in and laughed.

"You two look like you're on a mission," she said, and winked at Andy.

"Well, this growing boy here needs more sustenance." Hank grinned as he motioned toward his son.

"And your excuse, sir?" she said as she patted Hank's cheek. He laughed and allowed her to pass to the open door of the movable feast.

"I've taken care of all my correspondence for the day. What would you two like for lunch?"

"Whatever you put on the table will be fine with me," Andy said. "Everything you make always tastes so much better than what I fix." The men both grinned and nodded, backing away. "I'll set the table. Dad, I think your furry friend is waiting for you to take a walk with her if you feel up to it."

"I'm good, son. Come on, Lady, let's see if you can find some creatures to harass."

Betsy laughed. "She does love to chase those squirrels and give them a run to their trees." She peered out the window at Hank and Lady as she smiled. "Okay, I'll just heat some soup and grill ham-and-cheese sandwiches then."

Andy set the table and sat by the counter close to his mother.

"Did you have a good visit with your dad?" she said as she put the griddle on to heat and ladled homemade chicken noodle soup into a saucepan.

"Yes. He gave me a lot to think about, and most importantly, hope." His eyes turned downward.

She looked up and saw the sorrow on her son's face. His

pain likely reflected in her expression. One of her greatest gifts was that of empathy. She recognized and felt a person's pain. It was her compassion that drew people into her world.

She set the pot on the stove, covering it and wiping her hands on her apron. She stood beside Andy and gave him a hug. "I can't even begin to know, son, but your pain is palpable," she whispered. "You can always talk with us, Andy. But don't forget, when you're far from us, He's always there. He's just a breath away."

"I know, Mom. Thanks." He raised his head and looked at her. "I don't talk to Him often enough, but when I do, I can feel His strength. It's just been rough this year."

"All things are possible..." She left the passage open for her son to complete in his own time. She returned to the stove and assembled the sandwiches as she stirred the soup.

Andy nodded with a contemplative expression and watched in silence for a few moments before he spoke. "What do women want? I mean, what is it about Dad that has helped you love him all these years?"

His mother smiled and turned to him. "Those are enormous questions. Do you have lots of time?" She cocked her head and lifted a brow in thought. "The first word that comes to mind when I think of the many years I've known your father is respect."

It was quiet for a second, and then they burst out laughing. "Well, yes, Aunt Estelle and I taught those boys a lesson in respect, but this is much deeper." She grinned as she gained her composure. "This is the respect a man shows a woman, without which love struggles to grow. Love and respect go hand in hand. When a husband shows his wife respect, she feels safe both in his arms and in his love.

"That's what all women want—to feel safe. They need

to know their heart won't be broken by harsh, angry words or disregard. Love is respect, faithfulness, loyalty, and dedication to keeping her heart safe. A wife needs to be shown kindness above all others. Love is a verb and fights all enemies that battle the heart. Love doesn't falter or waiver." She thought for a moment. "It takes conscious effort to stay the course and to commit daily to your relationship. Does that make sense?"

He nodded. "Yes, what I hear is treasure and guard your wife's love and her heart, right?" he said as he watched his mom cooking. She turned and smiled at him. Pride filled her eyes.

Betsy continued, her voice earnest. "And you need to always show her she's the most important person in your life and the most beautiful woman in your world. Remind her daily with your words and often with small gifts of flowers or handwritten poems you know she likes. It doesn't have to be extravagant. Just show her she is never far from your thoughts. Know her. Listen to her."

Betsy rested her hands on the counter and looked directly into her son's eyes. "You must secure in her mind that you will not betray her trust, not when she's young and not when the years have grayed her hair and wrinkled her face. As you guard her heart, you must guard your own. There are beautiful women everywhere and you'll be tempted to allow your thoughts to wander. But remember, your thoughts are stored in your heart. So what you sow in your mind will also grow in your heart. It won't take long for those weeds of desire to block the joy and overtake the love you once had for your wife growing there. Don't let your mind lead your heart astray. Love is true and truth. Love needs to be maintained and never taken for granted." She wrinkled her brows. "Did I answer your question?"

Andy smiled and thought about an answer. "Yes, and you've given me a lot to think about. In one sentence, I'd say I need to treat my wife just as I want to be treated. Right?" he grinned at his mom.

Betsy laughed. "Yes. But love her even more than yourself. Okay, class over," she said with a big grin. "Please call your father in to eat now."

He stood up, but stopped before he got to the door. "Thanks, Mom. You're the best. What you and Dad shared should help make me a better man."

The men came in with Lady, who bounced up and down and bounded through the house and back to the kitchen. Her pack laughed at her enthusiasm.

"After we eat, we'll go out and tend to our fur and feathered friends in the barn," Hank said as he looked at his son.

As they ate, they discussed the ups and downs and the highs and lows of married life as they knew it. Several times, Hank or Betsy would reach out and pat the other's hand and they'd share a smile.

"Love is work, Andy," Hank said as he leaned back in his chair.

"And love is often compromise," Betsy added, and winked at her husband.

Then they looked at each other for a second or two and said in stereo, "Love is worth it."

Andy laughed. "And that's what happens when you've been married for such a long time."

CHAPTER EIGHTEEN

Andy carried his dad's small suitcase to the Bronco. Lady followed him and bounced around the vehicle, excited and looking for an invitation to join the suitcase.

"Sorry, Lady, but you can't go with us this time." As the furry face stared at him, his tone of voice stopped her wagging. She dropped her head at the rejection and sat. She wasn't often left at home alone.

"I know, girl, but you need to stay here." He crouched down and stroked the sides of her head with both hands. "It's going to be a long wait today." She licked his face in forgiveness and bounded back to the house. She seemed eager to check on the rest of her family inside. When Andy opened the house door, she ran straight to Hank and laid at his feet and stared up at him.

"Is there anything else I can do?" he asked when he met his mother in the kitchen. He sounded anxious, but then he'd never taken his father for surgery before.

She put her hand on his shoulder. "Sit. Relax. We still have a few minutes before we need to leave. You have time for more coffee." As she filled his cup, her hand trembled.

Hank was in the other room on the phone for several minutes. "Okay, Ben. We'll see you at the hospital in about an hour. And thanks—for everything."

Betsy set her tea down and walked to the corner of the kitchen where her memory box still sat on the counter. "I'm glad I left this downstairs. I almost forgot something." She opened it, reaching in and pulling out an envelope. She slipped it into her purse as she closed the lid.

Her husband walked into the kitchen and gave her a long hug. She wrapped her arms around him, laid her head on his chest, and lightly rubbed his back.

"Have I told you today how beautiful you are? And how lucky I am?"

She smiled. "I think you just did," she whispered back to him.

Her words made him smile as he released his grip. "Ben is going to meet us at the hospital. He wants to wait with you while I'm in surgery."

"He's always been such a good friend." But her smile didn't have the usual brightness. "We can always count on him."

"That'll be good," Andy said. Ben had been a member of their family as long as he could remember, and they relied on his strength in trying times.

"Your case is in the Bronco. Is there anything else I can do for you, Dad?"

"Just keep your mother company and make sure she eats something." He winked at his wife. "I've also instructed Ben to make sure you're fed."

"I'll be fine, you silly man." Her eyes expressed her gratitude for her husband's concern about her well-being.

He turned to look for Lady. She was within reach. He knelt and put his face next to hers. "Take good care of our family," he whispered in her ear. She thumped her tail on the floor and licked his cheek. He wrapped his arms around her shoulders and patted her side. She swished her tail back and forth in acknowledgment. "You're the best, my sweet Lady."

He stood up and put his hand on Andy's shoulder. "You're the keeper, son."

Andy stood up and gave his dad a tight hug. "I love you, Dad. And I'll keep everyone safe and the home fire burning while you're gone."

"I'm confident in that," his dad replied, "and that's a comfort to me."

"It's time to leave, but before we do..." Betsy held out her hands to her two men. They joined hands and bowed their heads.

Estelle was waiting in the hospital parking lot for her sister and family. She wanted to be close by during Hank's surgery to offer moral support. He was like the brother she'd never had and was part of her family even before Betsy married him. They had all shared so many memories. She said some prayers for Hank that morning because she didn't want their time with him to end, not yet. She'd spent weeks away traveling for business. Now she needed to let Hank and Betsy know how much she loved them and how dear Hank was to her. He'd been so good to Betsy all of these years and she appreciated how happy he'd made her sister. She got out of her car to let them know she was there and always would be.

"There you are," Andy said as his aunt walked up and hugged him.

"Of course. You know I'd be here for my family." She smiled at her nephew. "I swear you look more like your father every time I see you. And with that same trademark crooked smile. It's like you're thinking of some crime to commit—or you've already done it." Betsy and Hank laughed as they climbed out of the vehicle.

"Good morning, Estelle," Hank said as he wrapped his arm around her shoulder and squeezed. He looked at her and they shared a loving smile. "Thanks for coming."

"I'd say good morning back to you, Hank, but I'm not sure if the surgery disqualifies that." She grinned at him and then at her sister, who reached over to hug her.

"Good morning, sis," Betsy said as the women held each other for a moment.

"I'm here, Betsy," she whispered in her sister's ear. She smiled as a tear fell on Estelle's shoulder. "It's going to be okay," she said and patted her back.

Andy grabbed his dad's small suitcase. "I have your bag."

"Well, let's get me checked in then," Hank said. He looked at his family members and smiled.

Ben arrived at the hospital just before they put Hank in a wheelchair to go into pre-op.

"Good, I'm here before you go in." Ben wrapped his enormous arms around Hank's chest and squeezed. Hank couldn't see the worried look on his friend's face.

"You mean the world to me, you know that, right Hank?"

"Likewise, Ben." He hugged his friend back with the same amount of love.

"Is there anything else I can do for you?" Ben asked as he looked his friend in the eyes.

"One last thing. Take good care of our Betsy, will you?" His voice was strong, but his smile hinted at his fear.

"Always, my friend. You know I cherish her, too. Where would we be without her?" He grinned and looked at Betsy, who stood close by.

"I think you both would be in a world of trouble," she said, and looked at Estelle. "Right?" They all laughed when Estelle nodded and grinned.

"Well, I guess you two would know better than anyone," Ben said as he grimaced.

"I seem to remember they acted as accomplices a few times," Hank chimed in, and grinned. From behind him, a nurse cleared her throat. "I think that's my cue. I love each of you. Don't worry—I'll see you soon," he said when he sat in the wheelchair. As the nurse wheeled him down the hallway, he held up his hand with the victory sign. They all smiled. That was Hank alright.

The group walked to the waiting area where there was a table with coffee, tea, and packaged snacks. Estelle followed close behind and eyed the choice of teas.

"There," Betsy said as she pointed out the table to her male guardians. "I will be fully nourished while we wait. So you needn't worry about feeding me."

The men laughed. "That's not exactly what Hank meant, and you know it." Ben said as he shook his finger at her.

"A mere technicality, Mom."

"Okay, if I get truly hungry, one of you can go to the cafeteria for me." She conceded with a nervous smile.

"I got this, boys," Estelle said with a voice of authority and a look that caused the men to step back and grin.

They hadn't been seated for very long when the surgeon came in. "Good morning, Betsy." He had a confident smile.

"Good morning, Dr. Chandler. Let me introduce my sister, Estelle, my son, Andy, and our dear friend, Sheriff Ben."

"Good morning. Nice to meet all of you," the doctor said as he looked with astonishment at both women. "I knew you had a sister, but I'm amazed at the resemblance." His surprise was frozen on his face. "Forgive me, I'm not used to seeing double. A pleasure to meet you, Estelle." He recovered and turned toward Andy. "I'm glad you could come home. Your folks told me you might get some leave time. And lastly, Sheriff Ben, good to meet you. Your reputation precedes you." The doctor smiled and extended his hand.

"Only believe the good stuff." Ben shook his hand and grinned.

The doctor turned his attention to Betsy again. "I know this is a serious operation, Betsy, but I'm confident I can remove the tumor in its entirety." He paused and took a breath, careful in his wording. "We found it in its early stages, fortunately, and it's in such a place that there should be little to no adverse effects afterward. Hank may need some minor rehabilitation, but he's healthy and should recover quickly."

She inhaled deeply and nodded. "That sounds good. And the operation will take about three to four hours, you said?" She exhaled and held her sister's hand.

"We won't know exactly until we're in there. But I think that's a reasonable assumption. I'll have the nurse come out and give you updates on our progress. Do you have more questions?" he asked. He took her hand in both of his. "I'll take good care of him, Betsy. And I want you to know—I'll have angels guiding my hands." The doctor gave her a warm smile and nodded before he turned to leave.

"That was unexpected," said Andy with a puzzled look.

"No, it's exactly as I expected," his mother said. "I knew your father would have angels with him in the operating room." Betsy smiled at her with certainty. His Aunt Estelle smiled at him as well.

"Does anyone want tea or coffee?" Betsy asked as she walked to the beverage table. She and Estelle shared some quiet words as they prepared their tea.

With her beverage beside her on the table, Betsy reached into her purse and brought out a small yellow envelope. She sighed as she pulled out a clear, laminated bookmark. She looked at it and a tear rolled down her cheek. The lamination had permanently protected a dried daisy. An inscription on white paper was below the flower. Estelle, Ben, and Andy all noticed she had taken something from her purse. But now her tears caused them concern.

"What is it, Mom?" Andy's brows knitted together. He put his hand on his mother's arm and waited.

"Betsy," Ben said in a deep, soft voice. He looked at Estelle for an answer.

Betsy looked up and smiled at them through her tears. She stroked the bookmark.

"This," she said as she held up the daisy, "is Hank's promise to me. He promised to always come back—and he did."

CHAPTER NINETEEN

"Please, Betsy, don't be mad," Hank said. "I've told you my whole life I wanted to join the military. It's a tradition in our family. My dad and grandfather both joined to fight for our country. It's my heritage. It's my du—"

"You said you spoke with your dad," Betsy interrupted, her words unfiltered. "He told you not to join just because he had. You were supposed to think about it." She glared at him. "You had said nothing for weeks since graduation. I thought I talked you out of going—because you loved me," she said with tight lips. She narrowed her eyes. "So you lied," she hissed.

"I've never lied to you," he replied. "Dad told me to think about it and make my decision, and that's what I've done." His eyes filled with tears. "Things are different now—now that he's gone. But I have to do this for me, Betsy. It's who I am," he tried to explain. "The recruiter was in town and because I signed up today, he offered me extra bonuses. This was the first chance I—"

But Betsy jumped out of the car and slammed the door

shut. She gripped her purse, her anger apparent as she strode down the sidewalk.

"Betsy, wait," he shouted as he leaped out of the car and hurried to catch her.

"And just why should I wait?" she said without turning. "Why should I ever wait?" She threw her hands in the air.

"Because it's getting dark and I don't want you to walk home alone." He held his hands out as he pleaded. "I couldn't forgive myself if anything happened to you."

She stopped suddenly and whirled around. Hank almost ran into her, but he caught himself and shuffled backward.

"So you do care for me." She sneered as her face reddened. "You don't want me to walk home alone in the dark," she said, "but it's okay for you to break my heart." Her face was flushed with anger.

"That's not true. I don't want to hurt you." His face twisted in pain at the sound of her words. "Just let me take you home. You don't even have to talk to me. C'mon, Betsy, please."

The streetlight had come on behind him. She walked around him and got back into the car. When Hank sat in the driver's seat, she looked straight ahead, lips tight and face emotionless. They rode in silence for twenty minutes.

When he parked in front of her house, he turned to speak to her.

"Betsy, I'm sor—"

But she was halfway out of the car and slammed the door on his words. Without looking back, she walked into the house and shut the door behind her.

He sat with his head on the steering wheel, and his shoulders slumped for several minutes.

"What have I done?" he whispered to himself. Misery filled the car as he drove home.

~

"Is that you, Betsy?" her mother said as she ran upstairs to her bedroom. "I saved some dinner for you, honey," she called out.

"Thanks, but I'm not hungry," Betsy said flatly. "I'm going to bed now."

"I wonder what's wrong with her," her mom said to Betsy's grandmother. "She's been pretty moody since Estelle left for college—I suppose that's it. This is the first time the girls have ever been apart. I knew it would be harder for her because she's more emotional." She sighed and shook her head. "Estelle, on the other hand, is more reserved and stoic."

"Well, Estelle is two minutes older, after all." Nana was the only one to laugh at her joke. "Just let her be," the older woman said. "Whatever it is, she'll work it out overnight. And if not, maybe she'll talk about it tomorrow."

Betsy walked into her room, locking the door and pressing her back against it. Her face was flushed with anger and hurt. She picked up the phone and called her sister, but there was no answer. Dropping the phone, she threw herself across the bed. Tears smeared her cheeks as she grabbed her comforter and rolled onto her side. She cried into the night before she fell asleep, exhausted from the emotional upheaval.

Hours later, there was a knock on her bedroom door. She sat up, the morning sunlight streaming across the room. Her mouth was dry and her eyes were nearly swollen shut from the long night of crying.

"Who is it?" She brushed her hair off of her face and squinted at the brightness from the window.

"Honey, it's Mom. Hank is on the phone. Do you want me to tell him you'll call back?"

"No," she snapped. "And tell him never to call me again."

"What? I don't understand." Her voice was shocked.

"Sorry, Mom, I didn't mean to snap at you. I just don't want to talk to him ever again."

"Oh, okay." She turned and hurried back down the stairs and picked up the phone.

"Hank, I'm sorry, but she said she doesn't want to—"

"... speak to me ever. Right?" he said, as he finished the sentence.

"Yes," she answered, hesitating before she spoke again. "Whatever it is, just give her some time to think about it, Hank."

"I told her I enlisted yesterday, and she's angry," he said apologetically. "But I really feel it's the right thing for me to do. I'm just sorry she doesn't understand."

"She needs time, but I can't say how much or what that will mean for you."

Hank lowered his eyes and slowly exhaled. "I don't have a lot of time," he said in a low, disheartened voice. "I leave in three weeks."

"It's been weeks, Betsy. You should at least speak to Hank to say goodbye. He leaves in just about an hour. You two have been friends most of your life. This isn't fair to him," her mom said, her eyebrows furrowed and her voice worried. She could not convince her daughter.

"Mom, please," Betsy said, her annoyance clear. "I don't care how many times he's sent flowers, stood at our door, or called. I don't want to see or talk to him."

"But—"

Her mom's words fell on deaf ears. Betsy had already left the room and was walking down the hallway when her grandmother called from the living room.

"Betsy. Betsy, honey, come here, please."

"Yes, Nana?" she asked as she looked at her grandmother sitting in the rocking chair. Harvey was on her lap, soaking up the warmth from a sunbeam.

"Come and sit down by me for a moment, please." Her grandmother's voice was loving, but firm.

"Okay." She pulled the hassock closer to her grandmother. Harvey lifted his head and yawned as she sat down. She reached out and stroked his head as he purred. Nana and Harvey spent a lot of time sitting in front of the large window. She watched the people, and he watched the birds. Occasionally, a squirrel sighting caused Harvey to jump to the windowsill. He'd stare with rapt attention as he swished his tail and his whiskers twitched.

Betsy put her hand on her grandmother's arm. "What is it, Nana? Are you alright?"

"Yes, but I'm concerned for you, my sweet girl," she said with a slight smile. "I have always been amazed by your determination once you've set a goal. You've been pretty fearless when you've decided on something, and you've accomplished quite a lot in your young life. But what I see in you now is not determination, but stubbornness. It's a fear of change that you can't control."

Betsy lowered her eyes as they welled with tears that rolled down her cheeks and dripped onto her shirt. Her grandmother had said nothing to her before now.

"Nana, I'm angry with Hank," she whispered in her defense. "He made a decision he knew I wouldn't like. I—"

Nana lifted her granddaughter's chin, looked deep into her eyes, and took her hand in hers. "This was not your decision to make, Betsy," the old woman said. "You need to see beyond what you want. Hank has goals and dreams, too. I'm sure you are part of those, but not all. He has an admirable sense of duty to his family's tradition and honor, even more so since his father's death. You can't expect him to walk away from that. It would be to deny him his integrity, something deep inside him by which to navigate his life. This is part and parcel of who he is."

She stopped and filled her lungs for a few seconds as she rubbed Harvey's back. She continued. "For him to walk away from his calling would crush his spirit and diminish his sense of self." She patted Betsy's hand. "You might have him, but it wouldn't be all of him. He would lose his valor." Nana drew a quick breath. "Some men need to fight to find their strength. Some men need to test their courage in order to grow. To deny him that would be to deny him his identity —his manhood. Could you live with that? Because he can't. For him, military service is his rite of passage." The wise woman stared at her granddaughter's face. "Without this, he will live a life of doubt in himself."

The young woman wept even harder, but she looked down again. "Nana, I don't know what to do."

Her grandmother smiled and said, "I think you do, child —and you better hurry. He leaves in less than an hour."

"Oh, no," Betsy gasped as her eyes darted to a clock on the mantle. She jumped up and turned, then stopped. She bent down and hugged her grandmother.

"Thank you, Nana. I love you so much. You're right. I have to hurry."

She ran to the kitchen and grabbed her purse before giving her mother a quick hug.

"I'm so sorry, Mom," she whispered. She turned and headed for the front door. "I'm taking the car to see if I can catch Hank before he leaves. Thank you, Mom. I love you," she shouted as she bolted out of the door that slammed behind her.

Betsy drove faster than she should. But now she was determined to see Hank and to apologize. Her grandmother's words had cut through the stubbornness that had hardened her heart.

She took a shortcut through town that would intersect with the road he'd be on. Once there, she parked on the side of the gravel road. She waited about ten minutes and soon a wave of worry hit her.

"Oh, no," she whispered, "I can't have missed him. Please—please, God, let him come to me. I've learned this lesson, I promise. Please, let me see him." She clasped her hands and pressed them to her lips.

Seconds later, a vehicle came toward her in the distance. As it got closer, she parted her lips and a smile crossed her face. Betsy leaped out of her vehicle.

"Yes, thank you, God," she cried out as she grinned and waved her hands and arms above her head. She jumped up and down and continued to wave at the oncoming truck.

The truck slowed down, and there was Hank, smiling. He turned on the blinkers and pulled up behind her car.

"Hank," she shouted as he jumped out of his truck. She ran toward him and he met her with open arms. She clung to him as she never had, and he wrapped her tightly in his embrace. Tears rolled down his face as he hugged her. He couldn't speak.

"I love you and I'm so sorry, Hank," she uttered, pressing her face against his chest. "I'm just a stupid, silly girl and I don't deserve your love. But please, forgive me and give me another chance."

He took a deep breath and wiped his tears. He lifted her face and looked into her eyes. "I can't give you another chance, Betsy," he said with his crooked smile, "because I haven't stopped loving you. My heart is still yours and always will be. In case you didn't know, I've always loved you."

She looked at him and a flood of relief wracked her body. She couldn't stop her tears and could only repeat his name as she sobbed.

"Are you still my girl, Betsy?" he said in a gentle voice, his arms still around her.

She regained enough of her composure to nod. When she found her voice, she said, "Always. I will always be your girl." She hesitated and whispered, "Please come back to me, Hank."

They stood in silence and held one another for several minutes. He looked over her shoulder. "Just a minute," he said, releasing her. He walked toward the edge of the road, bent down, and reached out his hand. He returned and handed her a wild daisy. The white petals danced in the breeze surrounding the radiant yellow disc.

"This is my promise to you, Betsy," he said. "As long as these flowers grow, I will always come back to you."

Betsy extended her hand and took the flower. She smiled up at him and stepped closer as rose on her tiptoes to place a gentle kiss on his lips.

"And I will always wait," she said, placing her hand on his cheek.

Hank smiled and looked into her tear-filled eyes. "Only you have a place in my heart, Betsy. Only you," he whispered and pressed his lips to hers. She met his kiss with all the love and fear her childish heart felt.

CHAPTER TWENTY

Betsy and her family looked up from their conversation when a nurse in blue scrubs walked into the waiting room. It had been over two hours since the surgery started.

"Mrs. Walker?" she said, smiling as she approached Betsy. "My name is Hannah. I'm an OR nurse. Dr. Chandler asked me to come and give you an update. Your husband's operation is going well and with no complications. The doctor expects to complete the surgery within the next two hours. I'll come back again with another update when that happens. Do you have questions?"

Betsy shook her head as she exhaled. Estelle and Ben each held one of her hands and smiled at the news. They exhaled as well and smiled at Andy.

"No, I—I don't think so," she said as she relaxed. "Thank you, and please tell the doctor thank you for us."

"I will. Is there anything you need? The cafeteria is on the first floor if you're getting hungry," the kind nurse said.

"Thank you, ma'am," Ben said with a smile. "That might be what we all need."

"Oh, wait," Betsy said as the nurse turned to leave. "How soon after surgery will I be able to see my husband?"

"Normally, it would be a few hours in post-op to ensure everything is going well and he's coming out of surgery correctly. But I'll have more details the next time I have an update," the nurse said. She turned and walked down the hallway.

"I think I'd like to eat something now." Although she smiled at her two keepers and Estelle, Betsy was still strained by her concern.

"Come on, boys, let's take a walk to the cafeteria," said Estelle. "I'll bring something back for you, Betsy. Sound okay?" she said and hugged her. "That was good news from the doctor, but I know you want to wait here. Try to relax for now."

Betsy nodded. "That sounds perfect," she said with a smile.

Betsy stepped out of the elevator and was startled as she almost ran into Hank's surgeon. A bit flustered, she blurted out an apology.

"Oh, excuse me, Dr. Chandler," she said as they stood mere inches away from one another. "I am so sorry."

"Actually, it's me who needs to apologize. Not only was I not paying attention, but I was on the wrong side of the corridor," the good doctor said as his face reddened. "I really drive much better than I walk." His humor melted any tension, and they both laughed, enjoying the respite from the seriousness of their relationship.

"I was just on my way to see my husband," she offered.

"As am I," the doctor said with a gracious smile. "Then Hank will have to contend with the pair of us. Shall we?"

They walked down the hall for only moments and entered Hank's room at the same time.

He opened his eyes at the sound of their footsteps and grinned with recognition. "Wow, I'm blessed with not one, but two visitors," he said. "The most beautiful woman in the world and the renowned brain surgeon, Dr. Chandler."

Betsy and the doctor smiled as they both approached his bed. She leaned over to give her husband a kiss. "Good morning, honey," she said, patting his arm. "Look who I almost bumped into." She glanced around at the doctor behind her.

"I hope you won't be terribly disappointed if I don't give you a morning kiss, Hank," Dr. Chandler said with a smirk. "I like you, but not that much. And my wife is a jealous woman." Hank and Betsy laughed.

She stepped aside and sat in a nearby chair to watch and listen.

"How are you feeling this morning, Hank?" Dr. Chandler asked as he stepped up beside the bed. He was known for his great bedside manner, besides his excellent surgery skills.

"Good morning, Doc," he replied. "I'm much better than a few days ago, not to mention a lot more coherent now that the anesthesia has fully worn off. My headaches aren't as bad today as they have been, either."

The doctor looked at the latest entries on the chart. "Headaches are to be expected for a while. Are they manageable with the medication?" he said as he checked Hank's bandages.

"Yes. In fact, I think I could even gradually back off of the meds today," he said. "I'm not feeling dizzy this morning and my appetite has improved. So I'd say I'm recovering just fine, wouldn't you?" He grinned at Dr. Chandler.

The doctor laughed. "I don't suppose you want to go home, do you?" he asked his patient.

"Well, in my professional opinion," he said, "it's well documented that patients recover from surgery much better when their beautiful wives are caring for them." He looked at Betsy and winked.

Dr. Chandler shook his head as he grinned. "Well, everything looks pretty good to me," he said, "and I know your wife has a lot of medical experience, so I'd be putting you in expert hands. I'm friends with Dr. Michaels," he said and turned toward Betsy, winking. "He speaks highly of her. She has quite the reputation for helping folks on your mountain." She smiled and blushed at the acknowledgment.

"Yep, she's a real blessing to me and our community," Hank said with pride and smiled at his wife. "So what do you think my chances are of being set free today?"

The doctor checked Hank's pupils with his penlight and put it back in his pocket.

"I see you've been up several times over the past four days and are able to walk to the bathroom by yourself now." Dr. Chandler glanced again at the chart. "Any numbness or balance issues when you get up?"

"The nurse assisted me and I took it slow like she said the first couple of days. Just some slight dizziness the first time, but my balance was okay. The second time was better, though, and improved each time after."

"I want the nurse to put a fresh dressing on your head and she'll report back to me. If everything looks good, you'll be able to go home by lunchtime," the doctor explained. "How does that sound?" Hank nodded and smiled. "Rest and walking are the best things to do for your recovery."

"I like the sound of that plan, doc," he answered with a grin. "Now where's the nurse?" He looked past his doctor and toward the door.

The doctor laughed. "I'll give her my instructions ASAP." He turned to Betsy. "And if any concerning issues develop, call me right away, okay?"

Betsy nodded as she exhaled, less worry on her face. "Yes, of course. Thank you.

"Questions?" the doctor asked, and looked back at his patient.

"Yes, when can I dance with my wife again?" Hank said with a serious face before giving the doctor a crooked smile.

The doctor grinned back at him. "I'll have to admit, you're the first to ask that question. I'd say when you're comfortable walking and turning with no dizziness or imbalance. You'll know, Hank." Dr. Chandler put his hand on his shoulder. "You're a wise man to keep the romance alive." The men laughed.

"It's a good way to keep your woman in your arms," Hank quipped with a grin and cut his eyes toward Betsy. "Thanks for everything, Doc," he said as he looked at him and nodded.

"Well, you'll want to be thanking your angels, too," the doctor said with a smile. "They were guiding my hands the entire time."

As Andy pulled the vehicle up to the house, Hank's welcome committee waited on the porch. Lady was too excited to wait any longer. She barked once and jumped from the top stair to the ground, where she spun in circles. She stayed near the stairs and out of the way of the

Bronco, but once it stopped, she ran to the first opened door.

Andy hopped out of the driver's side and she greeted him as she jumped up and down, just out of reach.

"Hi, girl. I brought someone home for you," he said and stretched out his hand to the ecstatic canine. Lady sat instantly for some strokes, but as soon as she heard another door open, she ran to the other side. She saw Hank and whined and furiously wagged her tail. She had never been without him or Betsy for more than a day. When she saw Andy come around, she moved out of the way and sat, waiting just a little longer.

"Hey there, Lady. Did you miss me?" Hank said as Andy grabbed his dad's arm to help him out. He stood up and patted his leg. "Come here, my sweet girl," he said. Lady sidled up to him and leaned against him as he stroked the top of her head. She whimpered and looked up at him as she licked his arm. "I know," he said. "I missed you, too."

"Let's get you inside, Hank," Betsy said and smiled. "You two can reunite more in the house." Lady ran up the stairs and waited for her pack.

Ben came down the stairs to assist his friend while Andy carried in his dad's case.

"Sure is good to see you, buddy," Ben said as he put a hand under Hank's elbow and one on his back. "I just want to make sure you get up here where you belong, my friend."

"Thanks, Ben," Hank said. "And it's mighty good to see you, too."

Estelle waited by the door, which she opened for them.

She reached out and gave Hank a quick hug before he went inside. "Nice to see you, Hank," she said. "We missed you. And we've entirely rearranged your house in your honor." She laughed. "Ben and Andy helped, too. We needed strong backs," she added.

"Hey, it was her idea," Ben said as he grinned and pointed at Betsy.

"What? What kind of scheme have the bunch of you devised?" he said with a smile. As he walked in, some embers were glowing in the fireplace and the library doors were closed. "Well, so far nothing appears to be catastrophic." He stopped in the living room and looked at Betsy and her partners in crime. Lady stopped and sat at his side, watching his every move. She knew to be close, but not in his way. Her tail rubbed back and forth across the carpet and her ears were perked up in anticipation.

"You've been up quite a while now," Betsy said. "We should get you settled in and off your feet. How's the head feeling?"

"Yeah, I feel pretty exhausted with just a slight headache," Hank said as he moved toward his recliner. "Sitting in front of the fireplace will feel fantastic right now."

As Hank neared his chair with Ben and Andy beside him, Estelle and Betsy walked ahead of him and across the living room toward the library. When he sat down, his wife cleared her throat as the women swung open both library doors.

"Ta-da," they said in stereo and made a grand sweep with their arms as if displaying what the contestant had won on a game show.

"And behind doors one and two," Betsy said as they giggled, "is our new, temporary bedroom."

Ben, Andy, and the women laughed at the shocked look on Hank's face.

He looked stunned for more than a moment. His mouth gaped opened as the others continued to laugh. Lady ran into the cavernous, bookshelf-lined room now dominated with bedroom furniture. She jumped up on the bed, lay down, and looked at him with a grin.

Hank closed his mouth and smiled. "My, but you all have been exceedingly busy. It's amazing how something can be reimagined." He scanned the room. "I think I like it."

Betsy hurried over to her husband and kissed his cheek. "Well, I decided that until you've fully recovered, we shall make use of our library as our new bedroom. The guest room downstairs is too small for our bed. Problem solved," she said. "This way, I won't be worried about you navigating the stairs. Besides, it's closer to the kitchen and the fireplace, two of your favorite spots in the house." She grinned and looked at her accomplices. "What do you think?" she said as she turned back to Hank.

"It's brilliant, my love," he said and held her hand. "And my thanks and gratitude to your moving crew as well." He looked at the others, now huddled together by the fireplace, and winked.

CHAPTER TWENTY-ONE

The next morning, Betsy brought coffee to their new bedroom suite. Hank had awakened early enough to hear his wife humming in the kitchen. His eyes lit up when she walked in carrying a tray with Lady trotting beside her.

"Good morning, honey," she said in a cheery tone as she set the tray down by the bed and kissed him. "I've missed you with my coffee in the morning."

"And I've missed that sugar with my coffee." He grinned before patting the bed. Lady jumped up and found a comfortable position next to him. Her tail swept the comforter as she laid her head across his knee. "And I've missed you, too, sweet girl."

Betsy adjusted his pillows so he could sit up and handed him his coffee. She placed her cup on the nightstand and walked across the room to open the drapes.

"I didn't notice the drapes last night. Are those new?" he asked. "I like them. You've done a lot to accommodate my recovery. Thank you."

"Estelle brought these back from her last trip to New

York. She had them custom made for this window. I thought it might be too bright in the mornings while you slept."

"It sounds like you ladies have planned this for quite some time." His smile conveyed his gratitude. "You never cease to amaze me. I'm pretty certain you two could conquer the world if you set your minds to it."

She grinned as she pulled back the drapes. "I don't need the world—I have you, my dear." The room was filled with a peach-colored hue as the morning sun crept above the mountain. The promise of a new day and new hope had been delivered. She stood still, her face washed in the glow as she looked over the meadow below. Deer grazed on the moist, fresh grass and birds announced the darkness of night had passed. She sighed as she turned to look at her husband.

"I can never thank you enough for this—all of this," she said. She glanced out of the window again and saw an enormous bird in the distance. Her expression changed.

"What is it?" Hank asked, his curiosity piqued.

"I just saw a bird, but it was too far away to know for sure what it was. It looked bigger than our hawks and it flew differently just above the treetops." She hesitated, uncertainty crossed her face. "I think it was an eagle."

"Really?" He was surprised. "I didn't know there were any in this area." He attempted to get up but groaned as he lay back down.

"What's wrong, honey?" She hurried to his bedside and laid her hands on his arms, troubled by her husband's distress.

"It's okay," he said, trying to soothe her worry. "I was so excited about the possibility of seeing my first eagle that I sat up too fast—my headache got a lot worse." His expression was pained. "I'll have to remember not to do that again." He took a deep breath, then exhaled and grimaced.

"The medicine hasn't quite started working yet, unfortunately."

"Well, if it was an eagle," she said as she pulled the blanket over his chest, "he'll be there tomorrow. Today, you just need to rest and let your body heal. No more jumping up." Her voice was stern but loving.

"Yes, ma'am." He flashed a crooked smile. "Earlier you thanked me for all of this as you looked out of the window. You're welcome." He picked up her hand and kissed it. "Thank you for all you do to care for me and all this." He stroked her cheek. "I'm the luckiest man in the world."

She leaned over and kissed him on the forehead. She burst out laughing. "I think this is how our morning started —my kissing you."

"I'd say that's a perfect morning then, honey."

"Well, you look better and sound more alert today," Betsy said, sipping the last of her morning brew. They had spent almost an hour in small talk as they drank their coffee and enjoyed the beginning of their day together.

"I'd really like for you to see that bird. I'm convinced it's an eagle." She had spotted the large bird only one other time in the past ten days. Again, flying low, but too far away to identify with confidence. She'd grabbed the binoculars, but it already landed, obscured by the treetops.

"You have me curious about it, too," he said. "Maybe you can mention it the next time you go to the feed store. It's possible someone else has seen it."

"That's a good idea." She picked up the tray. "Shall we take this to the kitchen, then?"

"I'd like that." He wrapped his robe around himself and

scratched the top of Lady's head. She jumped off of the bed, slowly stretched, and followed them.

"You know what day this is, right?" she asked as she led her husband toward the living room. She stopped and turned as he answered.

"I think it's Wednesday," he said as he sniffed the air, "because I'm certain I can smell the cinnamon rolls baking." He hesitated in front of the fireplace, where the embers of the early morning fire still warmed the room.

"Hmm, this feels good. Maybe I'll just drink my second cup of coffee in here, if you don't mind." Turning his back, he sidled up to the warmth. "Did I tell you today how beautiful you are?"

She walked up beside him. "I think you just did. And I want you to be wherever you are the most comfortable. You," she looked at their furry companion, "and our friend." The dog's ears perked up as they glanced at her.

Hank looked toward the kitchen and seemed a bit perplexed.

She laughed. "Those cinnamon rolls can find their way in here, too, if that's what you're worried about."

"You read my mind." He grinned as he settled into his chair with his legs propped up. "Ah, this is perfect. It's been ten days now and I'm glad the headaches have backed off a little." He frowned. "But I'm so fatigued most of the time." He rubbed and played with Lady's ears.

"The doctor said it would take weeks before you'd even feel remotely like yourself. So nap if you need to before Ben shows up. Because we know he'll be here." She laughed as she walked to the kitchen. Lady stayed by Hank and soaked up the attention.

Betsy busied herself with making the cream cheese

frosting. As she opened the oven door to check on the cinnamon confections, Andy came down the stairs.

"Good morning, Mom," he said and walked over to give her a kiss on the cheek. "Mmm, smells heavenly. Those always make my coffee taste better. I'm really going to miss this when I leave. Hey," he said with a laugh, "that means it's Wednesday. The good sheriff should be here soon."

"He's consistent." She nodded and pulled the large pan out of the oven. "These look perfect, but they need to cool a bit before I frost them. Ask your dad if he'd like more coffee, please."

"Sure thing." Andy strode into the living room and found his dad asleep in his chair. He grabbed the couch blanket and draped it over him. Lady watched and swished her tail when she made eye contact. He reached down and patted her back. "Good girl," he whispered.

"Dad's napping, Mom." Andy dipped a finger into the frosting on his way to grab a cup.

"I'm not surprised." She filled their cups with fresh coffee and sat down. "It'll be weeks, even months, until he regains his strength. That surgery was a major shock to his body, but the doctor's happy with how well he's recuperated in this short amount of time." She took a deep breath and exhaled some worry. "I'm thankful there hasn't been neurological damage."

"I wish I could be here longer for you," he said with sadness. "I still have two weeks, though, so what would you like me to do? How else can I help?"

"Funny you should mention that," she said. "I'd like to get the gazebo spruced up for your dad. He'll enjoy resting out there as it gets warmer and sunnier. And he'll be able to see the view all the time. That's medicine in itself."

"Sure thing. Just let me know where, when, and what. I

don't suppose Aunt Estelle is in on this, is she?" He grinned because he knew their history.

She laughed and nodded. "Absolutely. And I'll ask Ben for his help—before he gets any cinnamon rolls."

～

Hank stood in disbelief, his mouth open as he looked around the gazebo. Sunbeams glowed on the flower baskets and potted trees. The red patio recliner, with a blue-and-white blanket tossed over the arm, shined in the light. "I wondered what you were all doing while I napped this past week," he said with a grin as he turned to look at everyone. "You four should start your own home-remodeling business."

"Yeah, they're the brains," Ben said, looking at the women, "and we're the brawn." He slapped Andy on the back and laughed as Betsy and Estelle grinned.

"It was pleasant in here before, but you've outdone yourselves, ladies." Hank had a puzzled look on his face. "Why is the temperature so comfortable, Betsy? It feels great, but it should be cooler out here." He looked around but hadn't yet noticed the changes.

She pointed toward the window openings. "Estelle found these vinyl glass patio curtains to enclose this from the elements but still have the view," she said. "We'll be able to get more months of use from this area now." She smiled at her sister. "I knew he'd like this. Thanks, sis."

"Of course," Estelle said. "I'd do anything for my family."

"Yes, thank you," Hank said, and winked at her. "You've been an invaluable part of my wife's renovations and schemes. And now I think I'll give that chair a test drive."

He grinned at a large carved box next to him on the table. He looked at his wife as he rubbed the wooden top.

"We'll have lunch out here to celebrate our new old room," she said. "How does that sound to everyone? You boys keep Hank company, and we'll bring out the food and drinks."

They gathered around the red picnic table. With a smile, Hank looked at each person before he held up his glass. "This is to all of you for your love and support," he said. "I'm a fortunate man to have a family like you."

Time quickly passed as they enjoyed the food, and conversations filled with amusing stories. Andy watched and laughed as his elders teased one another with love and understanding. They embraced each other unconditionally, their friendships standing the test of time.

"Well, this has been wonderful. You are all such a joy to my heart, but I have some business that needs to be finished," Estelle said. "Sheriff Ben, are you ready to give me a ride back to town?"

"Your chariot awaits," he said with a wink. "Andy, take care of these two and make sure they stay out of trouble." He nudged him with his elbow and laughed.

"You got it, Sheriff," he said and grinned. "Yeah, they can get pretty rowdy. And it's possible you might find their photos on the wall at the post office, too."

"Hey," Betsy said in mock indignation, "you shouldn't mess with the cook. She just might forget how to bake those cinnamon rolls."

Ben widened his eyes as he shook his head. "Now that's not even funny," he said. "Be careful what you say, Hank, especially if it affects my Wednesday morning routine."

CHAPTER TWENTY-TWO

Hank basked in the warm sunlight as he napped in the gazebo. Lady lay beside him and kept watch. She lifted her head when Betsy walked in and sat down.

She patted her lap as she looked at their furry guardian. "Come, give me some love," she whispered to Lady. The dog instantly went to her, placing her front legs across her friend's lap as her long black tail fanned the air.

"You're such a good girl, my cuddle bug." She held the dog's head with both hands. "What would we do without you?" She rubbed the soft fur on Lady's ears and leaned forward to gaze into her eyes. "You know he needs you, don't you?" Lady nuzzled her arm and licked her face in response. She patted the dog's side as they enjoyed the contentment for several minutes more.

"Are you two thinking up some diabolical plan?" Hank's voice was deep and soft, his eyes still shaded by sleep.

Betsy looked up as Lady wagged her tail and returned to his side.

"Nope, not this time. She was just giving me some love."

"You two were nice to see when I opened my eyes." The

dog pushed her nose into his hand. He looked down at his four-footed friend and stroked her head as she stood with her eyes locked on his. When he smiled down at her, she sat and brushed her tail across the floor.

"This gazebo feels like a vacation to my body and soul." He inhaled deeply and sighed.

"It's been two months now and I almost feel as good as new." He looked at his wife. "You take such good care of me. Thank you."

"It's my way of showing you how much I love you." Her smile was affectionate. "This really is quite nice out here, isn't it?" She looked around at the newly designed space. "I'm so glad Andy was here for you, although it wasn't long enough." She took a long, slow breath and exhaled. "He helped so much with the house, barn chores, and even some small repairs. You've taught him well."

"I'm mighty proud of that boy. I think he got the best of both of us, don't you?"

She agreed with a nod before growing serious. "It was so much harder to say goodbye to him this time. He's in my prayers daily that he comes home safe." Her voice was faint as she looked down at her lap.

"Mine, too. That's the most we can do, honey—keep him in our prayers and make sure he knows how much we love him."

Betsy sat and gazed at the mountain, her worried look vanishing and replaced by a joyful expression. She turned to speak. "I forgot to tell you Andy got a call from Willie just before he left. Angela is expecting. Isn't that great news? Andy was excited when he told me. He said Willie is thrilled he's going to be a dad and can hardly wait to hold his baby. Hopefully, he'll be back from his tour in time for the baby's birth."

"That's wonderful news. Willie's a good guy and deserves his happiness." He thought for a moment. "I'm so glad Andy and Willie are in the same unit and already have that close camaraderie. They have each other to lean on when it's really tough and things seem impossible."

"I'm grateful for that, too. They trust each other with their lives, which they need now more than ever."

Walking to Hank's chair, she smiled down at him and reached out to smooth his hair. She bent down and kissed him, resting her hand on his shoulder.

"You've always known how to speak to my concerns, especially about our son."

"And you, Mrs. Walker, have done no less for me. Your love has been more precious to me than life itself." He placed his hand on hers. "Thank you, honey, for allowing me to love you and to journey through this thing called life knowing you were beside me." He kept his eyes on hers. "And I thank God for the extra time He's given me to be with you."

Her eyes welled with tears as she knelt down beside him.

"I can't imagine my life being any different from what it's been. You're my best friend. You've loved me even when I was unlovable." She smirked. "And I think that has been more times than I care to count."

"You've never been unlovable." He paused. "Although perhaps a mystery." He laughed and caused Lady to jump up from her sound sleep. She looked around, saw no danger, and lay back down.

Betsy stood as she laughed. "And thank you most of all for the laughter."

～

"That sounds wonderful. Thank you, Estelle," Betsy said. "I'll see you in a few hours." She set the phone down and walked out to the gazebo where Hank was resting in his chair. She grinned like a Cheshire cat.

"How's Estelle today?" he asked as he finished his tea.

"She's well and wants to bring a surprise dinner out for our anniversary." She shrugged, her eyes wide with innocence.

"Really? I'm surprised she remembered the date." He arched an eyebrow. "Hmm, somehow I think you're involved with her memory."

"Maybe." She gave him with a coy smile. "Estelle asked because she wanted to make sure we'd be home—and hungry. She'll be here later this afternoon to drop off the food, but not to visit."

"That's very sweet of her. So this being our anniversary, maybe we can watch our movie before she gets here?" he asked.

"Yes. Dinner and a movie, our romantic tradition with Sam and Ilsa." She beamed. "We'll make some fresh memories."

"In the meantime, I thought we could plan our next trip. How does that sound? The doctor said in a couple more months I should be able to travel with no problems."

Betsy was less enthusiastic about his proposal and hesitated, furrowing her brow slightly. She sat in the chair next to him and held his hand.

"Would it be terrible of me to want to stay home on the mountain and not share you with the world? Would you be disappointed?" Her eyes pleaded.

He placed a gentle hand on his wife's cheek. "I am happy anywhere, my dear, as long as I am with you. I only wanted to give you the chance for another worldly adventure." He paused and looked deeply into her eyes. "This is where I am happiest."

"Thank you, my love, and I'm so grateful for the many places we've been and the experiences we've shared," she said. "But now I'd like to enjoy more of what we have right here. I want to have picnics in the meadow, rediscover this mountain, and maybe try to find that elusive bird I've seen. I want more memories of us here." Her voice was filled with an enthusiasm he'd not heard in a while.

He pointed to her treasure box. "Why don't you find that bundle of postcards you have in there? We can take a trip around the world with our memories in the comfort of home."

Her face filled with excitement as she reached in and pulled out a stack of postcards tied with a purple ribbon. She held the postcards against her chest, closing her eyes and sighing. Her face was an image of bliss.

"We've ridden camels in Morocco, climbed Machu Picchu, eaten tapas in Seville, and stood at the pyramids and felt the rain of the Amazon forest on our faces," she murmured. "And I can still feel the icy wind on my face as we hiked the heather-covered highlands of Scotland. Mmm, with my eyes closed, I can see and smell the village foods in Thailand and hear the bells of the Tibetan monastery. Oh, and the glorious night lights of Paris from the top of the Eiffel Tower." Her eyes were filled with wonder as she looked at her husband. "We've seen more of the world than most people." She hugged him. "It's been a fascinating life we've lived."

He smiled at his wife's reminiscent review. "And we haven't even looked at the postcards yet."

CHAPTER TWENTY-THREE

Betsy wiped the tears from her eyes as she snuggled next to Hank on the couch. He tilted her chin up and gave her a passionate kiss.

"Here's looking at you, kid," he said with the crooked smile she loved.

She kissed him again. "We'll always have Paris."

As they laughed in each other's arms, Lady jumped up and ran to the front door. She didn't bark, but wagged her tail furiously, which meant she recognized the approaching vehicle.

"That must be Estelle. She always brings a treat for Lady," Betsy said as she walked to the door. "She's right on time, too. I don't know about you, but I'm hungry."

"Yes, I second that. It'll be nice to eat a little earlier this evening. That gives us more time for romance." He grabbed Betsy around the waist and hugged her as she laughed.

"Wait, honey. We should see if she needs any help. We'll continue this later." She gave him a quick kiss and opened the door.

"I come bearing gifts for your special celebration,"

Estelle announced with a broad smile. She brought the dinner into the house and placed it on the counter in the kitchen. She gave Betsy and Hank each a hug and then instructions.

"You two get changed for dinner while I take care of the food and arrangements," she said. "Now go. Shoo."

"Get changed for dinner?" Hank asked, a bit confused.

"Didn't Betsy tell you? Tonight is a trip back in time to relive a memorable anniversary." She turned and winked at her sister.

He glanced at his wife. "Ah, I see you two have been busy scheming again." He shook his head in resignation.

"We wouldn't want to disappoint you, my dear brother-in-law." She and Betsy laughed.

"Okay, honey," Betsy said. "I've laid out your clothes in the downstairs guest bathroom. We have time to shower and dress while she sets up."

"What does she need to set up?" he asked, still a bit baffled.

"Hank," Estelle said in a firm tone, "this is the part where you just say 'yes, dear' and do as Betsy says."

He held up his hands in surrender and laughed. "I should know better than to question either of you. You'd think I would have learned after all these years," he said with a sheepish grin. He looked at Betsy and said, "Yes, dear."

The ladies laughed as he walked down the hallway to do as instructed and dress for dinner.

"Do you have it all handled?" Betsy asked her sister.

"Now, when do I ever not have it handled?" she said and smirked. "Now it's your turn to go."

Betsy grinned and gave Estelle a quick kiss on the cheek. "You're the best—ever."

"That's what big sisters are for," she said as she winked.

Estelle knocked on the bedroom door. "It's me, Betsy."

"Come in, sis. I'm almost dressed, and I could use your help."

She paused as she walked through the doorway. "Oh, my—you look beyond beautiful, Betsy. The dress fits you perfectly and looks stunning on you."

"Thank you, but I'm sure it's just as lovely on you," Betsy replied with a curious look on her face. "We're the mirror image of each other, you know."

"No, really—you look absolutely stunning. It didn't look as good on me when I tried it on at the last fitting in New York." She studied her sister's silhouette. "There must be magic in that material or in the night—or it's the love in your eyes. But, really, it definitely looks amazing on you."

Betsy hugged her. "I can't thank you enough for doing this—all of this—for us. Hank will be so surprised."

"You're welcome. I'm honored I could be part of your happiness. I told Hank to wait in the bedroom until you came to get him. Everything is ready and waiting for you."

"I just need to be zipped, please." She turned and looked at her reflection in the antique, cheval mirror. Her breath caught in her throat as she stood still.

"This is exquisite," she said as she gently touched the fabric. "I believe tonight is the perfect time to have done this. It's waited all these years for its glorious moment."

Estelle nodded. "I'll let myself out. I hope you both have a magnificent evening." The sisters hugged and knew exactly what the other felt. It had always been like that.

"Thank you. I couldn't have done this without you."

～

Betsy opened the bedroom door. Hank sat in the corner chair as he looked out of the window. She smiled at him when he turned toward her. He was flooded with surprise and whistled as he stared, frozen in place. He was awestruck by the radiant vision in front of him. The setting sun gleamed through the tall window pane and reflected on his wife. As she slowly turned, the golden threads of the gossamer fabric glistened in the light, the purple and green flowers seemingly dancing against their ivory background. His wife's auburn hair glowed and her face shined with love.

After several seconds, he found his voice. "You look captivating. You and that dress are extraordinary. It transports me back to the streets of Morocco." He fumbled for words to describe what he saw. Instead, he walked across the room and took Betsy in his arms. "Thank you. I'm the luckiest man in the world." He kissed her with a fiery passion. "Let's hurry and eat dinner." He offered her a smile and a wink, taking her by the hand and leading her downstairs. As they neared the bottom, it was eerily quiet except for the subtle notes of a mandolin that drifted through the kitchen. The melody they heard was "Musetta's Waltz," music from a distant memory.

Confused again, he turned and asked, "Estelle already left?" He glanced around the empty room.

"Yes," she said with a small smile. "We're all alone, my love. Now let me lead you." She walked ahead of him, holding his hand. When they stepped into the kitchen, they saw a bright yellow-and-red sign above the French doors leading to the gazebo. The glass panes were now covered with bright red fabric.

Hank grinned as he read the sign aloud. "Trattoria Gino." He grinned at his wife. "Do I hear music playing? Italian music?"

They walked through the kitchen and stood at the entrance to the gazebo. Each one grabbed a doorknob and swung open the doors. Inside, Italian love songs and a fairy-land awaited them.

There were miniature string lights along the ceiling above the walls and around the potted trees. A small cafe table had been placed near the windows and covered with a white linen tablecloth. It was set for two, complete with candlelight and flowers. A note leaned against a wineglass. The tiny flames flickered an invitation to be seated.

Betsy read the note. "The wine is chilled and waiting for you. Happy Anniversary and enjoy! By the way, I think the moon tonight is filled with magic. Love, Estelle." She gasped.

"I didn't know Estelle so clearly remembered the details of our romantic evening in Italy." She looked at Hank with a huge grin. "She even found the same wine we drank that night." Her eyes welled with tears at how much effort her sister had put into their anniversary celebration. "She even surprised me tonight."

They lifted the dome covers from their plates and were greeted with an authentic Italian lasagna and warm, crusty bread lying in a basket beneath a linen napkin. Hank opened the wine and poured just a splash into his glass. He swirled the red libation a few times before he lifted the glass to his nose.

"Mmm." He smelled the aroma and took a sip. "It's as delicious as I remember." He poured wine into Betsy's glass and then his own. They lifted them into the air.

"Here's to us," he said with desirous eyes.

"And here's to love," she replied with a slow, sultry smile.

~

"That was delizioso." Hank laid his napkin on the table. "I'm not sure if it was the wine, the bread, or the lighting, but the lasagna tasted like it came directly from Gino's."

"I was thinking the same thing, and fully expected to see Anna carry in the dessert plate with her chef right behind her." She pointed to the corner near the doors. "As we came in, I noticed an envelope placed near the speaker. Estelle wrote on it to open after we eat."

"Well, then it's time to see what the next surprise could be. Let me get it, honey." He retrieved the note and handed it to her. "Here, you can have the honors."

She grinned as she read the message. "She says that it's now time for us to dance. And that you have your doctor's blessings." They laughed at her talent for details.

"She called my doctor. I guess she thought of everything, didn't she?" Shaking his head, he pushed a few buttons, and the familiar song of their love story played.

He walked toward Betsy with an outstretched hand. "May I have this dance, my darling?"

She turned and placed her hand in his. "Yes, this and all my dances."

They locked eyes as Hank wrapped his arm around her waist. She lifted her face. Their lips met in a tender kiss that expressed a lifetime of love. Their bodies entwined as they swayed to the rhythm of the familiar melody. She rested her cheek against his chest and they moved as one. When the next song began, he looked down at her and she met his gaze. Their eyes spoke what their hearts felt as they hummed with the music.

"Look," she said. "It's a full moon, just like that night in Italy." Her eyes reflected the moonlight and her joy.

"It must be filled with magic—just for us," he said and kissed her once again.

Song after song, unaware of time or space, they danced in a fluid motion, in tune with each other's body. He clasped her hand, placing it against his chest and over his heart.

"Can you feel my heartbeat?" he breathed. "My heart has only ever loved you." He kissed the top of her head. "I have only ever wanted you in my arms."

"Yes," she said, "and I have only ever loved you. Your arms have been my shelter and your love has been my strength." She kissed the hand that held hers.

Their bodies slowed to the familiar strains of the last song. They had listened and danced to that song for what seemed like an eternity, but felt like only yesterday, much like the story of their love. A kiss seemed like a million kisses.

They held each other tighter as they whispered the last words of their song with a sigh.

CHAPTER TWENTY-FOUR

Max threw his head up and pawed the ground when he saw Hank and Betsy walk into the barn. The bay gelding nickered with excitement at the sight of his good friend.

"Hey there, Max," Hank hollered. "I wouldn't forget you, buddy. I brought some treats for you, too."

The horse's ears pointed forward as he shifted his body and snorted several times. He leaned against the door with his neck outstretched as his man neared.

Hank stopped just in front of the gelding and extended his hands. The horse lowered his chin and placed his muzzle against his face. They breathed nostril to nose for several seconds. He wrapped his arms around the horse's neck and the gentle horse laid his head on his friend's shoulder. They had quickly bonded the moment they'd first met.

"I missed you, too, Max," Hank laughed, patting the horse. "It's only been overnight, you big baby."

The horse kicked the sawdust and rubbed his muzzle against his chest in response. Reaching into his pocket, Hank pulled out a carrot. "Here you go, my handsome beast."

He grabbed the carrot with his lips, barely touching Hank's hand.

"That's my good boy." He rubbed the horse's neck and slid his hand down the shoulder. Max crunched on the carrot, bumping his arm with his muzzle when it was gone.

"Oh, you want more, do you?" He laughed, pulling two more carrots out of his pocket. The well-mannered horse whinnied and nodded. He nudged Hank's chest with his muzzle

again.

"Okay, you win, Max." He handed the first and then the second carrot to him. Human and horse had an established a close relationship and had no problem communicating.

Betsy finished feeding the chickens, tossing more fresh hay into Gertrude's stall before she walked across the barn.

"I see you boys are getting along well this morning." Max stepped closer to the stall door and snorted as he nodded. She laughed and reached up to stroke his forehead. He lowered his head and breathed in Betsy's face as he'd done with Hank. She and Max were good friends, too. She'd taken care of him while her husband was ill and recuperating from his surgery. The horse had been a good listener as she shared daily reports with him about his health and any improvements. Although the horse had been happy to see her each day and greeted her affectionately, he would still look toward the barn doors with ears stretched forward in anticipation of another arrival. Max had missed his other friend, the tall, deep-voiced, and gentle man.

Lady had treed a squirrel earlier, just outside the barn. Once satisfied a threat no longer existed, she ran in to be with her pack. She moved with such energy that she skidded to a stop in front of Hank. She sat, happy to be reunited with her family again as her tail swept through the sawdust. Max nodded and snorted when he saw his canine friend.

"Good girl, Lady." Hank stroked the dog's soft fur. When he ceased, the dog hurried toward the horse and stretched her front paws up onto the stable door. The horse lowered his head as Lady's nose touched his muzzle. They sniffed and shared a breath. Lady's tail relaxed as it continued to wag in a slow arc.

"I'm still surprised at how well our four-legged friends have adjusted and become attached." He watched in awe at the exchange between the two animals.

"I can't help but smile each time I see them do this." Betsy paused. "I wonder what they're thinking?"

She had only finished her question when two chickens ran by. "Oh, no, I didn't lock the coop door." Two more chickens ran by, but in opposite directions.

She called for reinforcements. "Lady, come help me round up the girls."

The black-and-white assistant turned her head and bounded toward the wayward birds. By now, all twenty hens had flown the coop. As instructed from a previous escape, Lady guarded the barn door to keep the fowl in the building. Betsy ran to the bucket of chicken feed. If the birds saw the food, they might be more cooperative.

Hank threw his head back and laughed as his wife coaxed her chickens toward the coop. She shook the bucket, hopeful, but most of the birds were more interested in freedom than food since they'd already been fed. A few stopped for kernels of corn long enough for the hen catcher to scoop up the bundles of feathers and return them to their rightful place. Those who chose to stay on the run made it more difficult by locating a rafter or high bale of hay to settle on. The barn was filled with cackling, squawking, and flapping wings.

Lady barked any time a chicken ran in her direction, causing it to flee to a safe space. Even Gertrude, the cow, joined in with an occasional moo or grunt as she watched with interest and chewed her cud. Normally, there was not so much action in the barn. It was fortunate she had already been milked earlier that morning. Otherwise, production might have been affected.

Hank's interference would only add to the momentary pandemonium. He laughed at the fun diversion, happy to be in the audience.

Soon enough, all the craziness came to a halt. The chickens settled down, and it was quiet again. Gertrude returned to her peaceful grazing on the fresh hay. It hadn't taken long to capture and return all the errant fowl to their enclosure.

"Well, I'm glad we amused you," Betsy scoffed with a stern face as she walked toward her husband and his big grin. She laughed and sat on the hay bale next to him. "I bet that was entertaining." She shook her head. "I won't soon forget to latch that door."

Hank laughed all over again. "You and Lady make a great posse, or should I say, tag team." He wiped the cheerful tears from his eyes. "You really know how to show a guy a good time." He threw his head back in a big belly laugh as he enjoyed his own sense of humor and comedic timing at his wife's expense.

She slapped his arm with her glove and grinned. "I think I've had my exercise for the day. But at least we got close to a dozen eggs out of all that chaos."

Hank put his arm around her shoulders and gave her a quick kiss and a sincere smile.

"As I sat here, I realized that one of the best gifts you've given me is joy," he said. "You

seem to always make me laugh, no matter how hard life may be. And along the way, you also taught me how to laugh at myself. Thank you for that."

"You're welcome, but I need to thank you, too. You've given me every reason to find joy in this life. Look at this." She waved her outstretched arm in a half-circle. "You've provided for us more than I could ever have imagined. You took the simple picture of a Victorian house I'd torn from a magazine and multiplied it exponentially. This property on a mountainside, replete with a dream home large enough for a bed-and-breakfast, is all much bigger than I ever guessed possible." She shook her head, looking at their animals and grinning. "You've even given a home to our extended family, the ones with hair, fur, and feathers." They chuckled at the sight of their barnyard friends. When they looked at Lady, she wagged her tail and scooted closer for rubs.

"We did this—both of us. And it's been a fun challenge, hasn't it?" He looked at his wife, his question heartfelt and genuine. "I couldn't have built any of this without you and your dreams. Your trust and faith in me gave me the confidence I lacked. Just like that young boy you shared your cookie with." He reached for her hand. "You've believed in me even when I didn't. Thank you for that and all the laughter along the way. Your happiness has been my driving force—and my happiness."

She put her hand on his cheek. "You know you're my hero, right?"

Just as their lips neared, Max snorted and stomped the ground, causing them to turn and look. The horse nodded his head and snorted again. They laughed at the gelding.

"I think somebody's ready to go for a run and get some

sunshine," she said, grinning. "He and Gertie need their pasture time."

"I bet you're right. But wait, I need to finish something."

As she stood up, Hank grabbed her in his arms and kissed her. "In case you didn't know it, Mrs. Walker," he said, "I love you."

CHAPTER TWENTY-FIVE

Betsy stood at the kitchen sink as she washed the last of the dinner dishes. The summer days had grown longer and sunset came later. She looked out of the window and smiled at the sight of Hank walking on the path near the woods. Lady sniffed the ground and looked up at the trees as she searched for something new to chase. She ran back to Hank every few minutes to check on him and his well-being, then bounded off to ferret out any unsuspecting creatures. Her enthusiasm was endless and the sight of Hank's smiling face was medicine for Betsy's heart. His recovery had been better than expected, but they took nothing for granted—not time, nor each other.

"Come on, Lady," Hank prompted as he opened the kitchen door. A few seconds later, a blur of black and white flashed through the kitchen. Their furry friend ran to Betsy and sniffed her leg as she looked up with her soft brown eyes while her tail stirred the air.

"When she does this," she said with a grin, "I feel like it's a welfare check."

He laughed. "It probably is. She wants to make sure

everything was fine during her absence. She wants to know all of her pack is happy."

"I'm sure you're right. She's pretty keen on keeping us in her sights. I can't imagine how she'd react if I were ever really in distress." She dried her hands and grabbed one of Lady's ears and gave it a good rub. "I love you, too, my sweet."

Seemingly happy with their exchange, the dog ran to the living room and throughout the first floor of the house. She was always on guard for their safety. Once there seemed to be no danger afoot, she grabbed her squeaky squirrel and lay down under the kitchen table.

Hank walked out to the gazebo as his wife finished up with her kitchen duties. He turned on some music and peeked around the doorway. Her back was turned. He snuck up behind her, grabbing her by the shoulders and spinning her around.

Surprised, she squealed and laughed as he pulled her against his body and danced. He twirled her and shuffled them toward the music as she followed his lead. Once inside the gazebo, he grinned at her with a devilish look in his eyes.

"The chores can wait," he commanded in his deep voice. "It's time to dance, my love—doctor's orders."

Hank looked at the barren trees outside the window. It was the start of the second semester of his senior year, and he had a problem. Prom was only a few months away. He was desperate to ask Betsy to go with him, but he'd never learned to dance—really dance. Sure, he could his plant his feet and keep time with his arms and body, but at his height, he always felt awkward. But more than anything, he wanted to make her proud she'd chosen to be with him. He wanted to make Betsy feel special by being a good dance partner and making her the star of the show.

He'd watched his parents dance at home often for no particular reason other than they seemed to enjoy themselves while doing it. They'd turn on the music and dance and laugh until exhausted. He marveled at how much in love they seemed. Maybe that had been the secret to their marriage. But his mom no longer had her dance partner.

He turned his attention to her, busy taking her last batch of cookies out of the oven. He cleared his throat as he bounced his feet on the chair rung.

"Mom," he asked with some hesitation, "will you please teach me how to dance?" He stumbled over his words but blurted out, "If you don't want to, that's okay." He was worried and anxious.

Mrs. Walker's hands and body stopped. She caught her breath and turned. "Of course, Hank. Never be afraid to ask me anything," she said. "That's the way to win a girl's heart, you know." She smiled at her son, which eased his anxiety. "Are you thinking about the prom?"

"Uh-huh," he mumbled with a mouth full of warm cookie. He took a few gulps of milk and continued. "I want to impress Betsy. We've gone to a couple of dances together, but I just look like all the other goofy guys." He shook his head as if to erase a terrible memory.

"Well, we have time enough to get you dance worthy before the prom," his mom said with a loving smile. "And I'd very much like that. I think you'll catch on pretty quick. You just have to relax and have fun. That's what your father taught me"—her voice caught—"and he would have taught you, too."

"Good. Thanks, Mom." He grinned as he grabbed

another cookie on his way to the back door. He stopped and turned around. "Do you think we could start today?"

His mom finished putting the cookies on a platter and turned off the oven. "How about after you finish that cookie? Soon enough?" She smirked and raised an eyebrow.

Hank stuffed the entire sweet morsel into his mouth and nodded fiercely, unable to speak.

His mom laughed and pointed to the family room as she wiped the counter. "Wash your hands first, please, and meet me in there," she said with a smile as she left the kitchen.

Hank stuffed another cookie in his mouth and made quick work of it before he washed his hands. He beamed with excitement at the music from the other room.

The night of the dance, as Betsy shared girl talk about dresses and hairstyles and Ben went off to chat with the guys who also had no date, Hank planned. His dad had told him often enough, "You never get a second chance at a first impression, boy." He waited for just the right song and within fifteen minutes, just as Betsy came back to join him, was the perfect melody. He turned to her with a mischievous grin and a devilish look.

"May I have this dance, Betsy?" Before she could answer, he took her hand, a gleam in his eyes, and turned toward center stage.

"Why, of course." Betsy grinned at his formality.

He walked her out to the dance floor, slipped an arm around her waist, and gripped her hand. Surprised by his sudden move, she gave him a curious look. He winked and pulled her closer as he whispered in her ear, "Betsy, just trust me, okay? Hold on to me, I'll guide you—follow the rhythm of my body. And you'll be okay."

She looked at him, puzzled by his words, and her brows knitted. When he took his first several steps, her eyes widened as the impact of his words hit her. Within a few turns, she felt the rhythm of his movements and she clung to him. As she relaxed, they soon moved as one.

As the other couples danced in their stilted and clumsy movements, they noticed Hank and Betsy glide across the floor. Unlike them, the confident dancers seemed to float past in complete synchrony. One by one, embarrassed by their own lack of talent, the teens cleared the floor and watched, dumbfounded. The elegant dancers had even silenced the chaperones' chatter and garnered their attention. When the song finished, a group of girls surrounded them and each vied for Hank's attention, as they hoped to be his partner when the music started again.

"Sorry, ladies, but all my dances are reserved for the most beautiful girl in the world." Disappointment washed over the hopeful faces. He grinned at his date as he pulled her closer. "Right, Betsy?"

She stood in complete and utter shock, blushing as she nodded. The girls gasped in unison at the public display of affection. Envy was obvious on each girl's face. They walked away as they whispered to one another. With an occasional glance back, the young women returned to their tables, much less interested in the boys they had hoped to impress. Many of the young males stood in packs. Hank had just set an all-time high standard—one they'd never reach with their two-step shuffles or wild gyrations.

Hank held Betsy's hand and walked her to a table in silence.

"Did I embarrass you, Betsy?" He wore an enormous grin.

"A little—I think," she sputtered. "But mostly I'm surprised at how bold you are tonight. I'm stunned by your newfound skills out there." She pointed and glanced at the dance floor. Her eyes grew wide as she shook her head. "And where in the world did you learn to do that?" She stood speechless, shook her head again, and waited for an answer. Hank just grinned at her. She seemed impressed and proud—and confused.

Before Hank could answer, the music played again. He laughed as he grabbed Betsy's hand. "C'mon, I'll tell you out there."

CHAPTER TWENTY-SIX

Hank and Betsy sat on the front porch as they enjoyed the mid-morning sun and the stunning view. The meadow was lush with wild flowers and teaming with wildlife and berry bushes heavy with fruit. The deer had feasted earlier that morning and wandered back into the shelter of the tree line. It was late summer, but the evening temperatures had already cooled off a bit. Soon leaves on the surrounding trees, with a hint of yellow on their tips, would announce fall. When the nights grew cool and crisp, a full palette of fiery-colored foliage would appear. Max and Gertie were in their pasture and content with each other's company as they nibbled on the fresh grass and swished their tails. The air was filled with the sounds and songs of life on the mountain.

"I think we're going to have an early winter this year, honey," Hank pondered as he sipped his tea and munched on the last cookie.

"Mmm, I actually like the sound of that. I miss sitting in front of the fireplace with you, mesmerized by the flames," she said and emptied her cup. The small dish was bare. "Do you want me to get a few more cookies for you, my love?"

"Well, if you're going that way." He grinned from ear to ear and offered her the plate. "Yes, please."

"I'm getting more tea, too. Want some?"

He nodded eagerly. "You're too good to me, Mrs. Walker."

Lady jumped up when Betsy stood. "It's okay, sweet girl. Go back to your nap." The dog lay down, but this time rested her head on Hank's boot.

Amused, he laughed. "She wants to make sure I don't sneak away."

When Betsy returned, her husband was speaking on the phone.

"Of course, Mr. Sato. We'll be home then. We look forward to visiting with you. Thank you and drive safely."

Hank ended the call, placing the phone beside the plate of cookies. "We have a visitor coming by in about an hour. Mr. Sato's bringing something for us, but wanted to keep it a secret until he got here." Hank shrugged. "I'm mystified by what the gift could be. His voice was unusually cheery, too."

"It's been a while since we've seen him. Hmm." She paused as she thought. "Oh, when he came to visit you in the hospital." She was pleased she'd remembered as she sipped her tea.

He stopped mid-bite on a cookie. "Yeah, that's right. It was such a pleasant surprise that he came to see me. I felt honored by his presence. He's such a humble person." He contemplated his words. "What an exceptional human being, and so generous with his time and talents." He gazed at the meadow as though lost in thought. "He was really close with my dad and took it hard when he died." His face grew sad with the memory. "I should make time to visit Mr. Sato more often. He's not getting any younger." A shadow of remorse fell across his face.

She noticed and waited to reply. "He's a tremendous asset to the community and always the first to volunteer his services," she added. "It's unbelievable what he did to create the park in town. The landscaping is breathtaking and visitors always comment about its beauty. We've had guests come to stay here that actually asked where they could find the Japanese gardens." She slowly shook her head. "I'd say that man breathed life into those empty public spaces. And I see him frequently tending to and adding plants along the streets."

He agreed as he finished his cookie. "He's done more to beautify Parsons than anyone who's ever lived here. And, you know, if there's money in the coffers, Mayor Flemming calls him for advice on how else to improve the town's appearance. Over time, our little town has developed a unique personality and charm. Yeah, old Flemming has a master plan to draw tourists in." He chuckled.

"That's pretty wise on the mayor's part." She reflected on her next words. "I think he must also realize it's more than just about beautifying. More than just what's seen. These projects bring the townsfolk together for a common purpose. It helps people take pride in their community." She laughed. "Also, who wants to argue about their differences when they're planting flowers?"

Lady barked and ran a short distance down the driveway. She stood guard and waited. Within a few minutes, a familiar red truck appeared.

"It's okay, Lady," Hank yelled. "He's a friend." And with those words, the dog returned to the porch and wagged her tail. "Good girl," he said in a gentle voice, and scratched the top of her head. She sat between them, her eyes intent on the approaching vehicle.

They walked down to greet their guest, waving as the truck pulled up and parked. A short old man with a broad smile and white hair sat in the driver's seat. He could barely see over the steering wheel. He got out and walked around the front of the vehicle. A much younger man opened his door and dropped from the passenger side. He nodded respectfully at the strangers.

"Hank and Betsy, it's good to see you," Mr. Sato said, his voice filled with affection.

"And it's even better to see you out of that hospital bed." His grin was infectious.

"It's sure great to be out of it, Mr. Sato," he replied with his crooked smile as he shook hands. The old man reached up and patted his shoulder.

"You look good—real good," their guest surmised.

"It's such a pleasure to see you again," said Betsy as she stepped forward and extended her hand.

"I think I should prefer a hug if you don't mind," the good-natured man said. "I haven't hugged a beautiful woman in years."

They all laughed. "It's a privilege then," she said and gave him a quick embrace.

"Let me introduce my grandson, Aaron. He's here because he has a strong, young back." It was obvious Mr. Sato enjoyed his own humor as he grinned.

"Hi Aaron, glad to meet you. This is my wife, Betsy." They all exchanged smiles.

"So, Hank, I've brought you and your lovely wife a gift. Actually, two," said Mr. Sato. "From my family to yours."

They walked to the back of the truck and Mr. Sato looked satisfied as their faces lit up. It was obvious his gift pleased them, and that clearly very much pleased him.

"These are magnificent," Betsy said as she admired the two ten-foot trees lying in the truck's bed, propped on the tailgate and supported with large bags of compost.

"I've grown these from my original Yoshino cherry trees I planted for my wife many years ago when we first moved here. They were in honor of her wisdom and my love for her." He took a deep, slow breath. "She enjoyed the Japanese tradition of Hanami, which welcomed spring. Each year, she prepared a special picnic meal which our family ate under the cherry blossoms. Her joy filled my heart as I watched her inhale the indescribable beauty of the flowers."

Mr. Sato gazed into the distance and his voice softened. "I've planted a cherry tree each year now since she passed. I feel her presence most when I stand among the trees, especially during the season of cherry blossoms." He looked at Hank and Betsy again. His smile was borne of sadness.

Betsy wiped her eyes. "That's beautiful, and it's so very kind of you to share that with us—and these." She took one of his hands in both of hers and held it. "Thank you, Mr. Sato. You've touched my heart."

Her husband was moved as well by the words and story, his eyes conveying that he understood the meaning on the deepest level.

"Hank, your father was an excellent friend to me. He and I spent many years sharing the stories of our lives, struggles, and triumphs. These trees are in memory of him and the honor your family has brought to this mountain. I pray that many future generations of your family will sit beneath the cherry blossoms."

Hank was too choked up to speak. He just nodded and looked at Betsy as she wrapped her arm around his waist. Lady seemed to sense his emotion, leaning against his leg and looking up at him.

The old man continued. "The cherry blossoms represent more than spring. Lasting only a brief time, the exquisite flowers serve to teach us the fleeting nature of our existence. The beauty of the flowers is short and sweet. They symbolize both life and death and illustrate the importance of embracing each day and each season. The blossoms remind us of the brevity of life and to enjoy—with fervor—each moment we spend with those we love."

Hank cleared his throat before he spoke. "I can't thank you enough," he said, "and if you don't mind, I'd like to give you a hug, too." With moist eyes, Mr. Sato nodded. The men hugged and patted each other's back, a symbol of their history's bond.

Aaron had stood in silence and respect behind his grandfather as he'd spoken.

Now the time had come for him to move. He lowered the tailgate and hopped into the back of the truck, waiting for his grandfather's instructions.

"Good boy, Aaron. Just push the container out while we hold the trunks."

With the help of Aaron's strong back, the trees were lowered to the ground. He grabbed a shovel, but Hank reached out his hand to take it. The young man relinquished, releasing it with a nod.

Hank and Betsy dug the holes with the elder man's guidance. Before the first tree was lowered, Mr. Sato spoke.

"Kobayashi Issa said, 'In the cherry blossom's shade

there's no such thing as a stranger.' And I say with the deep, fertile soil of love, these trees will bring much joy."

The trees were planted in love and with a new hope.

CHAPTER TWENTY-SEVEN

Betsy walked out to the gazebo and set a tray filled with fresh coffee, hot biscuits, butter, and jellies down on the table.

"That's perfect, honey. Thank you." Hank's smile was weak. "I'm not very hungry this morning."

Her cheer turned to concern. "Are you feeling okay otherwise?"

"Yes, but I didn't sleep well last night. I'm not sure why." His brows furrowed, his eyes filled with sadness.

She refilled her husband's cup. "Have you had any headaches lately?" She searched his face.

He sipped his coffee and picked up a warm biscuit. As he split it open, he answered, "No, not that I can remember. I just feel a bit tired."

She sat down, filled her cup, and buttered a biscuit. She still looked worried, but her husband was now focused on the assortment of jellies. When he looked up, Betsy was staring at him. She held her cup up to her lips but didn't drink.

"I'm okay, really. I plan to rest today and that includes a

nap with my favorite girls," he said with a grin. "If I still feel this way in a couple of days, you can make a doctor's appointment for me, okay?"

"Yes." She sighed. "Maybe it was all the digging we did yesterday."

He took a bite of his biscuit and nodded. "Mmm... this is good." He paused and looked past her for a moment. "I thought of that, but I wanted to be part of the ceremony," he said. "It was all so beautiful and filled with generations of meaning. I had to take part... for myself and the men in my family before me."

"I know," she said and set her cup down. "I felt the same way for all our families." They lingered on the expansive view.

"Those trees perfectly frame the meadow, don't they?" she said, her eyes filled with wonder.

"Yes, they do. And when they bloom, it will be magnificent and—" His voice trailed off as he stared out, his eyes teared with pain.

"... and so poignant," Betsy added. She reached across the table and put her hand on his. He looked at it and then into her eyes, his expression softening. She was always there for him.

"It's okay," she said. "You've been thinking about your dad, haven't you?"

"I guess that's the reason I couldn't sleep last night. It wasn't a conscious thought, but perhaps it was churning in the back of my mind," he replied. He looked at his wife's face. "It seems incredible to me how much I still miss him after all these years."

"That's not a bad thing," she said. "It's a measure of just how much you love him."

"But it still—" He choked, his voice giving a sound to his pain.

"Hurts? It probably always will, but not to the same agonizing extent," she said. "Our minds have a way of tempering that pain by reminding us of the wonderful memories." Her eyes filled with love and compassion. "We don't forget those we love. We just don't hurt as much. Each time we share their story, with cause to laugh, the anguish that consumed us slowly turns to sorrow. Day after day, memory after memory, we heal. And one night, as you lay your head on your pillow, you realize you didn't cry that day about your loss. The love remains, lasting forever, as a balm for the heartache. But that doesn't mean you won't have moments."

Hank squeezed his wife's hand and looked into her eyes. "You are the greatest possible gift any man could ever hope for," he said. "I can never thank you enough for all the years of love and your ability to speak to my heart." Almost in a whisper, he said, "Thank you for teaching me how to cope with my anger and sadness."

Hank was in the garage working on the bookcase he and his dad were building.

"I'm going to the hardware store for more sandpaper and wood stain. I'll be back shortly," Mr. Walker said as he headed for the door. He halted and turned to look at his son. "I want you to know, Hank, how very proud I am of you." He smiled for a moment before he walked out.

Hank grinned at his dad in response. "Thanks, Dad." He beamed.

He stepped back and admired their latest project as he

began again to sand the fine-grained wood. His dad had hired him as an apprentice carpenter, and he'd worked the last two summers and school breaks learning how to build and remodel homes. When Hank had completed the wooden box for Betsy, his father commended his talent. He even told him he had exceptional skills. That's when he decided he wanted to become a contractor, like his dad. Mr. Walker was ecstatic his son was going to follow in his footsteps, and Hank saw the same look of pride on his dad's face. The time they'd spent together, as he learned at his father's side, bonded them with a new rapport and respect.

The screen door of the house opened, and his mother coughed. He stopped as he listened.

"Hank," she called. Her voice sounded unfamiliar. "Hank, come here, please." Her words were serious and strained.

"I'm coming, Mom," he yelled as he ran across the yard and into the house. He was shocked at his mother's tear-stained face and the sheriff standing in the kitchen. He had been to their house several times for meals and had always been pretty cheerful and laughed a lot, but not that day.

Mrs. Walker tried to speak, but her voice cracked as she covered her face and sobbed. She made no attempt to stem the tide of her tears.

"Mom, what's wrong?" he asked as he rushed to her side. Fear washed across his panicked face.

The sheriff's expression was grim as he cleared his throat and spoke. He put a heavy hand on the boy's shoulder.

"Hank, son, there's been an accident," he said. "I'm afraid your father's been killed." Before the sheriff could say anything further, Mrs. Walker fainted, collapsing into her agony. He grabbed her before she hit the floor. "Help me, boy. Grab your mother's legs."

"Mom!" he shouted as he wrapped his arms around her legs and they carried the unconscious woman to the living room and laid her on the couch.

He fell to his knees and shook her by her shoulders. "Mom," he cried, "wake up. Please, Mom." The boy buried his face on her shoulder. Seconds passed before she moaned and placed her hand on her son's arm.

"Get a glass of water for her, boy," the sheriff said as he bent over to look at her grief-stricken face. She opened her eyes and tears spilled down the sides of her cheeks, lost in her hair. A sob caught in her throat. She choked and coughed as she slid her legs over the side of the couch. With shoulders slumped, she couldn't brace her body with her hands.

"Please," she said, "please tell me it's not true. How can he be gone?" she pleaded.

The sheriff helped her sit up as her son returned with a glass of water and held it out to her. She bit her bottom lip as she stretched out a shaky hand for the glass. Her hand trembled as she gripped her drink. Water splashed out, but she managed to take a sip.

Hank knelt beside his mother. He looked at her anguished face, something he'd never seen before—ever. Tears coursed down his cheeks and fell into the darkness of his grief as he laid his head on her lap. Mrs. Walker continued to cry in silence as she stroked the top of her son's head. His body shook as he released his despair.

The sheriff sat down with the expression of a man who'd brought such news to too many loved ones and friends. His eyes were red, but he sniffed and held back the tears. He waited for the shattered family members to process what he'd told them. He could wait—he'd waited before. There was time for them to ask about the person who'd never come home again. His shoulders sagged as he leaned forward and rested his forearms on his legs. His face was haggard from the weight of his job.

Minutes passed before Hank lifted his head, his face blotchy and his eyes red and filled with anguish. His mom cradled his cheeks and kissed his forehead. She looked over her son to the man across from her as she wiped her face and straightened her back. Now she was in charge of the family. There would be much to do and arrangements to be made. There would be time to cry later.

"Sheriff, please, tell us—what happened?" Her hands in fists beside her body, she exhaled as she controlled her breath and words.

"I can't tell you how sorry I am to bring this kind of news to you, Julie. My heart is broken for you both." His voice caught in his throat. "Andrew was a good friend to me and so many other people in this town." He stopped to draw in a slow, big breath before he continued. "It looks like he was headed back this way when another vehicle ran a stop sign. The other driver was speeding." The sheriff choked up but steeled himself. "We don't know this guy. He was just passing through, and he was drunk. Your husband was killed instantly. Nothing would have saved him. The other driver is in critical condition at the hospital in Oakville."

Hank jumped to his feet, his face now contorted by anger. His hands opened and closed involuntarily as they hung at his sides. He glared at the man who spoke the words of his father's last moments.

"He's still alive?" he shouted. "My father survived war and lived with shrapnel in his body," Hank said as he shook with rage, "only to be killed by some drunk?" Veins protruded on his forehead with beads of sweat interlaced.

The sheriff held his hand up as he spoke. "I know, son. It's not—"

"You know nothing," Hank snarled as he narrowed his eyes. His words cut off the sheriff's attempt to console with the unfairness of life.

"Hank," his mother scolded, "the sheriff is not to blame." She stood and reached for him, but her son turned and bolted for the kitchen door.

"Wait," she screamed at his back. She ran behind him, but he'd already escaped into the woods, his fury guiding him.

The sheriff wrapped a gentle arm around her shoulders.

"Let him go, Julie," he said. "The boy needs to deal with this on his own terms."

"I'm so sor—"

"You have nothing to be sorry about," he said. "This is the most devastating news anyone can hear. You and your boy are my primary concern and worry."

His kind words released another cruel wave of agony, and she sobbed into his chest. There was nothing else he could do but hold her and her grief.

In the distance, a flock of birds took flight as an excruciated scream filled the air. A carpenter's son sank to the ground and grasped at dead leaves and the image of his father as he'd left for the last time.

CHAPTER TWENTY-EIGHT

"Do you want more coffee while I'm up, honey?" Hank asked when he stood and stretched.

"Yes, please, my love." As she handed him the cup, he leaned down and kissed her.

"You look beautiful this morning, Mrs. Walker," he said. "How did I get so lucky?"

"I'm sure it was a shared love of chocolate chip cookies." She winked as she smirked.

"I think you're right." He burst out laughing and walked into the kitchen with Lady at his heels. Before reaching the coffeepot, the phone rang.

"Hello?" he answered. "Andy, my boy," he boomed, happy and animated. "It's terrific to hear your voice. I'm going to put you on speaker because I know your mother will be here any moment."

Betsy stood beside her husband in less than ten heartbeats.

"Andy, hi, honey. Oh, I miss you so much. Are you well?" Her words were a mixture of joy and anxiety as she clasped her hands, pulling them against her chest.

"Hi, Mom. I'm fine, don't worry. We're doing okay. It's been quiet here. Oh, before I forget, Willie says hi. Yeah, I just needed to tell you how much I love and appreciate you for always being here for me." Andy's words stalled. "We're moving out tomorrow, so you may not hear from me for several days." His voice lowered. "And I guess I'm a little homesick, too."

"We're mighty proud of you. You know that, right?" his dad reminded him, his face intent.

"We love you, son, and you're always in our prayers," his mom added. "You're stronger than you realize."

Lady followed them to the dining table as they continued their phone conversation. She laid her head on Hank's leg. As he rubbed her ear, her tail brushed the floor in a rhythmic back-and-forth motion. Her eyes were closed in contentment, with an expression akin to a smile.

They spoke for another twenty minutes, their demeanor and voices expressing the joy Andy brought to the beginning of their day. The dog lay down but watched as her ears rotated back and forth in perhaps an attempt to fine tune her understanding of their words. She was ever vigilant in assessing her family's moods in case they needed her for protection or play.

"It's always reassuring when he calls." Betsy poured more coffee into their cups. "I try not to borrow worries from tomorrow, but sometimes I find my thoughts wander into dark places." She looked up at her husband, standing nearby. "That's when I find comfort and peace in prayer." She brushed back a lock of hair and her features relaxed.

He wrapped her in his arms as he exhaled, slow and deep. "I know what you mean, my love." He kissed her forehead and picked up his cup. "How about we take this out to the gazebo?"

"I'm right behind you, honey."

Lady took the cue and ran ahead of them before they'd moved their feet. The sound of her nails clicked on the tile floor as she led the way.

"I swear that dog understands English." He shook his head in disbelief.

"Yes, she does, so be careful what you say." They laughed as they walked out to the sunny location.

"Ah, you've created a sanctuary out here." He lowered onto the soft, cozy loveseat. "I've said it before, but it bears repeating." His eyes were soft and warm as he patted the cushion for her to join him. "I appreciate all the hard work you and your wrecking crew put in to making this space more comfortable. It's been wonderful for my physical and mental healing."

"Anything for you, honey. And the gang was happy to be involved because we all love you." Her words made Hank smile.

Not to be ignored, Lady made her presence known loud and clear. She stood in front of them and looked from one to the other. Her tail swirled the air, causing the leaves on a nearby plant to flutter. She seemed poised to jump to whoever invited her first.

They laughed as they patted their legs. Lady seated herself between them with easy access to the double rubs. She panted and grinned, soaking in the love.

"I'm glad our boy's doing okay. At least that's what he says," Hank surmised. "I know how tough that life is and what he's going through. You not only have to fight to stay alive, but battle the loneliness that creeps into your soul." There was a tinge of recollection in his voice. She laid her hand on his arm.

Several seconds passed before Betsy spoke. "I'm glad

my letters give him some sense of home," she said, smiling. "And his instructions are to keep the cookies coming. I'm glad he shares them with Willie, our second son. That reminds me, I should call Angela and check on her now that Willie's gone again."

She reached down beside her chair for a bundle wrapped with blue ribbon. "Look what I brought from my hope chest." She held the stack of letters so Hank could see them.

He nodded and smiled. "Your letters kept me linked to you and this mountain, no matter where I was or what enemy we were fighting. It was you and your letters that got me home." He sighed, his face becoming solemn. "No one should have to see the things that war does and makes you do." His eyes turned toward the meadow. "It's hard to keep your soul protected and your mind well."

"Have you had any dreams recently?" Her voice was filled with concern. "You haven't mentioned anything to me in quite some time."

"No, it's been years since I've had any bad ones. There have been a few times when I woke up, though, and it was like a dark shroud covered me. It had no features, but I know it was memories from the war. Memories, perhaps, of just the pain. But nothing for a while now." His demeanor changed again. "Maybe it's a good thing, now and then, because that's when I pray the hardest. But it's nothing like the battle we fought together when I came back. It's hard when war follows you home." He reached out and took his wife's hand. No words were needed. Love had healed the wounds.

They sat in quiet repose as Lady napped between their chairs. Hank closed his eyes and laid his head back, falling asleep. His slow, deep breathing conveyed that he, too, was asleep. Betsy smiled as she watched the slow, rhythmic rise and fall of her husband's chest. Her eyes welled with tears. Before her sat the man she'd loved almost her entire life. A life filled with trials and triumphs, tears, laughter—and love.

"Thank you, God, for giving us more time," she whispered.

She pulled the ribbon from the stack of letters and cautiously opened one, careful not to disturb her husband. Lady, ever aware of her surroundings, lifted her head but saw no immediate peril and returned to her slumber.

The corners of Betsy's eyes crinkled as her lips curved up slightly and she read the letter from the young man she'd fallen in love with a lifetime ago.

Dear Betsy,

I can't begin to explain how important your letters are to me. This has been an especially difficult time, as we've constantly been on the move. But somehow, your letters find me and they are exactly what I need at the time I need them most.

It's hard to sleep at night. But I close my eyes and memories of us float through my mind. I smile at the thoughts of when we laughed and played as children. And the many spring picnics we had among the irises. Those were such wonderful times and are now some of my most precious recollections of our lives together. We were so young, weren't we?

I feel like it's been an eternity since I last saw you, the good people of Parsons, and our mountain.

How are you? How are you doing in school? I always knew you'd be a nurse. You were constantly taking care of

Ben and me. It seemed we were always getting injured. I guess it's true that when you're young, you really think you're invincible. I guess we didn't always make the best choices, did we? We should've listened to you and Estelle more often. I don't recall you two wearing bandages nearly as often as us.

Have you seen or heard from Ben and Estelle lately? Give them my regards. Is Estelle in Europe on her apprenticeship program yet? By the way, if you see Ben, punch him in the shoulder for me. Make sure it's before he graduates from the Police Academy, though.

I'm sorry I haven't written as often lately. I hope to come home on leave in a couple of months when this deployment is finished. Keep your fingers crossed.

Betsy, I miss you dearly. I carry your photo with me everywhere I go. I keep it in your last letter, next to my heart. It makes me feel closer to you. I long to hold you in my arms, touch your beautiful face, and watch the sun shine on your hair. You are my world, my sweet Betsy.

I love you, Betsy Parsons. Thank you for your letters and for keeping me in your prayers.

One last thing... are you still my girl?

Love always,

Hank

A squirrel chattered nearby and Lady jumped to her feet, running to the door. She bounced around, waiting to be given access to her nemesis.

As Betsy stood up, Hank jerked awake from all the commotion.

"It's okay, honey," she said and patted his arm. "Lady

just needs to answer the call of the wild." She released the black-and-white rocket from the luxury of her confines. Within seconds, the dog had located her adversary. The chase was on.

Hank sat forward with a smile. "That little nap was just what I needed. So what have you been up to while I slept, my dear?"

She held up the letter. "I'm reading some of our letters. It brings back so many memories. It was a time when we all went on different chosen paths but stayed loyal to our childhood bonds." She paused. "And we've remained inseparable from each other and this mountain. It never ceases to amaze me how our lives have always been intertwined and yet so differently transformed."

He reached out and took her hand. "And you never cease to amaze me, Mrs. Walker," he said with pride and admiration. "In no small part, you are what has helped hold us all together."

"And you, Mr. Walker, are my rock." she said and kissed his cheek. "Reading these letters reminds me you're the bravest man I've ever known." She tilted her head. "And have I told you lately that you're my hero?"

"I don't know that I'm brave, but if you asked me to move this mountain, I guess I'd somehow figure it out." They laughed.

"Well, I won't ask that of you, but how about a cup of tea?"

"That I can definitely do," he answered with a wink.

As she prepared their tea, he reached over and picked up the bundle of letters. He chose the one he'd received from her that helped keep him through the darkest moments of his life.

My dearest Hank,

Today I miss you a thousand times more than yesterday. I long to look into your eyes and feel your heartbeat beneath my fingers. I know for certain it has only ever been and will forever be you, my love. My heart belongs to only you.

I hope and pray you are well and safe. You are the bravest man I know, and you have made your family proud. You have brought honor to the memory of your father, grandfather, and your family name. I can't begin to even imagine your life now as you know it there. Please be careful and come home to me. I can barely wait until I'm in your arms once again.

I'm busy with school and will soon take finals. I'm nervous, but Professor Henry has given us a lot of advice on what to study. He's an alright guy and seems to want all of us to succeed. At least I made it through chemistry, which we both know is not my strong suit. Nursing school has certainly been challenging, but I can see the horizon now. And should you ever need any medical care, I will be well equipped. (smile)

After a year of criminology classes at Oakville Community, Ben is now close to completing his Police Academy training. Our schedules and locations are so varied, but we've managed to have lunch together a few times. I'm sending along his well wishes. He calls at least once a week for any news. He misses you, too. We all do.

Estelle was home for a week during semester break. It was wonderful to spend time with her, but it was over too soon. I feel like half of me is missing when she's away, but I know she'll come back to stay when she's finished with school. I'm really glad she's happy, though.

Last week, Tom Lester's bull got out of his pen and somehow made it to town before anyone noticed him missing. I was at the post office buying stamps that day when I heard horns honking and people yelling. There was an angry bull chasing Sheriff Richardson down Main Street as I walked outside. I didn't know our sheriff could run that fast. He escaped from harm but is still being teased by everyone in town. He thought Tom's bull would listen to reason, but apparently the animal was enjoying his newfound freedom far more than expected. Fortunately, it was all resolved when Tom persuaded his bull to get into a trailer and it was trucked home. The story had a happy ending. Well, except for our sheriff's suffering pride.

I have to study, so I'll close for now. I know it's hard for you to write, but that won't stop me from sending letters to you every day.

I love you, Hank, and I'll see you in my dreams.

Forever and always your girl,

Betsy

CHAPTER TWENTY-NINE

Hank and Betsy sat at the kitchen table finishing their coffee. Lady lay asleep beneath the chair, her paws twitching and the occasional muffled woof escaping.

"What time do you want to leave, honey?" Betsy asked as she took the last sip of her morning nectar.

"It won't take me long to get dressed, but I should look out in the barn before we go," he said. "Maybe in about an hour. That should give us plenty of time to drive to Oakville."

"Okay, sounds good to me. Is Miss Lady going, too?" As soon as the words were spoken, their fur friend jumped to her feet. As she cocked her head to one side and stared at Betsy, she wagged her tail in anticipation.

Hank smiled and looked down at her. "Of course. No way we'd get out of the house without her now." They laughed as Lady posed at attention with her ears perked up.

"Okay, you get ready, and I'll take our friend out for a short walk." As she stood, the dog bounced in a circle and dashed for the door. "I think I just said more of her favorite words," she said and laughed again.

"And I think her list of vocabulary words is getting longer every day." Hank laughed and took their cups to the sink before he headed up the stairs.

~

Dr. Lewis walked into the small but bright office. His countenance was cheerful, and it preceded him. Given that he often had to impart the worst news possible a person might hear, his congeniality remained intact. He was a tall man who walked with shoulders back, giving a heightened presence to his already sizable stature. A shock of thick, black hair adorned his head, and gold-rimmed glasses accentuated his pleasant face.

"Hank and Betsy," he said with a huge smile. "I was looking forward to speaking with you today." He reached for Hank's outstretched hand as he patted Betsy's shoulder.

Hank smiled back at him. "It's always a good sign when your doctor walks in with a grin."

The doctor sat down and picked up a chart, briefly glancing at the contents as he arched an eyebrow. He nodded and looked up at his patient.

"I looked at this a few days ago," the doctor said, "but just wanted to reassess. I'm pleased to tell you that all the follow-up tests show no recent growth."

"That's great news, Doc," Hank said as he looked at his wife and squeezed her hand. She hadn't realized she was holding her breath despite the doctor's smile. She exhaled and smiled at her husband and back again at the cordial man across from her.

"I can assume there have been no additional issues then since our last appointment? Headaches? Balance, okay?"

"No, no, and yes to your questions," he answered with a

grin. "I'm feeling better every day, almost back to my old self. But I still tire easily if I exert myself for too long. I'm doing my best to rebuild my stamina at a slower pace. I try to monitor myself and if I don't, you can bet she does." He grinned at his wife. "She's nursed me back to life on a few occasions." His face reflected his love for her.

"That's good to hear, Hank." Dr. Lewis said as he turned to Betsy. "So, Nurse Betsy, has our patient been as good as he would lead me to believe?"

She grinned and nodded. "I'd have to say he's been pretty exemplary these past six months. With the exception, perhaps, of some hole digging." She turned to look at Hank as the doctor pursed his lips and wrinkled his brows toward her husband.

"Digging holes?" the doctor questioned with pursed lips. "I'm sure there's a story behind that. So tell me—how long, how deep, and how did it make you feel?"

Hank was sheepish as he answered. "We have great soil up at our house. I'd say it took me about twenty minutes to go two feet deep by two feet wide, and that cherry tree looks spectacular. She helped plant one, too. They should bloom next spring." He wore a look of pride after his story. "I didn't overdo it, though. No headaches and just some fatigue the next day."

Dr. Lewis laughed. "Well, as long as you understand your limitations, I'm fine with your activities." He looked again at Betsy and spoke of his patient as if he wasn't there. "I'd keep him tethered for a few more months to make sure he is fully healed from surgery. And I'd say bull riding is no longer an option for your husband."

They all laughed, Betsy and Hank breathing enormous sighs of relief.

Hank leaned forward as some anxiety crept across his face. "When do I need to see you again, doc?"

"I think I'd like another MRI in six months and we'll see you when I get the results. My nurse can set that up and call you with all the details. Of course, I expect you to call me if there are any changes or concerns. Questions?"

The couple looked at each other with smiles and then back at the doctor.

"None that I can think of," Betsy said. They still held hands.

Dr. Lewis smiled as he said, "You've taken superb care of him, Betsy. I'm sure that's why he's looking so well."

She smiled at the doctor. "Thank you, Dr. Lewis. I plan on him staying around a while longer."

"Let's grab some lunch to eat at the park," Betsy said while she waited for Hank to unlock the Bronco. Lady stood on the back seat whimpering her greeting, barely able to contain her enthusiasm. When they were in their seats, she gave a quick sniff and lick on each of their cheeks. Then she sat back and grinned at them, her eyes sparkling.

They laughed and reached out to rub her head.

"We missed you, too," Betsy said. She held her hand out with palm up and the dog moved forward to rest her head on it. "You're such a love, my sweet girl." Lady thumped her tail on the leather seat as she soaked in the attention.

"How about we grab some burgers?" Hank paused and looked at their furry companion. "For all of us?"

Betsy laughed. "That's good for me, and I know she'll be thrilled." They were cheerful and relaxed as he pulled out into traffic.

Within twenty minutes, they'd walked to a park bench. There were about a dozen people and three other dogs enjoying the late autumn sunshine. Lady noticed the other canines but was focused on the delicious smell emanating from the bag her man carried.

"This looks good, don't you think?" Betsy said as she set her purse down.

"Yep, and just in time. I believe our little friend here is drooling."

As they looked at Lady, she instantly sat and awaited her treat, her eyes glued to the crinkling container and mesmerized by the aroma.

After they ate, they strolled along the many walkways and gravel paths. Lady was content to walk with them, happy to be out among the many intriguing scents and sounds. She often stopped and stood motionless with her ears erect. As she listened, she searched the trees with her eyes for any sign that her nemesis could be hiding. After a moment, she'd be content again to walk with her friends. No squirrels had been detected.

"This is beautiful, isn't it?" Betsy said, sighing. "Who would have thought there would ever be a Japanese garden in Parsons?" They stopped near the small bridge over the pond. Hank had kept half of the bun from Lady's burger and he tossed pieces of it into the water. Several ducks noticed, and they swam fast and disorderly as they competed to retrieve the offerings. They paid little attention to the black-and-white dog, who stared at them and lay motionless next to the water.

Once the tasty morsels were no longer pitched in their direction, the ducks turned and lazily meandered toward the other shore. As Lady watched the birds, intent on their every movement, she darted her eyes back and forth, causing her brows to jump up and down. The fowl exited the water and waddled toward the security beneath the bridge. There they settled in to enjoy the warmth of the sun. Now and then, a breeze would hint at the coming of winter. But all the people and creatures were content to embrace the comfort and hospitality the day offered.

"I remember when there was nothing here but trees, wild grass, and us," Hank said. "Parsons was just a speck on the map and a good place to turn around."

"We've lived a lot of life since then, haven't we?" Betsy sighed and closed her eyes as she faced the sun. As she parted her lips, a gentle breeze danced in her hair.

He looked at his wife and smiled. He glanced at the sun glistening on her auburn hair. "You're just as beautiful as the day we married." He placed a tender kiss on her lips.

She slid her hand around his waist and smiled up at him. "Thank you, my love."

They stood on the red bridge and looked at the water below as they held one another.

"I always know when winter is just around the corner," Hank said as he looked up at the snow-covered peaks.

"Your shoulder?"

"Yep, my built-in barometer," he said, "and a reminder of forgiveness."

"Betsy," the head nurse called from the doorway. "You have a phone call. He said it's important. I'll take over for you." Betsy was surprised and confused for a moment before she let the other nurse continue with the patient's vitals.

She rushed to the nurses' station and grabbed the phone while others looked on, concerned about her emergency.

"Hello, this is Betsy." Her voice was anxious and her eyes wide. "What? How bad? Tell me again, Hank, where are you?" She gripped the phone and held her breath. "Hank? Hank, I can't hear you, honey." She listened for several seconds to the voice on the other end before she visibly relaxed. The color returned to her face and her breathing deepened as she regained control of her body.

"He'll be okay, then? When? Are you sure?" She didn't blink as she asked her questions in rapid fire. "Alright. Yes. I'll be back home in about two hours and I'll wait for your call. Thank you, Lieutenant. Thank you so much. Please, will you put the phone next to Hank's ear now?" She spoke again, but this time with her voice modulated in a soothing tone. "I love you, Hank, very much. Hang in there. You're going to be alright. I know they'll take good care of you. You'll be home soon, in my arms and in my care. I'll be praying for you, my love. I'll see you soon, honey." She cradled the phone and leaned her back against the wall behind her. Tears rolled down her cheeks as she stood there. She stared ahead at nothing.

"Betsy," the desk nurse said, her face contorted with concern. "Has something happened to Hank?" She got up from her chair and walked over to wrap her arms around her distraught friend.

Betsy took two deep breaths and exhaled to a count of four before she answered. "Hank was on a mission and shot while under siege. He's being treated at a field hospital and will then be flown to Germany for further care. They're taking him into surgery right now before they fly him out. He's in stable condition. That's all I know." She covered her face, overwhelmed by her own words, as she slid into a crouched position. Her shoulders sagged as she sobbed.

The head nurse came down the hallway in time to see

Betsy cover her face and slide down the wall. She looked at the desk nurse, who frowned and shook her head as she held the slumped body. The elder nurse knelt beside the overwrought woman.

"Betsy, honey," she said. "We've got this covered. There's no need for you to finish your shift. You should be at home with your family. Are you okay with driving? I can call someone if you need me to."

Betsy looked up with makeup-smeared eyes as she wiped her nose on a tissue. "Thanks, Sue. I'm sorry—I kinda lost it." She stood up and straightened her uniform and smoothed her hair. "I just need to wash my face in some cold water and I'll be okay to drive home."

"No need to apologize. I know his being over there has got to be nerve-wracking. I want you to go home and take care of yourself now. Surround yourself with family and let them help you through this. Soak in a tub of hot water. Maybe have a cup of tea or a glass of wine. Okay? Call me and let me know if I need to adjust the schedule. We'll handle it."

She hugged her supervisor, who'd likely had more than her share of these types of calls over the years. She'd been a military wife for two decades and had lived with the uncertainty.

"Thanks, Sue. I really appreciate it. Lieutenant Hall said he'd call me with all the information and updates in a few hours."

"Whatever you need, hon, don't be afraid to ask. Okay?"

Both nurses hugged her and assured her of their prayers before she left her station.

When she stepped out of the elevator, she made a few calls before walking out to her car. The visitor's phone in the far corner was available, so she walked across the lobby. She called her sister first. Estelle didn't answer, so she left a message and asked her to pray for Hank. She dialed again.

"Ben, this is Betsy. Hi. I need to tell you that Hank's been injured. He's in surgery right now." She listened for several seconds and responded. "They said he's in stable condition and I'm supposed to get an update in a few hours. Yes, I'm on my way home now. Come over when you can, please."

She dialed another number. As the phone rang, her lip trembled. When her mother answered, all she could do was cry for what seemed an eternity.

"Betsy? Honey, is that you?" her mother's panic-stricken voice shouted. "Betsy, tell me what's wrong. Are you okay? Have you been in an accident?"

After a few guttural responses, she composed herself enough to explain she was coming home early and why. She made it brief so she wouldn't create an onslaught of tears again. Her mom confirmed she would go straight away to Hank's house to sit with his mother. Mrs. Walker would need the prayers, strength, and support of friends.

When she got into her car, she exhaled as she closed her eyes and leaned her head back. It was a tremendous relief to be on her way home. But before she turned the key, she said a prayer out loud for the love of her life, who lay hurt on the other side of the world.

After two weeks in the hospital stateside, Hank was home on convalescent leave. He'd been lucky. The bullet could easily have destroyed his shoulder. The surgeons repaired the broken bones with the aid of small plates and screws. With physical therapy, his prognosis looked good. Betsy had spoken with his therapist and assured him she could assist Hank while he was home. She helped him daily with wound care and stretches to increase his range of motion. He'd been happy to be home again, but soon became sullen and distant. She said nothing because he was in great physical pain. He didn't seem to notice his words were harsh and he had become unpleasant toward her, more so every day.

"You're doing good today, honey," she said as she held Hank's outstretched arm. "I know it's very painful but—"

"You don't know anything," he said in a surly tone. He pulled his arm out of her hands. "I'm done for today." He didn't look at her or see her eyes grow moist. He put his arm in the sling. "Sorry, Betsy. I'm tired. I'll see tomorrow."

"Oh," she stammered. "Okay. Uh, I'll call you later then." She gave him a quick kiss on the cheek and turned so he wouldn't see her tears. It wasn't until she started toward the doorway that she realized Ben was standing there and had seen it all.

"Oh," she said, startled by his appearance. "I didn't know you were here."

"Hi, Betsy. Yeah, I just got here," he said without smiling as he looked in Hank's direction, his brows knitted together. He turned toward Betsy as she walked by and they smiled at each other. He touched her arm for a moment and appeared concerned.

"Be careful driving home, Betsy," he said in a deep, gentle voice.

"Thanks, Ben. I will," she said as she reached for her purse. "I'll see you later."

Her words were cut short as he turned and walked into the family room. He looked over his shoulder to watch her walk out of the front door. He took a deep breath and exhaled as he sat in a chair across from Hank, who only acknowledged him with a nod and a scowl. Without a word, both men took a defensive posture.

"We've been friends a long time, Hank, and we've always been honest with each other," Ben said in a slow, deliberate manner. He planted his hands on his knees and leaned in.

Hank tilted his head slightly forward and looked at Ben with a fixed gaze as he gripped the arms of the chair.

"Is this going to take long?" Hank said, his voice filled with disdain.

Ben squinted his eyes at his defiance. That gave him the impetus to continue.

"We've all been going out of our way to help the wounded soldier," Ben started with sarcasm, "but I gotta call it as I see it. You're being a jackass right now and have been for the past two weeks. You've been a jerk to Betsy on at least several occasions that I've witnessed. She hasn't said anything to me—or to you. She's been nothing but love and kindness." His voice caught as he took a breath. "She's the most compassionate person we both know and you don't deserve her with this kind of attitude."

Hank stared at his friend. He tightened his jaw muscles., and he looked like he wanted to punch someone. Ben noticed.

"You want to punch me? Go ahead, but don't you dare speak another harsh word to Betsy or I'll take you down myself. She's too nice to say anything to you, but I'm not." He looked with certainty at Hank, whose hands were now clenched.

"Where," he emphasized, "is Hank Walker? Because the guy sitting in front of me is an imposter." Hank stood up as his friend glared at him and braced himself for what might come next.

Instead, Hank turned his back to him and walked to the window. He stood motionless and stared out for a while. The tension mounted before he returned to his seat and spoke. He looked up at the ceiling before he directed his eyes at Ben. He took a deep breath, and as he exhaled, he relaxed his body and softened his fists into hands.

"I really wanted to hit you a minute ago," Hank said, shame written on his face. "But you're right. I've been a jerk. I could feel it happening, but I couldn't stop it." His tone was commensurate with his confession. "I'm angry with myself, Ben, and I have no right to take it out on anyone else." His expression reflected his remorse. "I'm sorry."

"I'm really glad you realize it, but it's not me you need to apologize to," Ben said as he scolded his friend. "I don't suppose you noticed Betsy was crying on her way out just now?" he added as a slight accusation with a lot of sarcasm.

"No, I didn't," Hank said with pain in his eyes, as if his heart had just been impaled.

"That's because you and that other guy in your head are too wrapped up in yourselves," he said. "So you wanna tell me what the malfunction is?"

Hank squirmed a bit, struggling with that imaginary guy Ben mentioned.

"Come on, Hank, you know you can't keep it from me," he said wryly. "You forget, I know how to interrogate people now." His smile soon disappeared under the weight and enormity of what needed to transpire.

Hank offered a weak smile and relaxed. A counselor had visited him in the hospital to ask him if he needed to talk about what happened in the field the day of the siege.

He couldn't and didn't want to think about it then, let alone speak about it to a stranger.

He leaned forward, careful not to put pressure on his injured arm. It took him a few breaths before he gathered up the courage to speak his truth to the one man who dared confront him with such raw words of blame.

"When I got shot, I was trying to pull two other guys to safety. I couldn't do it. I tried and tried, but I only had one arm. Before I could get them in a safe place, they were both killed. I failed them. I failed my team." He hung his head in shame and defeat. "I failed myself."

Ben had never seen his friend so devastated. He knew there was only one way for Hank to deal with this. Days earlier, he'd already changed his prayers for his friend.

"Hank, I've known you almost my whole life. In fact, you even rescued me from certain death. If anyone could have saved those guys, it would've been you." He stopped to let those words sink in. The way I see it, you're fighting another enemy right now—and that's the enemy of your soul. He'd like nothing better than to have you live the rest of your life filled with guilt and self-pity," he said, careful to choose his words. "He'll try to convince you you're not worthy. But we know that's a lie. You're bigger than that."

Hank looked up with worry-filled eyes. "What can I do, Ben? This is tearing me up. And it's destroying my relationship with Betsy. If I'm like this now, what will I be like after I've served more years? How could she love me? I don't love myself. She'll hate me," he said, pausing as his brows furrowed even deeper. "I don't want to hurt her. You know that." Dejection flooded his face as he cast his eyes down at the floor.

Ben got up and sat next to his friend. He took a deep

breath and put his hand on Hank's good shoulder. Hank flinched at the contact and then settled into it.

"Well, the first thing you gotta do, Hank," Ben said with compassion as he squeezed his friend's arm, "is ask for Betsy's forgiveness. After that, you can work on forgiving yourself."

CHAPTER THIRTY

Betsy was basting the turkey when Lady jumped up from beside Hank's chair and ran to the front door. She barked once and circled twice before anyone could react.

"I bet that's Ben," Betsy called out. "Lady knows the sound of his truck and that's her happy bark."

Hank laughed as he walked to the door. He reached down and patted the excited dog.

"Okay, Lady, go give them your best welcome," he said and put on his coat. "I'm going outside, honey."

"Okay," she answered. "I'm tied up with Mr. Turkey at the moment. And he's a handsome bird indeed." Satisfaction and joy filled the kitchen with a side dish of happiness.

Hank laughed as he stepped out onto the porch. It had stopped snowing, and the temperature was still mild enough to be enjoyable. He glimpsed Ben's truck through the trees lining the driveway. As he waited, he looked out over the meadow—their meadow—that was now covered in a layer of white. The sun peeked through the clouds and glistened on the snow. Etched on the white canvas, the trails and tracks of the woodland creatures created abstract art.

Hank took a deep breath and exhaled the cold air as his body relaxed. They loved their small piece of this mountain. They had called Parsons home all their lives. Any brief time they'd been gone, the mountain always welcomed them back with whispers of seasons, friendships, love, and a sense of connection to something and someone much grander than themselves.

As the truck pulled up, Lady bounced around beside the driver's door. She jumped high enough to see Ben eye to eye. He laughed at her enthusiasm. It had been a long time since he'd had that amount of energy.

When the passenger door opened first, the furry hostess ran to the other side. She barked and wagged her tail furiously, almost beside herself with excitement. She danced about as if on hot coals, surprised by the unexpected guest.

"How ya doin', my fair Lady?" Andy grinned. He reached out his arm as he knelt down and Lady immediately stood still to accept his rubs and hugs. She licked every inch of his face before he stood up. He laughed and dried the love.

"I wasn't expecting a bath so early in the day," he joked. "Hey, Dad, good to see you." The men hugged long and hard, saying what words couldn't. It had been several months since Andy had been home. His absence was felt every day, but he was home again, so for now, it was time to celebrate.

Lady heard the other door and raced around to greet the sheriff. "I thought you forgot me, girl." He bent down and hugged his four-legged black-and-white friend. "Yeah, I missed you, too, but let's take this loving reception into the warm house, huh?" Everyone laughed and helped carry in the food he'd brought.

In the distance, a car honked, but Lady had already

heard Estelle approaching and was in place to greet more family.

"Good girl," Hank said. "I'll be right back."

As they walked inside the house, Betsy was on her way across the room with her arms extended, her face glowing with excitement.

"Andy, my son, it's so good to see you," she said, her eyes brimming with joyful tears. She held him like she never intended to let go.

He laughed. "Okay, Mom, let me set this stuff down so I can give you a proper hug." He protested, but not very hard. He kissed the top of her head.

She grinned, but seemed hesitant to release him. She kissed his cheek before she him let go. "Okay, but I'm holding you to your promise." Everyone laughed and continued into the kitchen with their packages.

"Hey, how 'bout me?" Ben said with a downturned mouth and a look of mock hurt.

"Oh, you big baby," she snickered. "You know you're going to get a hug." He grinned and wiggled his eyebrows. "I swear the townsfolk wouldn't believe what a big teddy bear their sheriff is."

"Aunt Estelle is just pulling up," Andy shared with his mom as she hugged her big friend.

"Oh, wonderful. She's bringing her special pies. I think I'll just skip dinner and go straight to dessert," she said with a wink.

"Yeah, let's start a new tradition—dessert first." Ben nodded, elated by the suggestion. "I brought whipped cream," he shouted.

Everyone laughed. It was well known that Sheriff Murphy had the biggest sweet tooth on the mountain. And the townsfolk kept him well supplied.

They gathered around the table filled with food, heads bowed and hands joined as Ben said the blessing. He was seated between the two most important women in his life.

"Thank you, Heavenly Father, for this food set before us and for your daily grace. Bless this food to our bodies and may we be reflections of Your light and love."

"Thanks, Ben." Hank nodded to his friend and stood to carve the turkey. With knife in hand, he said, "While I do this, why don't we each say a few words of what we're thankful for today?"

"I'm thankful I'm not that turkey," the sheriff said with a smirk as he watched the knife slice into the golden bird. The others joined him in laughing. "Seriously, though, I'm thankful to be here with all of you—you're my family and I love you more than I could ever tell you." His eyes welled with tears as he continued. "You've been with me through the good and the bad, the happy and sad. You held me in my darkest times and brought me back." He wiped his eyes and looked up with a smile.

Betsy sat next to him and squeezed his hand. "And I'm thankful you're all here. I love cooking this meal for my family. Not just once a year, but every day my heart is filled with gratitude for each of you. You make my heart and my life complete. I love each of you dearly." Her eyes expressed the depth of her love.

Estelle and Andy looked at each other and grinned. She hugged him and patted his cheek.

"I'm so grateful for this boy right here," she said, "I mean, young man. It fills my heart with pride to have watched you grow into the amazing human being you are, Andy. I know there are wondrous things you'll accomplish with your life. And I hope to be around to see them."

"You better be," he scolded his aunt and grinned. "I'm

grateful and feel fortunate to have you and Mom as two of my teachers. You've taught me so much about being a gentleman and especially about how women think."

Ben and Hank tried to hold it in but burst out laughing. When Hank could contain himself, he said, "Sorry, son, I just couldn't stop myself." He wiped tears from his eyes.

Ben laughed longer and finally said, "Maybe you could give me a refresher course, Estelle, about how women think." He looked at Hank and they started laughing again.

"Oh, you two," Betsy said, smacking her husband's shoulder and shaking her finger at the other instigator.

"Andy," the sheriff said, "that class is one you'll be in for the rest of your life."

When the two older men continued to laugh at his last words, Andy must have realized the humor in what he'd said. As he grinned at his mom and aunt, he joined the male chorus in the moment's hilarity.

The women looked at each other in mock indignation and shook their heads.

"And like I've always said"—Estelle motioned her hand toward Ben and Hank—"men are just big boys." The two women now had their own reason to chuckle.

Hank's laughter wound down, and he looked around the table at the cheerful faces of the people who he could most count on to love and accept him as himself, in good times and bad.

"I'm grateful for the abundance of laughter and joy we share," he said. "And I want to let you know just how healing that can be." He laid the knife and fork down and glanced at his wife. He faced the others and said, "I've been waiting for this day and this time to tell you all." He took a deep breath and exhaled with a big grin. "I got a clean bill of health from the doctor a few weeks ago. I guess you all are stuck with me a while longer."

"I knew you were hiding something from me, Betsy." Estelle grinned with wide eyes at her sister. "Oh, Hank, I'm so happy to hear it." She got up, walked around to her brother-in-law, gave him a big hug, and then hugged him again.

"That's terrific, Dad." Andy nodded as he grinned, his voice intense and emotional.

Ben reached his big hand across the table to his best friend and shook his hand. "I've been waiting for good news, buddy. Thanks." His eyes welled up again, but these were happy tears. He had no better friend than him and he'd been worried.

"And thank you for your prayers—and your gift of love." He picked up the cutlery once again and with a wave of the knife, said, "Okay, let's eat. What's my bid for this perfect piece of bird?" They all laughed and began passing the bowls of food around.

When Betsy picked up the candied yams, she handed them to Ben, who snickered and eyed Hank. "Oh, don't you do it, Ben Murphy," she scolded, but it was too late. Both men burst into laughter to the extent it caused the sheriff to choke and cough. "Well, it serves you right," she said. "I guess I'll never live it down, will I?"

Hank stopped laughing long enough to grin at his son and said, "Andy, my boy, that was one of your mother's finest hours. Let me tell you a Thanksgiving story."

CHAPTER THIRTY-ONE

"Okay, you two can't hover over us while we cook," Estelle said as she stirred the gravy and worked on mashing the potatoes. "Shoo, both of you. We'll let you know when it's time to eat. You boys will not starve to death." She opened the window above the pies to help them cool in time for dessert later. It had been a mild winter and the fresh air felt good.

Hank and Ben turned their eyes to Betsy, who waved her hand at them as if to scoot them out from underfoot. They looked longingly at the marshmallow-topped yams that sat by the stove, ready for their final bake. The men gave the women a forlorn look and retreated to the small living room.

"It won't be long," she said to the backs of the hungry and disgruntled dinner guests. She turned her attention to the turkey she was basting. She smiled to herself. "I think we're on track, don't you, Estelle?" Her sister nodded as she juggled her tasks.

"How 'bout a walk outside?" Hank said as he grabbed his coat. "This is their first attempt at a Thanksgiving dinner, so it might take longer than expected. And I have a funny feeling it will not go as planned with those two." They grinned and nodded in agreement.

Ben stopped midway to the front door. "Maybe we could just sneak a couple of rolls." With a gleam in his eyes, he turned around. He'd seen them on the counter as they'd exited the room of delicious aromas. He tiptoed back to the kitchen and peeked around the doorway. Both women had their backs turned. He rushed in and grabbed three rolls with a quick thrust of his hand before the cooks even noticed. His accomplice stood with the door open for a quick getaway and Ben's coat draped over his arm.

"Here ya go." Ben handed one and a half rolls to his buddy as they walked out into the brisk November air. They stuffed the rolls into their mouths, and with satisfied looks, nodded in unison.

"Mmm, if Betsy hadn't decided to be a nurse," Ben said with his mouth full, "she'd have made one heck of a terrific baker."

"Yes, she would," Hank replied. "I'm pretty sure I could live on her chocolate chip cookies." They both laughed. "She's been sending me care packages."

"And I could live on these rolls." Ben smacked his lips. "I'm glad we could all be home at the same time for the holiday. So, how's your grandma doing?"

"Mom called this morning and said she's doing better. She'll be able to come home in a few days. I told her the girls were cooking dinner at our house today as a surprise and she was happy about that. She felt bad she wasn't here to fix dinner but thought it would be good practice for them." Hank picked up a broom and cleared the light dusting of snow that had fallen on the front steps overnight.

"Glad to hear your grandma's doing better." Ben

finished buttoning his coat. He stopped and looked at his friend. "I've missed these times together with you and the girls. But I know when we all get finished with school and the military, we'll be back together again."

"Yeah, I've missed this, too." Mr. Gilbert was walking his dog on the other side of the street.

Ben turned to look. "Holy cow, that dog's a beast. I think it's the biggest German Shepherd I've ever seen."

Hank laughed at his assessment as he waved at his neighbor. "Hello, Mr. Gilbert," he shouted. "Brutus has really grown since the last time I saw him."

"That he has, Hank. Hope you boys have a nice Thanksgiving." The white-haired man strained to hold back his dog on the taut leash. A few more months and Brutus would take Mr. Gilbert for a walk.

"Thanks, you too." Another neighbor came out of her house.

"Hey, how are you boys doing? Happy Thanksgiving," Mrs. Grady said from her porch. She lived next door and had known Hank and Ben since they were just little boys.

"Happy Thanksgiving, Mrs. Grady." Hank waved and smiled at his elderly neighbor. "Do you need me to clear your sidewalk for you?"

"No, but—" Her words were cut short by the shrill sound of smoke alarms. Mrs. Grady's eyesight was not what it used to be, but her hearing was better than that of her miniature poodle, who sat by her feet.

"Oh my," she shouted, "is that your smoke alarm?" She widened her eyes and her face paled as her poodle, Roxy, threw back her head and howled loudly and incessantly. Mrs. Grady shuffled as fast as possible back into her house, leaving her pint-sized, curly-haired warning system to alert the residents nearby. "I'll call the fire department," she shouted, but her words went no further than the marching band's music of the Macy's Thanksgiving Day parade on her television.

Hank and Ben looked at each other and raced back through the front door, not bothering to be sure it was closed behind them. Hank almost tripped over Boots, his mother's cat, who was fleeing from the kitchen. He didn't know Boots could move so fast given his age and girth.

"Betsy? Estelle?" Hank cried from the front doorway. "Is there a fire?"

In just a matter of steps, the two men stood at the edge of chaos. The once warm, inviting, and aromatic kitchen had become the scene of a great battle. Before them on the tile floor lay the golden-brown turkey in a state of repose with a trail of stuffing. The dining table was littered with a gooey lagoon of candied yams and very burnt marshmallows, all having escaped their casserole dish, which sat upside down. The table setting was in complete disarray, with flowers strewn across plates, napkins, and silverware. An empty vase sat perilously close to the edge—much like Betsy and Estelle.

The women stood in shocked horror with hands covering their ears. Meanwhile, when Roxy saw the cat burst out of the house onto the front steps, her howls turned into a rapid succession of high-pitched barking. The yapping bit of fluff jumped from her porch and ran through the picket fence in pursuit of Boots, who was sprinting toward the street.

Roxy's howls and barking had gained the attention of Brutus. The big dog jerked his leash free from his owner, who almost fell to the ground. The giant German Shepherd turned and galloped toward the exciting sounds of a chase.

Boots outran the little dog, but nearly crashed into a

hairy hulk named Brutus at the intersection of the mailbox and sidewalk. The cat did a swift about face back into the house with both dogs intent on his capture. The cat and dogs did furious laps around the living room, up over and under furniture, small tables, and a tall bird cage. Hank's grandmother had a mild-mannered parakeet, Billie Bird, who was transformed into a shrieking ball of flapping wings and flying feathers.

Without warning, Brutus left the chase and ran into the kitchen, grabbing the still-warm, perfectly bronzed turkey with his enormous jaws and running out of the front door. Roxy smelled the cooked bird and ran in hot pursuit of a snack. Boots, not taking any chances, lay down on the top of the drapes. Billy Bird huddled wide-eyed in the bottom of his cage, holding his feathers tight against his slight frame. He didn't blink even after the dogs left. There was another set of eyes fixed on him.

"Where's the fire?" Hank yelled above the deafening smoke alarms. "Betsy, are you okay? Estelle?" She nodded, but her sister was frozen in place.

"What in the world happened in here?" Ben said, his mouth gaping as he assessed the damage.

"There's no fire." Estelle paused. "Any more. We're okay. Just make the alarms stop, please." She had regained her composure but still wore a look of disbelief as she sighed and shook her head. She attempted to speak again, but there were no words. There was only complete ruin.

"Ben, there's a ladder in the hall closet," Hank ordered. "Pull out the batteries."

Betsy stood looking at the scattered food disaster. As Estelle walked over to her sister, a wall of water came through the open kitchen window, drenching the pies and splashing onto the food-littered floor.

"What in the world?" Hank yelled. He ran across the room to the back door and yanked it open. There stood Mrs. Grady's six-year-old grandson with an orange plastic bucket in hand—an empty bucket. His huge, proud grin showed several missing teeth.

"Grandma said your house was on fire," the boy said, "and I saw smoke coming out of the window." After his explanation, he grinned with satisfaction at having been a junior firefighter. It just so happened the fire chief had visited his school the week before.

Hank shook his head and sighed in resignation. "Thanks, Neil. You can go home now, okay? Happy Thanksgiving."

As he closed the door, he spun around to look at Betsy, who began wailing, not comforted by anything her sister had to say.

"It's ruined," she cried. "It's all ruined. The turkey," she said and motioned to where two drowned pies sat on the counter under the kitchen window. "And now the pies." She sat on the floor and bawled again when she saw the relish tray with cut veggies lying in a puddle of ranch dressing on the chair in front of her.

Outside came the siren of a fire truck as it pulled up to the house. Mrs. Grady heard it, too, and ran to look out of her front window.

"I may be old, but I can still help," she said and grinned at her grandson as she handed him a piece of pumpkin pie loaded with whipped cream.

∾

When the firemen were convinced there was no emergency and the calamity once-called Thanksgiving dinner had been cleaned up, the friends sat down to eat what had survived.

"Well, this has been quite a day to remember," Ben said as he took a bite of mashed potatoes with gravy. "I'm happy this was still on the stove." He grinned at the women, who looked exhausted, exasperated, and lacking in humor.

"Hey," Hank said, "this is plenty enough for us to eat, and the house is still intact." He glanced at Ben and they both grinned.

Betsy and Estelle threw their rolls at Hank and then took aim at the other grinning face. They all burst out in laughter, finally able to see the humor in the myriad of events, also known as the domino effect and a Rube Goldberg. The girls couldn't have performed it any better that day.

"So, let me get this straight," Ben said in his best policeman's voice and caricature. "You, Ms. Betsy Parsons, were attempting to brown marshmallows by broiling them. Is that correct?"

She bit her lip and nodded as she brushed back some stray hairs from her face and settled them into the mayhem of her auburn tresses.

He continued, "But being preoccupied with cutting vegetables, you forgot about the marshmallows until smoke filled the kitchen. And once you opened the oven, the smoke alarms went off. Would that also be correct?" He grinned at his male cohort.

She shook her head again. Exhaling and rolling her eyes, she nodded her guilt.

Hank joined in the mock interrogation. "So please, Ms. Parsons, tell us again what happened after that. I want to be sure I fully grasp the details."

She put her fork down as her cheeks flushed once again. "I grabbed the casserole with the yams and burning marshmallows and turned to put it on the table because the stove top was full. The table was closest. But when I turned, I stepped on the cat's tail. That made me lose my balance and the dish with the yams flew out of my hands." Betsy widened her eyes as she extended her arms and held out her empty hands.

"Estelle had just put the turkey on a platter and was setting it on the table at the exact moment the yams flew through the air." She clapped her hands together as if they'd exploded. "The yams crashed into the turkey and fell on the table," she said as she took a deep breath and continued. "And Mr. Perfect Turkey flew onto the floor, complete with a stuffing streamer."

The men burst into laughter. Ben looked at Hank and grinned. "I'd say there were mass casualties, wouldn't you?"

Betsy pouted and squinted her eyes at them. "But I had nothing to do with the demise of the pies," she quipped with a smirk.

"Hmm," Estelle said. "Perhaps in a roundabout way, don't you think?" She arched a brow and grinned at her twin.

"Et tu, Brute?" Betsy picked up another roll and tossed it at her sister, narrowly missing her head.

Estelle laughed and winked at the men. "Betsy always loved a good game of knocking down dominos."

"By the looks of the living room," Hank said, "I'd say we missed quite the circus act."

"How's Billie Bird?" Ben asked. "He may be the only bird who survived today."

"Other than being caught up in a tornado, he's fine."

Betsy snorted. "I straightened his cage, fixed his food and water, and covered him. He should feel better tomorrow."

Estelle giggled and shook her head. "Boots is still perched on the drapes, staring at the front door. I'm sure he won't be tempted to go outside again, ever."

Hank laughed. "Yeah, I was impressed with his speed and agility."

Ben held up his glass. "Let's toast to burnt marshmallows and the Great Chain of Events Thanksgiving."

They all looked at Betsy and laughed as the glasses clinked.

"What?" she protested and rolled her eyes.

CHAPTER THIRTY-TWO

Betsy and Hank sat in front of the fireplace in quiet contemplation and sipped their first cups of coffee. The glow from the fire cast dancing shadows on the walls. Lady was asleep on the floor within quick reach of her human family. It was early Christmas morning and their mountain world still slumbered, blanketed in winter's darkness. The heavenly scent of cinnamon hung in the air as the lights on the Christmas tree twinkled to the rhythm of the crackling fire.

Hank took a sip and turned to his wife, and she gazed at him with gentle eyes. He smiled at the woman with whom he'd shared most of his life and dreams.

"Have I told you how beautiful you are in the firelight? Your hair has a lustrous, copper sheen," he said with a crooked smile. "I'm sure I fell in love with your hair first." He winked.

"Thank you, my love." Her eyes glimmered. "And I'm very certain I first fell in love with that crooked grin of yours." She coyly batted her lashes at her husband, causing him to laugh.

"There's been no one else but you and your glorious hair," he said. "Although Estelle has the same color, it's not as brilliant."

She laughed. "Well, I think you may be biased."

Lady, roused by the laughter, sidled up to Betsy's leg and laid her head down on the silky robe.

"Merry Christmas, my sweet Lady," she said as she reached down for the soft fur.

The dog thumped her tail on the carpet. She closed her eyes as she enjoyed the soothing strokes on her head. Hank smiled as his two girls share a loving moment.

"I think I'm almost jealous," he said and laughed. "Although she may be the best surprise gift I've ever given you."

"I'd have to agree with you. She's such a cuddle bug. I've cared for animals before, but I love her in a way that fills my heart—almost as a child does. She's so intuitive and intelligent." She smiled down at Lady and they locked eyes. "I'm sure any day now she's going to just start talking to me in actual words. That might sound foolish, but she just knows things—and me."

"No, that's not foolish. She's a mind reader if there ever was one." He grinned, and the dog walked over to him and put her paw on his knee. "See? She knows we're talking about her skills." They both laughed as her tail swished through the air.

Betsy stood and reached for Hank's cup. "I'll get more coffee, my love."

"Thank you, honey. We'll just sit here and enjoy this warmth." The dog had rested her body against his leg as he rubbed her soft ear.

When his wife left the room, he reached into his robe pocket and brought out a small gold box. He tied it around

Lady's neck with a red velvet ribbon and smiled at his partner. His fur friend took it all in stride as being part of their pack.

He bent down as he held the curious dog's head. He looked into her eyes and whispered. "Now, when she comes back in, I want you to sit in front of her. Okay?" She blinked and wagged her tail as if accepting her mission and panted in reply.

Betsy returned with their coffees and set them on the small table between the chairs.

"I think there's a light snow out there now. I hope it doesn't drop too much on the road." She sighed as she sat down. "I'm glad Estelle is riding out here with Ben today. His truck is good in any weather." She turned to look at Hank, who hadn't responded to her.

He was looking at Lady as he flicked his finger in front of her face toward Betsy. But she just sat there with her head sideways and ears perked up as she gazed at him. Several seconds passed, but she moved just as Betsy spoke.

"What are—" Her words fell away as Lady promptly sat in front of her and placed a paw on her knee. Their friend opened her mouth and panted a grin as she swept her tail back and forth across the carpet.

"What is this?" she said when she noticed the shiny little box that dangled from the ribbon. She turned and looked at her husband. "Could this be magic?" she asked with a raised eyebrow. She held Lady's face in her hands as she stared into her big brown eyes, excited by the attention. "Or the work of a sneaky man and his furry associate."

Hank slapped the chair and laughed. Lady jumped up and raced around their chairs before she ran into the kitchen and back again. She stood in front of her people as she panted and waited for more reasons to express her happiness.

"You better grab that before she takes off again," he said with a grin when the black-and white-sprinter crouched as if at the starting blocks of the next race.

She patted an invitation on her leg. The furry athlete was happy to oblige as she trotted over and placed both front legs on her person's lap. She closed her eyes as her head was rubbed. Betsy untied the ribbon and held the box up for inspection.

"I guess it's time to open presents?" she asked.

Hank smiled, his eyes bright with anticipation and his face glowing with love. "Yes, please, my darling," he said with a childlike anxiousness.

With much care, she untied the gold string and lifted the lid. A purple velvet pouch enveloped the surprise inside. She opened it and turned it into her open hand. She gasped as an exquisite gem fell into her palm. The deep purple amethyst flashed blue and red in the firelight as she held it up by the silver chain. With wide-eyed wonder, she was transfixed as the pendant swung gracefully. A delicate sterling silver iris attached the gem onto the necklace. She was at a loss for words. As she looked at her husband, her lips parted, but no sound came out.

"Like it?" he implored, his eyes excited and his face expectant.

Before she could answer, he dropped to one knee in front of her chair. He took her hand in his and stared into her eyes.

"Will you marry me, Betsy—again?" He held his breath.

She was stunned by his proposal. "Oh, Hank," she said through her tears. "Yes, I would marry you a million times more." She leaned forward and wrapped her arms around his neck and covered his face with kisses. She placed her hands on his cheeks and smiled into his eyes. He gazed back at the desire of his heart, his one and only love. On their faces was the excitement of the years yet to come.

She handed him the necklace and lifted her hair as she leaned in closer. Hank kissed her forehead gently as he reached back and fastened the clasp. She touched the gem and smiled at her husband, the flickering lights reflected in her eyes.

Their lips met as if for the first time. The years melted away, and they were young once again. In that moment, gone were any heartaches and tears. Only their love and joy abounded. And they would pledge to honor and love, through sickness and in health, for richer or poorer—once again. There were no truer hearts or a more loyal love than theirs.

"Hello, Hank, this is Betsy's mom. Yes, she went shopping with Estelle and should be gone for more than an hour. It's safe for you to come over now."

"Did Hank tell you why he wants to talk to us?" Mr. Parsons said as he set down his newspaper. His wife shook her head. "Curious." He picked the paper back up to finish reading the financial section with a slight smile.

"Perhaps he needs some help to buy her a Christmas present." Mrs. Parsons said with a grin as she walked back to the kitchen. Her cheerful expression continued as she sipped her tea at the dining table. When she got up to set her cup in the sink, the doorbell rang.

"I'll get it, honey. I'm already up," she said to the back of the newspaper.

When she opened the front door, she was greeted with a big grin by her favorite soldier.

"Good evening, Mrs. Parsons," Hank said as he held out a bouquet to her.

"These are lovely, Hank. I will give them to Betsy. Come on in."

"Uh, no, ma'am, those are for you," he said before he walked into the living room.

"Why, goodness, thank you." She patted his arm as she grinned her appreciation for his thoughtfulness.

"Good evening, Mr. Parsons. I hope I'm not interrupting," he said as the men exchanged smiles.

"Hi, Hank. Nope, we've already eaten and we're just waiting for the evening news to come on."

"Have a seat, dear. Would you like something to drink? I have tea or water."

"Thank you. Water would be great," he replied with a smile to the kind woman and sat down on the couch nearest to Betsy's dad.

The newspaper was set aside. "How's your shoulder and arm? I hear the therapy's been pretty tough for you," the elder man said as he glanced at the young man's shoulder sling.

"Well, at first I wasn't so sure I'd have full use of the arm, but with Betsy's help, I'm gaining more range of motion. I don't know what I'd have done without your daughter." He shook his head. "I'm not so sure the military docs would've cared for me like she has."

Mrs. Parsons placed a glass of water on the table in front of him. "She's a genuine treasure alright," she added as she sat at the other end of the couch. "She's always had a tendency to nurture both animals and people alike. I know they all love her at the hospital." Her face filled with pride as she leaned back into the soft cushions.

"I'm lucky they granted permission for me to continue my physical therapy through the hospital in Oakville," he said. "I have the prettiest nurse around." He grinned and laughed nervously.

They smiled, and the room fell silent as Betsy's parents looked at him and waited. He squirmed a bit.

"So, I'm sure you're wondering why I'm here," he said with just a hint of anxiety in his voice and a slight tremble in his hands. "It's about your daughter." He looked from one to the other as he straightened his posture. As he drew his breath, there was a slight smile on Mrs. Parsons' face. He relaxed as he uttered the most important words in his young life.

"Mr. and Mrs. Parsons, I'd like to ask your blessings to marry Betsy," he blurted out before he gained control. "She is the kindest, most compassionate person I've ever known. And she's also my best friend." He cast his eyes down and his voice took a serious turn. "When I came back injured, I wasn't the easiest person to be with, but she managed to love me despite myself." He looked up again as he cleared his throat and continued. "I had allowed my anger at myself to cause her heartache." He directed his eyes first to her father and then to her mother. He took a deep breath. "I had no excuse to hurt the most wonderful person in the world. I have since apologized and made a promise to never again let my frustrations be a source of pain for her."

Mr. Parsons studied Hank's face and could see the young man's remorse. He'd known this man who sat before him since his daughter was in third grade. He'd watched the two grow up together and share their joys and sorrows over the years. But he'd also seen how their trials had strengthened their bond. They were adults now and needed to find their own way, and Hank wanted them to find it together.

"Hank, first let me say it takes a big man to not only recognize when he's wrong, but to admit it. And that you've made amends, I commend you for that." Mr. Parsons sat closer to the edge of his comfy chair. He leaned forward and placed his forearms on his knees, his hands relaxed with his fingers intertwined.

"I've known for years you two were not only in love, but meant for each other. You complement one another with your strengths and weaknesses. We all know how strong-willed our sweet Betsy can be, but we also know she's fearless and not a quitter. You are steadfast and courageous. I have no doubt you will protect our girl." He stopped to let his words sink in both for Hank and his wife. "I've had the advantage few fathers have of watching you two together for most of your lives, and I see you are both willing to stop and think about your actions. More importantly, you are both willing to say you're sorry when at fault." He looked at Mrs. Parsons and nodded so she could speak.

Her gentle smile caused Hank to exhale in relief. She scooted closer to him and took his hand in hers. He smiled back, as he had a thousand times in the past. She held a special place in his heart. It was her chocolate chip cookie recipe Betsy had learned to bake.

"Hank, I think you already know how I feel about you and your relationship with my baby. I have no fear that you will do all that you can to take care of her and to provide for her. My only concern is for you to ask yourself if you will love Betsy for a lifetime. Will your devotion to her withstand the test of time and temptation? Your love is strong now, but it will need constant attention to grow deeper and remain unbreakable. Will you remember why you love her?" She squeezed his hand and blinked back her tears. "Will you love and treasure her as she should be?"

"Yes," he said and placed his free hand on top of hers. "I promise to always put her before myself because I know she does that for me. She is the most remarkable human being and I don't deserve her love. But I will, every day and in every way, prove my love to her and show her she didn't make a mistake. Loving Betsy has made me a better man."

Betsy's mom reached up and placed her hand on Hank's cheek. "Remember to never end a day with anger." He nodded. "With that promise, Hank, you have my blessing."

Mr. Parsons stood up with a big smile as he extended his hand, much to the young man's relief. "Hank, my boy, you have my full blessing." He laid a hand on his shoulder. "Thank you for the respect you've shown us now and through the years." The men exchanged smiles as Betsy's mom wiped her tears and stood beside her husband.

"Thank you," Hank said. "Both of you. You've been like a second family for me, and I feel very fortunate to have you in my life. You've raised an incredible daughter and I'll do everything in my power to make her happy."

Mrs. Parsons stepped forward and gave him a hug as she whispered, "We know you will."

CHAPTER THIRTY-THREE

"Okay, we'll get there before sunset at about four-thirty. I'm glad the weather's cooperating. Thanks for calling and getting everyone in place, Estelle," Hank said. "You're the best big sister ever."

Estelle laughed along with him. "Hey, that's what big sisters are for. I can't wait. Bye."

"See ya there. Bye."

He walked into the kitchen where his mom was locking the back door. She smiled at him when she turned around.

"This is going to be so exciting, Hank," she said with a huge grin. "I can hardly wait."

"I just spoke with Estelle and she's on her way to pick you up. I'm leaving now to get Betsy. We're gonna stop for burgers, so that will give everyone a chance to get in place," he said with a huge grin. "This is kinda fun, being sneaky." He hugged his mom as they laughed about their devious plans before he grabbed his keys and coat. "I'll see you soon." He stopped at the door and turned around. "It's good to see you so happy, Mom."

She smiled at him, her eyes filled with joy. "You make my heart happy, son."

~

"I'm really glad you came with me, Betsy. Thanks," Hank said. "Mom wasn't sure I'd pick out the best tree. She said the job needed a woman's eye." He glanced at her and grinned.

"Of course. I'm happy to help," she said. "Besides, I love this drive. It's so beautiful this time of year with the new snow."

He slowed at the bright red sign and turned onto the narrow side road leading into the tall, snow-covered stand of pines. The trees gave way and as they approached a clearing, she gasped. It was late afternoon and a portion of the blue sky had turned a shade of orange as the sun hid behind a cloud, casting sunbeams in all directions.

He stopped the truck as they stared at the scene before them. Through the red gates, rows and rows of Christmas trees as far as the eye could see surrounded an old red barn whose roof was glazed with snow. In front of the barn stood a red-and-white sleigh with two reindeer waiting to take the next visitors through the winter wonderland.

"It's—it's like a Norman Rockwell painting," she cried. "The sky is breathtaking. It's all so magical. I wish my mom could see this."

He grinned at her words because her mom was probably seeing the same sky at almost the same place.

"Are you ready?" he asked, not wanting to rush her but knowing others waited.

"Yes. Thank you for this moment. I'll remember this for the rest of my life," she said, mesmerized by the view.

His grin even made the corners of his eyes crinkled.

There were only a few cars in the vacant lot and some children running through the rows between trees. He parked and ran around to open the passenger door. He smiled as the love of his life slid down from the seat.

"Thank you," Betsy said with a coy smile. She saw that in his hurry, his coat had slid off his injured shoulder and arm. She reached over and covered him. "How are you feeling?" Her expression was one of concern.

"They don't hurt a bit," he said with a grin. "In fact, it all feels fine—really fine."

She gave him a curious look, but before she could say anything further, a man approached from the barn. He wore a Santa suit complete with big black boots, a red hat, and a huge smile framed by an enormous white beard.

She grinned over Hank's shoulder and he turned to see his old friend, with arms outstretched, walking toward them. His face lit up.

"Hank," Santa said in a loud, welcoming voice. He quickly noticed the young man wore a sling. "I was gonna give you a big hug, but now I can see what got injured. How are you doing?" the man said as he patted the uninjured shoulder.

"Great to see you, Dan," he said as he shook his head. "I was lucky—real lucky. But I'll be okay, thanks to medical science and my girlfriend's help." He turned and looked at his companion. "Betsy, I'd like you to meet an old family friend, Dan Foster. Dan, this is my wonderful lady, Betsy."

The young man beamed with joy and Dan smiled at the knowledge of what was soon to happen. He would later tell folks about the grand conspiracy he had taken part in.

"So glad to meet you, Betsy. You're just as beautiful as folks say." He gave her a big hug, catching her off guard.

She blushed after the friendly greeting and compliment. "Thank you, Dan," she said and composed herself. "How is it we've never met? I've been out here lots of times before."

"Just my bad luck, I guess," he said and laughed loud and hearty, surprising the young couple. He chuckled at their expressions. "I need to practice my Santa laugh before all the families show up. We've just opened, you know. I'm glad to see you, son," he said and paused. "So, how's your mom these days?"

It almost looked as if Dan had winked, but perhaps it was the sun in his eyes. It had come out and from behind the clouds, and as it slowly sunk to the horizon, the snow shimmering in the golden light.

Hank couldn't have grinned any bigger as he answered, "She's well, thank you. I'll tell her you asked about her." He nodded. "This is going to be a good Christmas for her. I can just tell. She seems joyful this year. The happiest since dad died."

"Good, good. Come over to the barn with me and I'll get you set up to find a tree."

When they got to the barn, Dan handed her a furry red Santa hat and a yellow tag on which he'd written Hank's name.

"Put this hat on top of the tree you like and attach this tag to a branch," he said. "I'll have my boy come and cut it down for you. Take your time and enjoy the trees. It smells wonderful out there and the temperature is perfect—for just about anything, maybe even some magic." He burst into a loud, hearty laugh again.

"I can hardly wait to walk among your trees," Betsy said, surprised by his enthusiasm.

"Thanks," Hank said. "Maybe we can go for a sleigh ride later?"

"Sure thing. The sleigh will be ready and waiting for you. I think it's going to be a special evening. I can feel it in the air."

As Hank and Betsy walked through the trees, she stopped occasionally to look at and surmise a tree's possible candidacy.

"He is a really nice guy, but I guess you'd have to be if you're wearing a Santa suit," she said and laughed.

He grinned. "That's a good point, but yeah, he's great."

"It almost sounded he was talking in code a few times. Like there was an inside joke," she said as she completed her circle around a tree.

"Oh, he always has a few jokes rattling around in his head," Hank said with a smirk. "I just don't think the punch lines all come out at the right time." He quickly pointed to a handsome and structurally appealing pine. "Hmm... how does this one look to you?" He grabbed her hand and lead her to it.

She was quickly distracted and forgot about her suspicions as she began her inspection of the winning pine. "This looks good," she said and handed him the red hat as she attached the yellow tag to a branch.

"But let's keep walking. He's right, it's wonderful out here."

As they strolled, they held hands and enjoyed just being in each other's company.

"I think we're alone out here now. I haven't seen any other customers," she said.

Hank stopped and gently pulled her closer to him. "I think we are, too. And that sunlight is glorious in your hair." He smiled and lifted her chin. She wrapped her arms around him. He studied her face for a moment before he spoke.

"I love you, Betsy Parsons, with all that I am and with every beat of my heart. I am yours forever."

She looked into his eyes and smiled, a smile worth a thousand words and a lifetime of love. Her lips parted as he gently placed his lips on hers and his hand on the arch of her back. Their kiss lasted for several moments as they breathed in each other's essence. She laid her head on his chest, his heartbeat steady. He caressed the back of her head and stroked her silken hair. No words needed to be spoken.

As they walked back toward the barn, they stopped to watch the sunset behind the mountain. The evening glow reflected on their faces. In the distance, the birds chirped their goodnight, and a muted clicking could scarcely be heard through the holiday trees.

"I told you it would be special," Dan said from behind them, and they spun around. "I've just turned on the tree lights and decorations. Come on in." Santa grinned and waved his arm at them in a welcome. "You'll be the first to see this year's display."

As they walked into the barn, Betsy stopped short and gaped at what was before her. She blinked several times. Earlier, there had been a long canvas curtain stretched across one of the far corners. It had hidden a tall, magnificent Christmas tree decorated with gold and red ornaments, white angels, and glowing with hundreds of colored lights. On the rafter above, long, pine garlands were draped and tied together with bright red and gold ribbons. Twinkling white lights hung like icicles in varied lengths. Beneath the tree were mounds of what appeared to be fluffy snow. A faint sound of sleigh bells drifted through the air.

Hank held Betsy's hand as she strolled toward the tree, the lights glowing in her eyes. Her smile was one of child-like amazement. She looked at them. "This is unbelievable."

He led her to within touching distance of the tree and he leaned in for a closer look at the ornaments.

"Isn't this beautiful?" he said as he pointed to a red bulb with gold engraving.

She nodded and gently touched a porcelain angel. "These are gorgeous."

"What do you think of this one?" he said as he reached out.

When Betsy turned to see what he was speaking about, he took a small, heart-shaped box off of the tree. Her brows wrinkled in disapproval as if he'd done something wrong.

Before she could protest, he opened the box and dropped to one knee in front of her. She looked down and suddenly realized what he was about to say. She covered her mouth as she gasped. Betsy stared at the diamond ring he held up and glanced into his eyes without blinking. She held her breath with an intense expression of expectation.

"Betsy Parsons, will you marry me?" he asked as his hand trembled. His eyes pleaded for an answer as he held his breath. The sound of a shutter clicking went unheard, masked by the subtle jingle of bells.

She nodded, breathless and unable to speak. She found her voice. "Yes. Oh yes, Hank," she said through her tears. He took her hand and placed the ring on her finger. As he stood, they wrapped each other in their arms and kissed with a desire they had not yet known.

Without warning, there were cheers and applause as all their family and friends came out from hiding. The cheerful noise rang through the rafters, along with Santa's booming laughter.

Betsy released Hank and turned in disbelief at their surprise appearance. Her mouth fell open and her eyes mirrored her shock. She shook her head, stunned at not just one immense surprise, but two. She grinned at every person and turned to Hank with hands on her hips as if to scold him. He was too busy laughing to take her seriously.

"You had this planned all along, didn't you?" she said to him through her grin. Then she pointed to Estelle. "And I know you were definitely part of this, big sister." She laughed and cried as she ran to hug everyone.

Someone she hadn't met stood in a far corner unnoticed by her. With a camera to her trained eye, the *Oakville Tribune* photographer had recorded all the precious memories of the young couple at the Christmas tree farm. She captured their kiss among the trees, the golden rays of sunset on their faces, and the look of surprise when Hank knelt and slipped the ring onto her finger. On the front page of the *Oakville Tribune*'s Sunday edition was a photo of the newly engaged couple in Santa's sleigh.

CHAPTER THIRTY-FOUR

"I'm finished with all the barn chores, honey," Hank said with a cheery tone as he walked into the kitchen. "All of our hairy, dairy, and feathered friends are happy as can be. Max and Gertie are in the pasture enjoying the new grass."

Not waiting for an answer, he walked up behind his wife at the sink and wrapped his arms around her waist, kissing her on the back of the neck.

She squealed and laughed as she turned around and gave him a quick kiss on his lips. "It's springtime on our mountain," she said, her face excited and eyes bright with anticipation. "So give me just about fifteen minutes to get ready, please."

"Take all the time you need, my dear. I await your command," he said with a grin and a grand bow. "I'll take Lady out again before we go," he said. At the sound of her name, the dog jumped to her feet and ran to the back door. She was always eager to search for more chatty squirrels. She buried her nose in the door's crack as if to smell for the little critters.

"Okay, my love," she said as she headed for the staircase.

"I can hardly wait to see the valley and meadow. Spring is early this year. The irises should just be blooming." She looked at her husband as they shared a smile.

"I love that we'll spend some time today visiting the place where our life together began," he said, his voice filled with decades of love and trust.

"And I love you for that very reason." She winked before she ascended the stairs.

Spring on the mountain was nothing less than spectacular. Just above Parsons, off the beaten path and at the end of a narrow road, was a view and meadow that most of the townsfolk considered sacred. It was a sanctuary for the soul, a haven for the heart, and a place for new beginnings. During the peak of spring, the meadow brimmed with wild flowers, a plethora of grasses, and a sea of purple irises. The majestic flowers stood tall above all the other growth and beckoned the eyes as far as a person could see. A small path led to a large outcrop of granite which overlooked the breathtaking view. It was on that large, level rock that Betsy and Hank exchanged their vows so long ago. The irises were a perennial reminder of constancy because of its reappearance year after year. Ceaseless and undying, the flower lived beneath the harshness of winter as a testament and witness to the endurance created by abiding, faithful, and unfailing love.

It was here that Betsy's ancestors had discovered the new land they would call home. And the place where angels would live and miracles would touch the lives of those who settled on the mountain. They had been brought here by a dream—a vision of a mountain of green with a living sea of purple. They said a prayer of thanksgiving and asked for blessings on their family and future families.

Hank and Betsy held hands as they walked the familiar path of their past. They shared a glance and a reverence for this place as they stepped upon the granite rock. A cool breeze filled with the fragrance of moist earth and new life ruffled through her auburn hair. As they strode across the stone surface, the meadow and valley came into full view. They stopped near the edge of the ancient magma tabletop, which overlooked the mountain's beauty below. Hank squeezed her hand and slid a lock of hair from her face. Her eyes smiled at him.

"I don't want you to miss any of the view," he said as he wrapped an arm around her shoulders and they gazed at the wonder before them.

She inhaled deeply as she put her arm around her husband's waist. He bent down and kissed her forehead. In their silence, the gurgle of a creek lost in the trees and the echoes of birds calling in search of mates could be heard in the distance.

"It seems like the first time—each time I look at this," she whispered. "It's amazes me." She fell silent for a minute and inhaled the fragrance of life. "And it inspires me to be a better person. This must be holy ground. I can feel heaven right here on earth." She stared into the distance, still and barely breathing.

"I can feel it, too," he said in a hushed voice.

A slight gust of wind seemed to answer questions that may have occupied their minds. Their bodies relaxed and their faces reflected a radiant peace. They stood in silence for a moment, or perhaps an eternity, as the breeze passed over and around them and into the surrounding trees. The rustling of newly formed leaves spoke of spring's arrival.

She was the first to speak. "It seems like only yesterday we stood here and exchanged our vows." She looked up at her husband.

He thought for a moment and looked at her with a grin. "That is, until we see Andy." They both laughed at how the measure of time ebbs and flows, how years are lost and gained.

"I guess it truly is all relative," she said and gave him a tight hug.

On the ride home, they reminisced about their wedding day and about how young and how much in love they were.

"It's funny how nervous we were and yet we'd known each other for so long," she said and laughed. "I just wanted it to all be perfect, I guess. And I prayed it wouldn't rain."

"And I just wanted to be able to speak," he said as he shook his head with a grin. "But when I saw you step onto the rock and walk toward me—" His words caught in his throat. "I knew I'd find my voice at the right time." He reached over and took his wife's hand. "Once I saw you, my heart was flooded with peace. The most amazing woman in the world was about to tell me she wanted to spend her life with me. At that point, nothing else mattered."

She smiled and placed her other hand on top of his. "And when I saw you, my heart jumped. I was just a few steps away from our forever."

They rode in a contented silence for a brief time and allowed their words to find a home in their hearts. She glanced at her husband. "I've given it a lot of thought," she said, "and I think I'd rather renew our vows standing above our meadow in our own little mountain sanctuary."

"Really?" he said. "I would really like that, honey. But what changed your mind?"

She thought before she answered, her face tranquil. She was at peace with her life.

"When we stood on that rock and promised our lives to each other, we were giving ourselves to one another for the first time. That place is where hearts are joined and a new life starts. And I believe God blessed our union on that altar of stone. He has been with us every minute of our lives, through our sickness and health—"

"And for richer or poorer," Hank interjected as he grinned. She nodded and smiled.

"He's blessed us with a home on this mountain and I'd like to offer our thanks to Him by renewing our vows to each other in the place where He settled us."

"I couldn't agree more, my love." His face showed the admiration he'd always felt for his wife, the woman who had stood beside him—loving him—for so long.

Betsy glowed with happiness. She reached up and stroked his arm as she had throughout the years. She didn't realize the impact of that simple act. Hank's face glowed, too.

CHAPTER THIRTY-FIVE

"I'll handle everything," Estelle said. "That's what sisters are for. Right?"

"Are you sure?" Betsy asked, surprised once again by the generous offer.

"Hey, I live for this stuff. You are my number one project—always. I'll make some calls and get some volunteers." She laughed. "I know a kindly sheriff who will be happy to help with the arrangements."

Betsy laughed and nodded. "He's a sweetheart alright." Her face lit up as she spoke the words. "I'll let you surprise us then, sis. Know it's with all of our love and gratitude."

"Of course. This will be fun. All you need to do is bring yourself and that hunky husband of yours."

The sisters giggled like teenagers and said their goodbyes.

"It sounds like you two have it worked out," Hank said as he looked up at his wife with a grin. "I'm always just a wee bit afraid of what you and your sister might cook up. I gathered long ago I just needed to be in the right place and follow instructions."

She bent down and planted a kiss on her husband's cheek.

"Oh, we're not that bad, are we?" she said coyly. She held her innocent expression as long as she could before she burst out laughing.

He grinned and grabbed her hand, pulling her onto his lap as she shrieked. Startled, Lady jumped up from her nap and joined in the revelry as she barked and ran around the recliner. After a couple of laps, panting and wagging her tail, she stopped and laid her head on Betsy's lap.

"Good girl, my sweetness. You'll rescue me." She grabbed the dog's soft ear and massaged it.

"No, you have that wrong, my love. I think it's me that needs to be rescued." He laughed long and hard at his words.

"And it's best for you to remember that, Mr. Walker." Her words came with a smug look. She laughed and snuggled her face into his shoulder as they sighed and enjoyed the moment. A moment they didn't take for granted.

"I'm thankful for every day I wake up and see you next to me," he whispered as he rubbed his wife's arm.

"As am I. And thankful for each kiss, each smile, and each touch. I love you, Hank." Betsy's lips were near the hollow of his neck. The warmth of her breath lingered there.

"I love you, too, Betsy, every minute of every day. It's always been you."

～

"Thanks for doing this with me, Ben," Estelle said as she got into the truck while he held the door. "Mr. Sato sounded honored to be included." She smiled at her friend. "I just had a feeling he should be part of their ceremony. He was close friends with our fathers for decades."

"It's a great idea, and they'll be pleasantly surprised."

"He said he has some ideas for designing the location, too. He'd like our opinions and input."

"He's a remarkable man and I really respect all the work he's done in the community. He's turned Parsons into a town that shouts welcome to our visitors," he said. "The man knows how to speak to nature and I'm pretty sure it talks back to him." He grinned at his passenger and turned his attention back to the road.

"I don't doubt that," she replied. "There seems to be such a sense of peace and joy wherever he's planted trees and flowers. I'm sure it must be therapy for everyone else in town, including me." They shared a grin.

As they got closer to Mr. Sato's house, they were greeted by masses of flowers and a spectacular display of cherry trees in blossom along his driveway and entrance.

"Oh, my," she gasped. "This is incredibly beautiful."

"You can say that again." He shook his head in disbelief. "It's no wonder these trees are revered."

A man stepped out from the porch as they neared and waved at them with a huge smile. That prompted them to smile back with just as much enthusiasm.

"Hello, Sheriff Ben," Mr. Sato said as he extended his hand.

"Mr. Sato, it's a pleasure to see you again. And may I say, you look even younger than the last time I saw you." He grinned and took his hand as he put his arm around the elder man's shoulders in a brief hug.

"You always make me feel so much better—and younger." The senior gentleman laughed as he patted the sheriff's arm. Ben opened the passenger door for Estelle and helped her down.

Mr. Sato's face brimmed with joy as he stepped up to his lovely guest and gave her a quick hug. She had known him her entire life and considered him family.

"But this young woman here is the one who deserves our close attention," he said, his face full of pride and with a wry smile. "She has the face of a queen and the mind of a general."

Ben was surprised by his words as he blurted out, "You are absolutely right. I couldn't have said it any better." They all laughed. "And never bet against her," he added with a grin.

Mr. Sato laughed out loud and slapped his friend's back. "I never gamble, Sheriff Ben." He winked and motioned them to follow him to a large greenhouse.

When they stepped inside, they were greeted with a warm, earthy fragrance. Estelle had been in it once, years ago, as a child. She was still just as enthralled by the profusion of plants and flowers.

"It smells wonderful in here," she said. "It's a banquet for your senses." She grinned as she bent over to catch the scent of a brilliant red blossom. Her eyes widened as she inhaled.

The sheriff stood in amazement as he slowly absorbed the magnificence of the greenery and flowers, each more beautiful than the next. "You are truly a master, Mr. Sato," he said in a reverent tone.

The older gentleman smiled at his guests' appreciation for the gift of his labors. "This is not work for me," he said. "It is merely a reflection of what my soul is trying to attain— beauty and peace."

"We were just speaking about that very thing and how

you've extended this beauty and peace to our town," the sheriff said, his eyes speaking his gratitude.

"And for which we all are eternally grateful," Estelle added as she placed her hand on Mr. Sato's arm. "We all feel you've helped to make the town our home."

The elder man bowed his head for a few seconds before he looked up. "I do it for my wife. She was my inspiration and I see her everywhere now," he said with a smile. "It brings joy to my heart." He sighed. "And I feel her presence with each bloom of color."

He motioned again for them to follow him through the greenery. He stopped in front of an explosion of purple and smiled as he turned to them. Before their eyes was a lavish display of potted irises. From one side to the other, the plants stood two to three feet tall. Behind the purple and green palette stood rows of small cherry trees loaded with pink blossoms. It looked every bit a painting from a master artist.

"The iris is a gift from our mountain. I do not sell them. I simply pass them on to those who live here." He bent down and straightened one pot. "I give them to people who need some hope in their lives." He turned and looked at his guests with eyes of empathy.

Their faces showed they understood the meaning of his words. Their eyes smiled as they nodded. They were in the presence of a wise and humble man.

He continued, "I thought, perhaps, we could use some of these plants as a walkway to the cherry trees where Betsy and Hank will exchange their vows. It can be a path from their home to the pink blossoms. What do you think?" he said as he looked into Estelle's eyes for an answer.

She held her hands as if in prayer against her chest as tears streamed down her cheeks.

"You will make a certain sister of mine beyond happy," she said as she wiped her face. "It will fill Betsy's heart with such joy." She smiled and hugged him. And then hugged him again.

"Thank you."

"I'm pleased you like the idea. I remember how beautiful the meadow was the day they were married, and I want to have that for them again," Mr. Sato said. "My grandsons and I can bring them up the day before the ceremony, if that's good for you. And then put them in place on the special day. Also, with your permission, we'll come back a few days after and plant them in their meadow."

"Of course. That will be wonderful."

"I can help as well," Ben said. "I'll call you and we can make the arrangements."

The old man nodded and smiled. "Come inside now, please, for some tea."

They nodded and returned his smile. "We would be honored and delighted."

CHAPTER THIRTY-SIX

"Hi, Estelle. Do you have more instructions for me?" Betsy said into the phone and laughed.

"I do, as a matter of fact. How'd you know that?"

"Because, my dear sister, you are ever the one for details and perfection."

"Oh, you know me well. But in my defense, it's all for you, Betsy."

"I know, and you're too good to me." Her voice was filled with love as she asked, "So, what do we need to do?"

"It'd be great if the two of you could leave the house for a few hours tomorrow. Say early afternoon? Maybe go to lunch or shopping."

"I know Hank would be all about the food, but not so much the shopping." They laughed. "Sure, we can do that. I take it there's an element of surprise involved?"

"Absolutely," she answered, "and no peeking behind the barn when you get home." She tried, but couldn't suppress her snicker.

"Well, now I am intrigued, but okay, we can do that."

Betsy smiled as she spoke. "And the other thing we discussed?"

"It's all taken care of and I'll have the paperwork for you after the ceremony. I think it's a fantastic idea and he'll really be surprised. I love it."

"Me, too. Anything further, General?"

"I'm glad to know you understand who's in charge." The sisters laughed once again with an easy, loving joy that was their relationship. "And, yes, there's one more thing," she said. "At noon on the day of your vows, please draw all the curtains and blinds facing the meadow. You are not to look outside until you open the front door at five o'clock."

"Wow, that's pretty specific—and mysterious."

"Okay, I need to attend to more secret stuff," Estelle said and laughed.

"We appreciate all that you're doing. You know that, right?"

"Of course. I do it because I love you and you both mean the world to me. Our sheriff is having a lot of fun with this, too."

"I'm really intrigued by Estelle's cryptic instructions," Hank said as he pulled the window coverings closed. "She's always had a flair for the dramatic, don't you think?"

They laughed and continued to shutter all meadow views in the house. Just then, Lady barked and they heard vehicles in the distance as they approached their house.

"Well, I know whatever she creates will be nothing less than spectacular. I can hardly wait to see it." She clasped her hands, her eyes wide in anticipation.

He wrapped his arms around her as he laughed.

"You've always loved surprises, haven't you?" He gave her a quick kiss.

"Mmm—I love that even more," she quipped and planted a long, passionate kiss on her husband's lips. "Let's save some of this for later." She smiled and winked.

He looked surprised and burst out in laughter. "After all these years, you still make me laugh," he said with a grin. "How'd I get so lucky?"

She flipped her hair back. "You never had a chance, Mr. Walker. Not a chance." She grinned. "I'll fix some grilled sandwiches and a salad. We can have a long lunch and a glass of wine before we get ready."

He nodded. "Yeah, that sounds good, and it just might distract me from all the noise outside. It sounds like an army of people and an awful lot going on out there." He shook his head as he sat down. "That's definitely not just Estelle and Ben. I thought this would be simple." He wrinkled his brows as he glanced toward the front of the house.

She laughed at her husband's curiosity. "Hush. How about if you put on some music while we eat?"

"That'll help." He walked back into the living room.

"Maybe some anniversary music," she called out as he disappeared around the corner.

He grinned as he put the vinyl on the turntable. He had already made his selection and within seconds, the familiar notes of their favorite love song drifted into the dining room.

"Ah, that's much better. That music soothes my soul."

"Yep, that was a great idea, my love. Now I can focus on just you. After my stomach stops growling. I'll set the table."

"Yes, please, and be sure to add a couple of wineglasses. Estelle brought us a bottle of our favorite Italian wine for our anniversary."

"She always remembers, no matter what," he said. "Last

year was our big Italian dinner night and this year we're renewing our vows. And she's doing all the work. Remind me to give her extra hugs."

She smiled as she set the food on the table. He poured the wine, and they lifted their glasses.

"Here's to us, my darling Betsy."

"Happy anniversary, my love."

There was a faint knocking on the bedroom door as Betsy applied her lipstick. She glanced at the clock. Hank had been told to get into position fifteen minutes before her.

"Lady and I are leaving now," he said. "We'll be waiting for you, honey."

"I'll be there shortly, my love. I can hardly wait." She moved a stray wisp of hair as she looked once again at her reflection. Sunlight come through the window behind her and she stopped in front of it. The once barren trees were now fully clothed in lime-green leaves. She sighed as she closed her eyes for a moment. Her lips silently moved. "Thank you. Amen," she said as she opened her eyes again.

She descended the stairs and took her place by the door. On the entry table was a lovely bouquet of purple irises, wild daisies, and baby's breath, all banded together with white ribbons of pearls. Her sister always remembered the details of her special memories. She picked up the flowers and stood at the ready. A few minutes passed before Lady barked. That was her cue to exit the house.

As she reached for the doorknob, the door slowly opened. She was speechless, her eyes wide and mouth open.

"Hi, Mom," Andy said with his father's crooked grin.

"But—" She couldn't quite find her words. Instead, she

wrapped her arms around him and held him with all her strength.

As her son laughed and hugged her back, he whispered, "I got here this morning." He bent his arm and held it out for her. "Come on, everyone's waiting." He kissed her cheek and moved a stray hair from her face.

Lady sat at the top of the porch steps and wore a lei of daisies around her neck. She wagged her tail when Betsy stepped outside, but pivoted her attention back to Hank. He had practiced hand signals with their furry friend for several months while he recuperated from his surgery. And now they would have the chance to show off their newfound skills.

As Betsy stepped through the doorway, she stopped again at the sight of dozens of faces smiling at her. They were friends she'd known for decades. Some she'd helped and others who had helped her throughout her life. She'd always felt their love and respect.

Her foot touched on an amethyst-colored runner that led across the yard to the twin cherry trees where her husband stood waiting. She slowly exhaled, her lips frozen in a half smile as she stood mesmerized by the incredible view. The purple fabric on the ground was lined on both sides by dozens of potted, blooming cherry trees and irises. Pink rose petals lay scattered on the path and lights twinkled in and among the branches and flowers.

Her eyes wide and filled with tears, she looked at her sister, who stood beside Hank, Ben, and Mr. Sato. Estelle blew her little sister a kiss and gave her a huge smile. The men grinned at the surprised expression on her face. She breathed in, quickly regaining her composure, and stepped forward. She and her handsome escort stood behind Lady.

Seemingly out of nowhere, the first chords of a familiar

song drifted through the air. A look of recognition swept across her face. Blocked from view, an orchestra of keyboard, violinist, and cellist softly played "I Can't Help Falling In Love." Betsy batted her eyes to hold back her tears.

Hank patted his leg, and Lady began a slow walk down the steps toward him. She seemed to play to the crowd, her head held high as she wagged her tail. Betsy smiled at the choice of flower girl as the dog kept her eyes on her human, ever ready for the next command. She glanced back only once and seemed to know she should be followed.

Estelle motioned to Betsy, and she and her son fell in line behind her flower dog. The air, still moist from an early morning, held the sweet fragrance of the cherry blossoms. The irises swayed in the gentle breeze as she walked past, surrounded by the people, sounds, and symbols of the love in her life. Her eyes focused on Hank as he watched her. Pride and adoration glowed across his face. Lady sat in front of him and with a flick of his finger she quickly walked behind and took her place beside him. He reached down and scratched behind her ear as her tail swished, his recognition of a job well done. He gave her the signal to lie down, so she'd be comfortable.

Betsy completed her walk and faced Hank as he turned toward her. The musicians played a new song, "Only You," as they exchanged smiles, and Estelle and Ben took their places next to them. Mr. Sato had stepped back a few feet and looked at all of them, his eyes filled with kindness. The group stood near the edge above the beloved meadow. As Betsy looked at the elder gentleman, she noticed purple plants below them that hadn't been there the day before. She smiled and glanced at Estelle as she handed over her bouquet. The looks they exchanged spoke volumes of the lifelong love they'd shared as sisters—as twins.

Hank reached out his hands for Betsy's and whispered, "I love you."

"I love you back."

Mr. Sato smiled and wiped his eyes. "Shall we begin?"

CHAPTER THIRTY-SEVEN

"Betsy and Hank, it is my honor to witness the renewal of your vows," Mr. Sato said. "I stand here today as having been a good friend to both of your fathers. Generations of your families have brought honor, dignity, and kindness to our town, and as their children, instilled those qualities in both of you. They also taught you about commitment." He took a deep breath and looked at the faces that surrounded him. He gazed for a moment at the couple, smiled, and continued.

"Your commitment to one another is the highest example of love. You've faced life's best and worst of times, always together and always with prayer. You've lived your life together with integrity, respect, and care. He smiled again. "And an abundance of patience, understanding, and forgiveness.

"These cherry blossoms represent a time of renewal and expectation but also speak of the fleeting nature of life. The flowers tell us to grasp all that each day brings, to see the blessings and beauty in each detail.

"Your marriage reflects that sense of awareness. I see it

in your eyes and the way your hands search for the other's hand. Your love is expressed in the quick response to each other's smile. You complement one another. You each are half of the whole your lives together have created. Your love has bonded you to each other, to this mountain, and to those whose lives you've touched. May you continue on this blessed journey ever mindful of each moment, living each day with passion and joy. And may these blossoms remind you that life is precious and filled with promise."

Mr. Sato placed his hands atop Betsy's and Hank's joined hands.

"And may God continue to fill your hearts and life."

The musicians had moved within sight and were playing "Only You." Estelle whispered in her sister's ear. Hank and Betsy turned toward their guests and were surprised to see a photographer as she captured the images of their special day. When the music softened, the couple turned to look at each other again.

Hank took her hands in his, lifted one of them, and kissed the back of it. Her eyes radiated love. "Betsy, you've always been the reason I wanted to be a better man, to be a man you could be proud of and a man you'd never make apologies for," he said as the corners of his eyes grew moist. "You've given me the best in you, even when you saw the worst in me. You are more precious to me than anything else. You are my world."

Betsy blinked back tears as she spoke. "Hank, you've taught me so much and shown me, by your example, the meaning of true love. You held my hand and led my heart with yours. You have always made me feel valued. And for that, I am so grateful. We've laughed and cried together." Betsy's eyes teared as she smiled. "Together is my favorite word."

Lady sat up and nudged Hank's knee with her nose. They laughed along with those close by. He reached down and rubbed her head as she thumped her appreciation.

They had written their vows as psalms. Hank stood and cleared his throat as he smiled at his wife.

"Without you, Betsy, I am but a ship tossed about, without hope, in a raging sea. Your arms embrace me. They are my warmth. Your smile pierces my heart. It is my joy. There has been no other who caught my eye, for your beauty and heart are my treasure." He squeezed her hands as he gazed into her eyes.

Betsy took a deep breath and spoke. "Hank, you are my everything, my heartbeat, and my breath. By day and night, you are my light and peace. You bring quiet to my soul. You give songs to my days. With you beside me, I am strong. No trials nor tears shall break me."

They smiled and, with deep intention, spoke their words together.

"Only you can quell my longing, my yearning for love. It is only you I cherish."

They smiled at each other and continued their vows together.

"Today, in the presence of our family and friends, I reaffirm my commitment to you. I promise to love you, honor you, and comfort you in sickness and in health, for richer and poorer, for better or worse, as long as we both shall live."

They grinned and Hank swept Betsy up in his arms and planted a long, passionate kiss on her lips. Lady jumped up and barked as she ran around them in celebration that she no longer had to stay in position. She then ran straight to Andy to greet him.

As the orchestra played their favorite song, "As Time Goes By," their family and friends clapped and cheered. Hank promptly took Betsy's hand, and with great enthusiasm, they danced on the purple runner and scattered flower petals in every direction.

"You look breathtaking, my darling," he whispered. "Perhaps we should visit Morocco one more time to fetch more fabric."

She tilted her head back as she laughed. "I already have other plans, my love."

When the song finished, Estelle motioned for them to follow her and Ben. Lady ran ahead to lead the pack. The happy couple hadn't seen the other surprise that awaited them. A short distance down the driveway and around a curve, a large, white tent materialized—seemingly out of nowhere. The procession of revelers came to a sudden stop as they clapped and cheered.

Hank's and Betsy's eyes were wide with amazement. She threw her hands over her mouth, unable to speak, as Hank shook his head in disbelief.

"How in—" he said. "When did—" He couldn't complete a sentence, distracted by the behemoth of white canvas.

Ben and Estelle burst into laughter as they leaned on each other, as if to keep from falling over. Andy laughed and pointed at his parents' perplexed faces.

"I think we got them this time, Estelle," Ben said as he slapped Andy on the back and continued to laugh.

She grinned and wiped her eyes. "By golly, I think you're right, Ben."

"Hey, son, grab that flap and help me open this up," Ben said. The two men pulled back the canvas doors and exposed the interior, complete with a crowd of smiling faces and more applause.

"What?" Betsy shrieked and covered her face, her cheeks flushed with excitement.

Hank couldn't control his laughter and moments passed before he gained control and could speak. "You two have finally outdone yourselves."

After many congratulations and hugs, food and cake, and dances and toasts, the festivities waned. People said their goodbyes and bid farewell with much affection.

Hank and Betsy sat at a table with Andy, Estelle, and Ben as Lady worked as the cleanup crew, vacuuming the wooden floor.

"It's unbelievable what you accomplished," Betsy said as she looked at her sister and Ben. "This has been nothing short of miraculous." She gazed at the decorations, flower arrangements, and the twinkling lights hanging from the ceiling. She smiled and reached her hands out to hold each of theirs. "Thank you sincerely," she said with a smile. Her expression conveyed her gratitude and love.

"Yes," Hank said. "You've made this a truly remarkable day—and memory."

"When word spread about today's ceremony," Ben said, "dozens of businesses, church members, neighbors, and friends contributed their time and resources to making this a success." He grinned. "It has to be the biggest secret this town has ever kept." They all laughed at the thought, given there were a few people known as unable to keep mum.

Estelle nodded as she added, "And the people of Parsons wanted to show you both just how much you mean to this community."

Ben held his wineglass up in a toast. "To Hank and Betsy. To love and friendship." They clinked their glasses and sipped the champagne.

Andy smiled and turned to his parents. "If ever there was an example of what love and marriage is, it's you two. Thank you for being you." He stood up and walked around the table to give each a hug. "You're the best."

"Thank you, son. Just remember to always make them feel beautiful and take every opportunity to hold them in your arms." He grinned and looked at his wife. "One last dance, Mrs. Walker?"

She stood up with a smile and held out her hand. "Of course, Mr. Walker."

As they swayed and spun to the music, she whispered in his ear, "Would you like to take a train trip across Canada?"

He stopped moving for a split second. "Really?" he said as he looked into her eyes.

"Yes. That's my gift to you. I decided I could share you with the world," she grinned. "I have our tickets. We leave tomorrow."

Hank hugged her and continued with the dance. When the music finished, he held her and leaned her back into a low dip. He pulled her up and into his body. As he pressed his cheek against her hair, he held her tight. He kissed her and looked deep into her eyes.

"Are you still my girl?"

Her lips parted as she smiled back at him and tenderly kissed his lips.

"Always."

The End

Thank you for spending your time and money on this book. I hope you enjoyed it. **If you could please post a review** on Amazon or Goodreads I'd be very grateful. Your reviews are critical to my success as an author and will help me write better books in the future. Thank you!

ABOUT THE AUTHOR

My life has led me from the foothills of Northern California, to Interior Alaska, the beaches of Kona, Hawaii and finally the high desert of Arizona. Along the way I've been a mom, wife, bookkeeper, camp cook at a gold mining operation, lay counselor, singer, entrepreneur, photographer and friend. I've tried to live a life of compassion, empathy and humor. I've done much more listening than speaking. (My children may disagree!)

Besides a story meant to entertain, it is my desire for you to glean hope, inspiration and encouragement from these words. Wherever you are in life, it is my wish that you walk among angels unaware.

"May you laugh till it hurts... and love till it doesn't."

--Eila Trent

ALSO BY EILA TRENT

The Christmas Miracle Bell

Dream Mountain

Visit my website at EilaTrent.com for the latest book releases.

ACKNOWLEDGMENTS

Many thanks to Misha Carlstedt for her excellent editing skills.

Cover design by Elizabeth Mackey.

 Created with Vellum